ST. MARTIN'S

MINOTAUR

MYSTERIES

Other titles from St. Martin's MINOTAUR Mysteries

ST. MARTIN'S PAPERBACKS is also proud to present these mystery classics by Ngaio Marsh

Praise for DONNA HUSTON MURRAY

"Murray always weaves an intriguing tale while also expanding our knowledge—in this case—of the art of textiles and antique fraud. I enjoyed LIE LIKE A RUG immensely."   —Robin Hathaway, Agatha-winning
author of *The Doctor Makes a Dollhouse Call*

"Thank heavens! A cozy with a brain! . . . [Murray's] characters . . . even the cameos . . . are all intensely real and completely realized. . . . The thing that also grabbed and held me . . . purely stylistic . . . is [Murray's] ability to turn a phrase that is insightful/graphic/or just beautiful in and of itself . . . to paint a whole physical and emotional gestalt with just a few, perfectly chosen words."
            —Ellie Miller, Independent Reviewer

"Definitely not your usual housewife detective."
            —Deen Kogan, Director/Organizer of Mid-Atlantic
Mystery Book Fair & Convention

"Very smart writing and a good enough plot to have kept me reading it pretty much in one sitting."
            —Carolyn, "Alice"
of Malice the Mystery Bookstore

"Pick a less than usually very busy week to start your reading. . . . "   —Lauren Bergold, for Rivergate Books

"An easygoing cozy . . . [it has] Murray's smart, often insightful first-person narrative."
            —*Publishers Weekly* on *School of Hard Knocks*

"A solid addition to the subgenre of amateur sleuths."
            —*Alfred Hitchcock Mystery Magazine* on
No Bones About It

"Intelligent, wise, with a full measure of pluck, Ginger Barnes is the sleuth and friend we'd all want on our team."
—Camilla Crespi, author of the Simona Griffo series

"Donna Huston Murray has whipped up a treat for all lovers of domesticated malice."
—Gillian Roberts, author of *In the Dead of Summer*

"A welcome new series!"
—Jeremiah Healy, author of *Invasion of Privacy* and *Spiral*

"Donna Huston Murray has given us a real treat in FAREWELL PERFORMANCE. Ginger and Didi are a winning team and those of us who have fond memories of slumber parties, girlfriends, and just being kids are going to really enjoy this one." —*Romantic Times*

"No major literary award for 'Best Chapter Endings' currently exists. The minute such a prize does exist, Donna Huston Murray will win it. Easily. Not content with merely writing excellent, cozy mystery novels . . . Murray seems to put extra thought and craftsmanship into the very last paragraphs of those chapters."
—*Rivergate Books*

"Murray knows the territory, and there's plenty of territory for her to cover. . . . Ginger Barnes will be around for a long time." —*Main Line Today*

"[Ginger] is practical and smart as she looks at things that need explaining and more self-aware than a lot of detectives. She has a good eye for description and insight. It is a pleasure to read of her adventures and her friends and easy to believe in her family. She is a breath of fresh air." —*Kate's Mystery Books*

St. Martin's Paperbacks Titles
by Donna Huston Murray

THE MAIN LINE IS MURDER
FINAL ARRANGEMENTS
SCHOOL OF HARD KNOCKS
NO BONES ABOUT IT
A SCORE TO SETTLE
FAREWELL PERFORMANCE
LIE LIKE A RUG

Lie Like a Rug

Donna Huston Murray

St. Martin's Paperbacks

LIE LIKE A RUG

Copyright © 2001 by Donna Huston Murray.

ISBN: 0-312-97897-9

Printed in the United States of America

St. Martin's Paperbacks edition / July 2001

St. Martin's Paperbacks are published by St. Martin's Press, 175 Fifth Avenue, New York, N.Y. 10010.

10 9 8 7 6 5 4 3 2 1

To Skip Graffam

. . . for lots of reasons

ACKNOWLEDGMENTS

This book would have been impossible without the generosity of two very patient people. Assistant U.S. Attorney Nancy Winter answered all my questions about federal court procedure so thoroughly that she enriched the book even beyond my hopes. I am indebted to her and most grateful. (To be fair, U.S. Attorney Michael Stiles offered first, and more than once, which prompted the federal trial idea. However, we didn't meet at a mystery convention, and he wasn't reading one of my books at the time.)

Linda Eaton, Curator of Textiles at Winterthur, also intrigued me when she said she didn't know of any mysteries with a decorative-arts background. Soon she was giving me tours and homework and checking my fictional experts for mistakes. I loved what I learned about her work, and I think readers will, too.

So many others added to the texture of this book, and I thank them all. Nancy Packer, Collections Manager for the Paley Design Center of what is now called Philadelphia University; James Glover and Pamela Pawl, both Technical Associates there; Freddie Ford in PR; Professor William Wolfgang; Lois Janney; and Acting President William D. Andrews were all valuable resources.

I also thank Janice Roosevelt, former Director of

Public Relations at Winterthur; Dilys Blum, Curator of Costume and Textiles at the Philadelphia Museum of Art; Trish Morrissey of Jack's Firehouse; the staff at J. M. Sorkin; Sandy Haas and Marion Smith from Keepsake Quilting & Country Pleasures; and particularly Ray Albed, who read about my project in the newspaper and was kind enough to add his polish to my expert's testimony.

—*Donna*

Chapter 1

Ryan Cooperman was fifteen going on thirty to life, and he was mine for the next couple of hours. I was just waiting for his mother to come out of my husband's office. He was trying to stare the skin off my nose.

Had he been a less formidable opponent, Muhammad Ali perhaps, I'd have told him "Stop it" forcefully enough to return the favor, but since this was the infamous Terror of Bryn Derwyn Academy, I chose to assert my authority in a more mature manner. I struck up a conversation about upholstery.

"Kind of worn," I remarked, rubbing my finger along a thinning edge of cording. We were seated on two blue sofas separated by a coffee table strewn with recent yearbooks. I had selected the furniture myself only two years ago, but the reception area of even a fledgling private school like Bryn Derwyn gets plenty of use.

"Maybe burgundy and light blue would look nice next time." A committee would probably redecorate now that the school had a larger community body, but that wasn't the point. The point was to show this surly mutt that he couldn't get to me.

Of course, it was possible that I simply knew too much about him; for example, why he had been expelled from his previous school.

Ryan Cooperman had stolen a pair of hundred-dollar running shoes from a kid who had saved months to buy them.

The proud owner, a track star who made the mistake of boasting about his purchase, had initialed the heels with big block letters; but that didn't deter Ryan, who simply unloaded his booty (for $20) on a runner from another school. Subsequently, the two track teams had a joint meet, the victim recognized his stolen property, and the new owner fingered our boy as the thief.

Ryan's only remark at his expulsion hearing: "The kid shouldn't have bragged."

I also knew that his Bryn Derwyn Academy application had been accompanied by three testimonials stressing his intelligence, young age, and willingness to learn from his mistake.

Unfortunately, the letters were true. Getting caught had taught Ryan to hurt others without incurring such a high price. Teachers were now insulted via double entendres, female classmates teased to tears. In and of themselves none of his many physical pranks merited expulsion; they simply earned him the title of Least Loved Student.

"What do you think?" I inquired mildly, referring to the upholstery.

The homely teenager sneered with exactly the deprecating superiority I had expected, so I countered with my Cheshire smile. Men, especially young men, hate that even more than they hate upholstery conversation, and this afternoon I would need any advantage I could manufacture.

For as soon as my husband finished talking to the boy's mother, Ryan and I would take a train into Philadelphia for a meeting with Federal Judge Gerald Rolfe. Rip regularly tapped Bryn Derwyn board members for their professional expertise—that was part of the deal—and when Ryan's latest questionable endeavor came to light (call it the second-to-last straw), Rip immediately thought of Gerry. A father of five boys as well as a hard-nosed proponent of justice, he was the ideal person to scare the hell out of an arrogant, self-involved erstwhile criminal.

The chore of escorting the teenage miscreant to his downtown appointment had fallen into my lap the usual way—I volunteered—but that didn't mean I was happy about it.

Married to the head of an understaffed, underendowed private school, I was dangerously susceptible to suggestion, especially when Rip got that crooked little wrinkle between his eyes, as he had last night at dinner.

"Why tomorrow," he groused, giving his mashed potatoes a wicked poke, "when everybody—and I mean *everybody*— is tied up with the midyear faculty meeting?"

"Any reason I can't take Ryan to Gerry's office?" I foolishly wondered out loud.

Rip's face had widened with endearing astonishment, but he tried not to sound too eager. "No reason at all. Can you spare the time?"

Unfortunately, we both knew I could.

So now it was Tuesday afternoon, the second day back to school after New Year's. Ryan and I were locked in a generational face-off, while Rip was busy correcting Mrs. Lawrence Cooperman's view of reality as it applied to her son.

Finally, the office door opened and a woman emerged. A winter-pale champagne blonde with no defining edges, Ryan's mother had chosen the stunned-speechless response to Rip's ultimatums when tears might have demonstrated a better grasp of the situation.

I did my best, her expression apologized to her son.

Not good enough, Ryan's tightly pressed lips complained. Glaring angrily, he deposited his book bag at her feet.

"We better get going," I remarked with a glance at my watch.

"After you," Ryan replied with a pseudocharming sweep of his hand.

I narrowed my eyes. Behind me the nimble teenager could duck out of sight in a second. Searching the school would cause us to miss our train and also Ryan's appointment with Judge Rolfe. To prevent this I crooked my arm around his bony elbow and aimed him toward the door.

We were Felix and Oscar, the oddest of couples, me a thirtysomething substitute authority figure with an acorn cap of nutmeg hair. I was dressed in leather boots, brown wool slacks, a fuzzy turtleneck, and an overcoat.

Ryan, my virtual opposite, wore an expensive, multicolor down jacket over the school-required khakis, white collared shirt, and emblemed green pullover. My height, about five foot six, he would never be considered a handsome boy—too much nose, too little chin, and a thick crop of woolly brown hair chopped into a wedge below his ears and bleached unevenly on the surface by both bottle and sun. He looked like an exotic, ungainly baby bird until he fixed you with those laserlike black eyes.

As I was not about to taxi him home after what was essentially a punishment, I told Mrs. Cooperman I would let her know where and when to meet our return train.

Her flicker of hesitation reminded me that she had a much younger daughter to care for, so I caved in and mentioned the local train station I knew to be more convenient for her than for me. At eleven and thirteen my own kids would be okay without me for a couple hours. They were also quite used to an erratic dinner schedule.

I jostled Ryan to get him moving. Left, right. Left, right. Joined as artificially as an usher and a wedding guest, we marched forward like two-thirds of a Three Stooges routine.

Loose on last-period errands, half a dozen other students paused to watch. I couldn't guarantee any were Ryan's friends, but they comprised an audience, so he smirked and wiggled his fingers good-bye over his shoulder. Three steps back mother dear tortured the strap of her Coach bag and bit her lip.

"Mrs. Barnes," she called just as we reached the door. She had extracted a twenty-dollar bill from the purse and now hurried to press it into my hand—for train fare.

Ryan snatched at the money, but I grabbed it back.

"Thank you," I told the boy's mother. The gesture had been an attempt to take some responsibility for her child, and I felt a pang of pity for the woman. No spine, this habitual screw-up for a son, and a husband too infatuated with his corporate success to care a fig about either of them. It was all in Ryan's file, not that the knowledge suggested any easy solution. If this afternoon's outing worked, anybody ever connected to Ryan would throw up his hat and cheer.

"That's very thoughtful of you," I added. "And please call me Ginger, or Gin." Ryan snorted at this, but his mother's features softened.

"Thanks," she said. "I'm Krystal."

I was mentally answering "Of course you are" when a sob and a ragged gasp of breath drew everyone's attention to the inner edge of the lobby. One of the teachers, Geraldine Trelawny, scurried by crying and biting her fist. She disappeared into the women faculty's rest room so swiftly we observers had to check each other for signs of a group hallucination.

Ryan Cooperman's eyes glinted with amusement over everyone else's concern. He actually laughed when I lifted his arm to hustle him along, and I began to gloat over the pleasure it was going to be to dump this kid at Gerry Rolfe's doorstep.

Outside, an unkind breeze stung my eyes and parted my hair with an icy comb. I dug gloves out of my pockets and put them on. Overhead a depressing roof of dirty dove-gray clouds promised an early twilight without the reprieve of snow.

My tan Subaru wagon waited in the school's front circle, so our walk was mercifully brief and silent.

"Seat belt," I reminded my charge before shutting him into the passenger seat. Even through the window I heard Ryan's derisive grunt.

His latest desperate bid for attention had been a departure from the usual peeing in somebody else's sneakers/tossing a cherry bomb onto the playground syndrome. It was a moneymaking scheme involving the Internet, not coincidentally the medium in which Daddy had made his bundle. A concerned eleventh grader confided to Rip that Ryan had been buying A papers from his fellow students for months. Five dollars cash. Any topic. The informant claimed that our young entrepreneur intended to sell these highly marketable documents via e-mail as soon as he owned a large enough selection.

Technically, Ryan would have been within his rights to resell material he legally owned; but since most of his customers would have tried to pass off the papers as their own, the morality of the scheme was a murkier matter—conspiracy to commit plagarism, perhaps. Ryan had learned how to get his forbidden cookies secondhand.

As I turned out of the school driveway, he fixed me with another, more curious stare. "You have kids, don't you?" he inquired.

"Yes," I answered. "Two."

"I bet they never get into any trouble," he goaded.

Not like you, I might have replied. Or just plain *no*, which would have been untrue but the safer answer. I suspected anything I said would be tailored into juicy gossip for Bryn Derwyn student consumption. But a couple years of sharing my husband's limelight had taught me that Rip's reputation would be much better off without the smear of Ryan Cooperman's fingerprints on it.

"Some," I replied ambiguously, accompanying the statement with an I'm-not-biting smile.

Ryan raised an eyebrow—and the ante.

"Boy? Girl?" he pressed, hoping to expose any exploitable weakness.

"Yes," I answered, which garnered a laugh.

"The girl as pretty as you?"

I ignored that trap.

My passenger pretended to scan the passing landscape, which consisted of large, elderly homes on mature, wooded lots. The town where Bryn Derwyn Academy was located offered a barren and boring facade in winter, but it never looked especially frivolous. Philadelphians, even the suburban ones, open their arms only to trusted friends. Individuality is protected inside exteriors that scrupulously conform. Such reserve preserves the luxury of choice, buys time to evaluate people, fads, anything new. Philadelphians are not cold so much as cautious, but if you stay long enough—you've arrived. I grew up on the wrong side of the river in a less pretentious, much more open environment, but even I have come to appreciate the wait-and-see approach.

The Radnor train station was on SEPTA's R5 run, formerly

the Pennsylvania Railroad's Main Line. If you're not a regular commuter, you park on either side of a long drive running out toward the turn off Matsonsford Road. Instructions insist that you park nose in to leave your license plate exposed. I briefly wondered why before I realized that the rule probably saved the police time searching for stolen vehicles or escapees of any sort.

Amazing. Half an hour with Ryan Cooperman and I was thinking like a cop.

After depositing three quarters in the parking meter, I hustled my charge through the chill down to the station, which was closed to ticket sales this late in the day.

We proceeded through an arched plaster and brick tunnel to the inbound track, crunching on rock salt meant to nullify the perpetual underground dampness. Brightened now by graffiti-style art, the tunnel remained a dungeon I'd never wish on either male or female after dark. Even periods of daylight felt uncomfortably isolated down there.

Ryan perceived my unease and grinned.

"So, you going to find out why Ms. Trelawny was crying, or what?" he inquired.

We had reached the train platform, and I turned and told him sharply, "That's none of our business."

Ryan smirked. "Maybe not mine. But you care about everybody, don't you? That's why you're here."

My blush was so sudden and hot that the wind on my cheeks felt good. Ryan the Kid had nicked me, and he knew it. I shut my mouth on what would have been too telling a denial.

Content with his victory, the teenager sat patiently at my side until just before the train was due.

I was thinking about how well metal benches conduct cold, musing on the rotten underside of the roof covering the far platform, or perhaps I was zoning out even more completely, because suddenly I became aware that Ryan was no longer beside me. He was twenty yards down the platform leaning over the track. Should the train have come through with him in that position, his entire potential would have been in his past.

"Ryan!" I called as I trotted toward him. "What are you doing?"

"Penny," he said, holding one up for my inspection. "If you put it on the rail, sometimes the train will flatten it. Looks really cool."

"Too bad," I said. "I'm not bringing you back here to find out if it worked."

"Oh, it works. Unless the vibrations shake it off first or somebody sees the penny and picks it up."

"That's swell," I said. "Forget it." I hooked his arm again and led him to a safe location behind the yellow line.

The train arrived, and we got on. I chose a seat that rode facing forward, one at the back edge of a wide oval window. When I had commuted to a downtown office job before our children were born, I discovered that only seats to the back of the oval offered you a view. Today I calculated that daydreaming out the window might save me from some of Ryan's boobytrapped conversation.

I paid the conductor and pocketed the receipts. Villanova Station came and went, and the few college students who boarded settled around the mostly empty car. Ryan observed them with bemused interest, then returned to peering at me.

"So do you work, or what?" he asked. The deep timbre of his voice was deceptively adult, even if the question was not.

"Certainly," I answered. I worked day and night, just not in a defined job.

"No," Ryan amended, reading my response for what it was. "I mean like in a career."

"I make hors d'oeuvres," I said instead, my favorite flip reply to what was essentially a prejudiced and rude line of questioning, especially coming from Ryan's orientation. He, and the others—mostly ignorant males—often sought to quantify my life in monetary terms. Relegating a non–wage earner to the bottom of their mental earnings graph allowed them to dismiss me before I wasted any more of their time.

"No, seriously," Ryan tried again. "What do you do?"

My mother's words came to mind. "You solve problems," she once remarked. "All day every day." She had done the same during my upbringing.

If Rip had had a less impossible job, I might have rejoined the commercial workforce, but running a school has been described as dancing with a bear. "You dance until the bear gets tired." Since Rip took on the struggling Bryn Derwyn Academy, my overriding goal had been to relieve my husband of anything I possibly could in order to allow for some sort of family life. However, this was nothing I saw myself sharing with a fifteen-year-old brat.

"What does your mother do?" I asked instead.

The boy's eyes narrowed. He was enjoying this. "Shops, I think. And whines."

And enables you, your father, and your sister to do everything you do, I wanted to retort. Even though Krystal Cooperman had struck me as a bit of a wimp, she clearly had the basics of maternal nurturing more than covered. If anything, her son seemed overindulged.

"Humph," I said. "Sounds like you ought to ask *her* that question sometime."

Ryan grunted with finality, and I finally got to daydream.

The rest of the Main Line backyards rumbled by, giving way to junk piled on scabby earth and desolate-looking buildings trimmed with either frozen laundry or industrial equipment. Welcome to Philadelphia's ugly edge.

The train wisely burrowed under it. Thirtieth Street Station led to Suburban Station and then Market East, our stop.

Most of the remaining passengers jostled through the doorways and down onto the platform. There they threaded through the waiting crowd and rejoined into two lines at the base of the nearest escalator and stairs. Others strode purposefully toward more distant stairs or even deeper into the building for exits more to their convenience. When I realized Ryan had left me again, my insides sickened, my mouth soured, and my skin became slick with sweat. My initial *He wouldn't!* response quickly became *He didn't. Did he?*

"Ryan! Where are you?" I shouted into the crowd, but this

time the teenager wasn't just twenty yards away. This time he was totally gone from sight.

Missing the appointment was no longer my primary worry. It was the city. Predators of all sorts spent their day hoping to snare strays, misfits like Ryan and me who didn't know what or who to avoid. Together we had the protection of purpose—a deadline and a destination. Wandering loose was another matter altogether.

I went up on tiptoe to scan faces. I scurried around clusters of moving people. I ran toward the next bank of stairs and back again. My purse weighed fifty pounds. My knees were made of pasta. My eyes burned and my head pounded. Where the hell was this kid?

"Ryan!" I called. "This isn't funny. Ryan! Come on. Where are you?"

In the space of two minutes the crowds thinned to a very few. Ryan Cooperman was nowhere among them.

Last I saw he had been behind me, but now I had to accept that he may have passed me without my noticing and taken the stairs. It didn't feel right, but the only place left to search was on the next level up. Yet my body didn't want to go, in part because my instincts said he was still on the platform.

A glimpse of bright cloth drew my attention to a wide post—Ryan's multicolor ski jacket. I wanted to collapse with relief; but as he was hiding from me, the battle was still on.

Hammering my boots loudly toward the bottom of the stairs, I shouted into the cavity, "Ryan Cooperman! Are you up there?" Ambient city noise deadened my voice before it reached the middle steps, but for my purposes that didn't matter.

Pivoting on my toes, I silently retraced my steps to the far side of the square, three-foot-wide post. Ryan was just turning to run when he smacked into me. His gleeful expression switched to shock. When breath returned to his lungs, he tried my name in a mollifying voice, but I reached out and pinched his earlobe between my fingers.

"Don't bother trying to suck up, you little worm," I said.

"You will never, and I mean never, do that to me again. Do you understand?"

"Oww," he complained. "Let me go. That hurts."

"Good," I said without releasing him. "Now I'm going to tell you what I think of you, Ryan Cooperman. You are a spoiled, very intelligent kid and you have no idea how lucky you are. Whole armies of adults are trying to stop you from destroying your life, but for some unfathomable reason you refuse to cooperate.

"Look at yourself. Listen to yourself. You're so angry at who-knows-what that you can't see what's really going on. You're in a nosedive here, and you're the only one who can pull you out of it.

"It won't be easy, but your mom, your dad, they'll get over whatever you do to yourself now. They'll move on because they'll have no choice, but at the rate you're going, you won't."

He had squirmed his shoulder around so he could stand more upright. As a result, he was probably even more uncomfortable, but I had his attention, and I had more to say.

"So, you will accompany me to the Federal Courthouse. You will keep your appointment, and you will not step one inch out of my sight until I turn you over to your mother back at Radnor Station, because if you do, I swear I will instruct my husband to find a way to make your school year—wherever you are—pure hell. If it means telling your father just how big a jerk you are, if it means getting a court order grounding you until the beginning of the next decade, I will see that it happens. Do you understand me?

"Do you?"

Ryan tried to nod without shifting his eyes from mine.

"Say it," I ordered.

"Say what?"

"Say that you won't leave my sight again."

"I won't leave your sight again." He said it singsong and whiny, but that was as much reassurance as I was going to get, so I let go of his ear.

"Jeez," he said. "I probably have a lawsuit."

"You would lose," I declared, not at all sure it was true. Still, I felt much better. I clapped the kid jovially on the shoulder.

"Let's go," I said. "We gotta hustle."

I steered him toward the exit up to the Galleries I and II, two attached urban malls stretching between Eighth and Eleventh on Market.

Eschewing the warmth of the indoor route for the speedier sidewalk, I guided Ryan up and out and away from City Hall. As we passed the Hard Rock Cafe, he pretended to try to go in; but I shot him a look so nasty he started to whistle and stroll in a silly circle around me.

For the rest of the way he entertained himself by gawping at the odd mixture of pedestrians, who ranged from your typical professionals to the quintessentially atypical professional bums.

When we reached the block of Market Street commanded by the Federal Courthouse, I automatically checked myself the way a driver who just spotted a police car glances at his speedometer. It seemed to me even the buildings stood up straighter, their windows scanning the wide brick sidewalk for strewn gum wrappers or passersby wearing furtive expressions. A row of trees growing out of tight squares of earth displayed NO STOPPING signs, "Temporary Police Regulation, City of Philadelphia." And yet two white squared-off police vehicles with light bars, blue trim, and door shields reading "Police/Federal Protective Service" waited at the curb.

Across the street a medium-blue banner pointed tourists toward Betsy Ross's house, Independence Hall, and Visitor Center Parking. Other "Historic Philadelphia" banners in red, white, and blue trimmed with four stars decorated the light poles. The United States Constitution, which guaranteed the right to a trial by jury, had been written a mere block away; and of the ninety-four federal courts currently in existence, I knew Philadelphia's to be one of the oldest, dating from 1789. Yet its housing was solidly modern—brick for the first floor, something darker and more austere for the second story and above.

Ryan apparently absorbed none of this, since he nearly walked right past.

"Hey," I alerted him. "We're here." And, thanks to all our rushing, we were early.

Entrance to the vast black marble lobby involved an airport-style metal-detecting arch and X-ray conveyor. Serious guards in serious clothing performed the expected duties. Ryan holstered a make-believe gun, and the black woman who had just cleared my purse rolled her eyes at me with what I determined to be sympathy.

"We have half an hour before his meeting with Judge Rolfe," I confided. "Is there an interesting trial we could sit in on until then?"

The woman reexamined Ryan with the detachment of a skilled professional. "We got a fraud just starting in 6-A," she decided.

"Perfect." I thanked her with a smile, but it wasn't returned.

Chapter 2

The hallway to Courtroom 6-A was empty of anything but the unrelenting angles of its long walls and infrequent doorways. In comparison, the railway station had been Club Med. Ryan and I traversed the hundred feet to the left indicated by a permanent sign with an arrow.

At the door opposite the courtroom entrance a female sentinel in a pink suit projected stern authority. Bleached hair puffed in the lingering style of a cliquey Philly neighborhood suggested an evening life quite different from her job. Hands at parade rest behind her severe suit jacket, she remained the only person in sight.

"Will we be intruding?" I asked, jerking a thumb toward the room where the fraud trial was being conducted.

"Nah, anybody's allowed in," she answered.

No sound could be heard coming from the courtroom. "You sure?" I pressed.

The blonde gave me a pitying frown. "It ain't like church. Youse can come and go."

I guess she perceived my trepidation as I braced to open the door, because her expression eased, and she added, "Anyhow, dey'se just startin'."

The room was smaller than the average church, with similar maple-colored paneling and intensely teal industrial carpet. After shrugging out of my coat, I slid into one of five long pews provided for spectators. Ryan seemed almost eager to join me, but whether that was due to genuine interest or his usual glee over someone else's misfortune I couldn't say.

"Yes, I was assigned to the case immediately after Officer Evans called us in," a menswear model answered into a microphone attached to the edge of the witness box.

The prosecuting Assistant U.S. Attorney, a spectacled man with dark hair going thin at the pate, nodded before asking his next question. "Agent Hoopes, please tell us how the FBI handled the investigation from there on."

"Certainly, Mr. Lloyd. First we visited the victim's house to take his statement."

The witness began to relate the victim's address, who was present during the complaint, and other details that meant nothing to me, so I took a moment to glance around the courtroom.

It looked like most of the stage sets I'd seen on TV with a few interesting additions, such as a large gold medallion set into the wall behind the expected Stars and Stripes. The jury sat in a raised section front right, and the judge was centered behind his even higher bench.

Also facing inward between the judge and the litigators' stations were two desks and a shared computer. I supposed the occupants to be the bailiff and the court stenographer.

The long left wall was trimmed with vertical strips of walnut and a portrait of some man. The high ceiling was covered by a gold grid that may or may not have been functional. The upper half of the walls were painted a soft off white and indented inward a foot on the left and as much as six feet over the jury's heads and above the audience. The architect's concept must have been to place odd-size blocks inside the confines of a larger box, but the result didn't seem worth the bother, unless the peculiar shaping had something to do with climate control.

At present Lloyd—Samuel Lloyd, if I remembered my local newsmakers correctly—stood at a microphone in front of his table where both the witness and the jury could most easily see him. The defendant and his attorney observed from the remaining table to the left.

The accused man, a soft-bodied senior with zinc white hair that included a short white beard, slouched in his brass-studded chair like marshmallows in a sack. Mostly I saw the side of his head; his face was obscured by the hand he held across his mouth and chin.

Something about his lawyer seemed familiar though. Just a little something, so I watched until the man reached farther sideways for the pitcher of water. Eric Allen. Jeez, I hadn't seen Eric Allen in years.

He'd been one of my husband's many high school chums. Those of us still living in the Philadelphia area had hung out as a group during the pretzel-and-beer years, the early early postcollege period when some of us were married and some were not.

I remembered Eric as sarcastic and cynical and very very funny. But I was newly in love, so I considered all of Rip's friends to be exceptionally clever.

Later I realized what they had in common was their prep school entrance exam, not money, as most outsiders automatically assumed. Immersed by then in the world of private education (literally living on a campus), I observed that how a student's tuition was paid—whether by check, installment plan, or financial aid—rarely meant much of anything to his peers. Once you were in, wit became your currency.

Off the playing fields, it was also the weapon of choice. Eric's humor ruthlessly preyed on the weaknesses of others. A hooked nose would spark a wicked can-opener comparison, an unexpected pregnancy half a dozen lewd one-liners. You laughed along with everyone else or risked the group's disdain. Taking yourself deadly seriously was a given, but showing it was not done. "A" types. Rip and I were acquainted with more than our share.

"So you took steps to determine that the rug Mr. Ignatowski bought was not as old as it was represented to be."

"Objection." Eric addressed the judge with the condescending tone of defense attorneys everywhere.

"Overruled. I'm sure Mr. Lloyd's next witnesses will clarify Agent Hoopes's statement. Am I correct, Mr. Lloyd?"

"Yes, Your Honor."

Eric pinched his lips, then threw up his hand in a "whatever" gesture. He wore a well-fitted gray-green suit that I knew would match his eyes. His tie, which he habitually stroked, would probably be thickly textured silk, although I couldn't swear to that at my distance. His wavy, medium-brown hair was stylishly perfect, his shoes shiny, his chunky watch masculine but not too butch.

The last I heard Eric had paid off his ex-wife with a house and a portfolio, left his center-city law firm, and joined another located in my suburban hometown of Ludwig. Had he adapted to the change in circumstances? Or had my old neighborhood welcomed him just as he was? I suppose even small-town rubes will join forces with a shark if life has taken a deep enough dive.

Meanwhile, the Ludwig connection made me wonder whether I knew the defendant. Since I hadn't recognized him, I looked for clues to his identity among my fellow onlookers.

To my immediate left sat a pear-shape retiree with no hair—not even eyebrows—wearing red suspenders over a white shirt. His companion had posed for the classic painting "American Gothic" in his younger years.

Two or three assorted adults gave off the diffident aspect of reporters.

One man in the back row wore a dark suit and a darker expression. Arms tightly crossed, his concentration on the speaker didn't lapse even when I twisted halfway around to stare at him. He had to be the wronged party, the victim of the fraud.

The only person left to scrutinize was a tiny woman positioned in the second row directly behind the defendant. She wore a plum-colored crepe dress and a matching sweater. Her hair had been hastily styled and appeared pinkish where her scalp showed through. Her back refused to rest against the pew, and her hands gnawed at each other like young cats on the verge of causing serious harm. The defendant's wife, of course.

Meanwhile, a few words the FBI agent spoke into the microphone got through to me like a hypodermic full of adrenaline. "Students," he said, followed by ". . . Philadelphia College of Textiles and Science."

Couldn't be, I argued with myself.

Could it?

Just then the defendant's wife turned her concern toward the jury, revealing enough of her face to confirm my fears.

I gasped, and Ryan Cooperman immediately asked, "What?"

I was too stunned not to answer.

"I know them," I said. "They're Birdie and Charlie Finnemeyer."

Ryan's inappropriate "Cool" reminded me who and where I was—and why.

My watch said five more minutes before the boy's showdown with Big Brother, so I slid along the bench a few feet to whisper a quick question to the suspender guy.

"What'd I miss?" I asked.

He showed no surprise at my question, but his wrinkles converged on each other in an expression of grave concern.

"This morning was just jury selection," he whispered, "which was inter-esting but not pertinent, if you know what I mean." I nodded, afraid to silence my most expedient source of information. "Then they had the cop that took the complaint." I nodded some more. I was close enough to notice the shine of spit on his lips and the smell of chocolate on his breath.

"Course, fraud of a certain dollar value bumps the crime up to federal status, so the cop called the FBI, and that's the guy we got talkin' now. You heard most of him."

I had and I hadn't, but I was certainly paying attention now. Unfortunately, there were about two minutes left before Judge Gerry would duck out for a cup of cocoa and forget all about the incipient computer criminal presently watching my every move.

I stuck out my hand for Suspenders to shake. "Ginger Barnes," I whispered earnestly. "I'll be right back."

"Jack Armstrong," he whispered congenially. "I'll be here."

I longed to inquire about the old man's connection to the

case and how he knew so much about law. Actually, I wanted him to hand me a synopsis tied up in ribbons explaining how my old baby-sitters had landed in this particular stew. The text would assure me just how Eric the Barb of Ludwig, Pennsylvania, intended to free the mild-mannered elderly professor, who would then be permitted to return to his wife and their reasonably comfortable and totally anonymous retirement.

Not too much to ask of a complete stranger.

Hadn't there once been a boxer named Jack Armstrong, *All-American Boy*? I knew the tag to be too ancient to refer to the man I just met, yet I tried to unearth the reference while Ryan and I waited for the elevator. Cartoon character? Myth? Movie legend? I was too young to get it right, but I liked the serendipity of it, allowed myself to smile until Ryan interrupted with another of his baited questions.

"So you knew the defendant in there, right?"

Technically, Birdie Finnemeyer had been my baby-sitter, the one my mother paid to look after me. But in reality her husband Charlie had become my playmate, my honorary "Uncle Wunk," my sweet-natured grown-up friend. For a certain period I had loved him nearly as much as I loved my father, until I evolved into a haughty eleven-year-old who demanded that she be allowed to baby-sit herself.

"Yes," I answered. "I knew him."

"He a relative or something?"

"No."

"Couldn't have been a friend."

"Why not?"

"Way too old."

I allowed my face to reveal what I thought of that remark. Ryan threw up his hands in surrender. "Okay, okay. But I'll tell you one thing."

"What?" I snapped as the elevator doors opened.

"He's in a shitload of trouble now."

Luckily one of the suits in the elevator said "Hey!" and the other said "Watch it, kid," because I was tempted to boot Ryan Cooperman where it would have done him some good.

*   *   *

Judge Gerald Rolfe nearly filled the doorway to his chambers. His expression made me gulp. Even Ryan held his ski jacket between his hands as if it were a hat.

"Judge Rolfe, Ryan Cooperman," I said, performing my primary function. "Ryan, this is Judge Rolfe."

The judge showed no sign of having eaten meatloaf at my all-purpose plank table. He seemed not to know me or even care to know me. He was Blind Justice. He was Ryan's executioner, or savior, or perhaps neither.

He glanced at his watch.

"Four-fifteen?" Gerry Rolfe was indicating that I should return for Ryan in half an hour.

"How about four-thirty?" I suggested.

Gerry's left eyebrow arched and his bulging brown eyes blinked. From my unexpected contradiction he discerned that Ryan Cooperman was a teenage miscreant of extraordinary scope. A future threat to society. An opportunity to prevent much misery and public expense.

The physically impressive judicant breathed a few gallons of air into his capacious lungs. "Very well," he said. "Four-thirty it is."

He arched an arm just above Ryan's shoulders and hooked him into his chambers without a touch. The door closed lightly in my face.

For a long moment I stood there willing prayerful energy to follow them into the room.

Then I sprinted back to the elevator and fidgeted all the way back to the sixth floor.

Chapter 3

After delivering Ryan Cooperman to Judge Rolfe's chambers, I rushed back to Courtroom 6-A and slipped into the pew beside my new acquaintance.

"Where's your friend?" I whispered into Jack Armstrong's ear while catching my breath. I referred to the other older man who had been observing the trial, the American Gothic look-alike.

"Huh? Oh, you mean Joe," Jack realized. We sat far enough from the action that our low voices couldn't be heard. "Place he lives serves supper four-thirty. He hadda get back."

Retirement-home schedule. My mother's older friends adhered to a similar routine. Although I couldn't ask, I wondered what was different about Jack's living arrangements that permitted him to stay. It was impossible to imagine him being younger than he looked.

Thinking of food had reminded me of the bite-size Hershey chocolates at the bottom of my purse. I nudged my companion and dropped three into his hand. For a minute we ate candy and silently smiled.

"So is Charlie Finnemeyer in big trouble, or what?" I whispered as soon as I could.

On the stand the FBI agent was still testifying in excruciating detail, something about canvassing the Finnemeyers' neighborhood. Apparently they no longer lived on Sixth Street in Ludwig, but then neither did I.

"You know 'im?" Jack asked, surprise multiplying the wrinkles on his brow.

"Used to be my baby-sitter," I abbreviated.

"No kiddin'." The candy had done it, we were buddies already, a club of two now that Joe was gone, brought all the closer because everyone else in the courtroom had come for reasons more legitimate than ours.

I remembered now that Gerry Rolfe once called regular spectators like Jack and Joe "roving jurors." They were retirees hooked on real-life drama, courtroom groupies who rarely missed a day.

"Yep. So what kind of trouble is he in?"

"Antique fraud. If you know the defendant, how come you don't know that, if you don't mind my askin'?"

I told him I hadn't needed a baby-sitter in a while.

Jack laughed. "Me either," he agreed, "but my niece threatens to get me one if I scare off any more of her boyfriends."

"Do you really?"

"Only the jerks."

I registered my alarm, and Charlie patted my hand.

"Not to worry. I own the house."

I released a sigh then tilted my head toward the proceedings. "Actually, I just wandered in here. Gave me quite a shock to see Charlie up there."

Jack rubbed his chin across his knuckles. "Guess so," he agreed, yet I was pleased to note an absence of any bias toward Charlie in the old man's attitude. This Jack Armstrong was no longer much of an All-American boy; but he appeared to be a kind and fair adult quite content to listen before forming any conclusion. No wonder he spent so much time here—the environment suited him.

"So what's Charlie's situation?" I asked again.

Jack pouted sympathetically. "So far we got him passing off an Oriental rug as an antique when it probably wasn't. That sound like your guy?"

That answer would require some thought, so I shrugged.

"Guess that's what we're here to find out," Jack concurred. We both turned our focus to the front of the courtroom.

Jack actually listened to the FBI guy's tedious testimony, but I continued to tune it out, preferring to revisit my childhood memories of Charles and Birdie Finnemeyer.

Most vivid was the vision of sunlit Saturday mornings prowling the yards of household sales, Charlie holding my hand in his big right paw and his even younger daughter's in the other. In and out of the milling crowds we wove, pausing occasionally while Uncle Wunk poked through a box of items waiting for the auction block.

There would be furniture, too, but this was of no interest to Charlie. As a professor at Philadelphia College of Textiles and Science, fabrics of any sort were his passion. Quilts and tapestries were favorite finds, but patterned rugs deserved close scrutiny, too. Lacy linens or old cross-stitch samplers also made his day. I learned later that he had a bit of a business going on the side reselling undervalued items he picked up at estate sales.

But when I was with him, I sensed no mercenary bent to Charlie's treasure hunts. Rather he was Peter Pan finding a useful bit of string, or a child on Easter morning searching for colored eggs. I caught his spirit of discovery and soon set off on my own explorations.

The kitchen of the soon-to-be-sold house almost invariably became the cashier's domain for the day. With steady traffic in and out all morning and afternoon, nobody bothered to stop a little girl from looking around the rest of the rapidly emptying house. Occasionally I overcame adults doing it, too, making comments like "This could be Rory's room," or "Not much closet space."

It wasn't until I was in my teens that I understood the loss behind those household sales, the death of the last elderly relative or the financial failure that precipitated the liquidation of every earthly possession until finally even the ground under our feet went to the highest bidder.

"And what did that portion of your investigation yield, Agent Hoopes?" the prosecutor asked into his microphone.

Two years younger, Karen Finnemeyer was her mother's child, a feminine, fussy kid who found our Saturday outings tedious. She was forever tugging on her father's pant leg begging for another brownie from the baked goods table or just plain nagging to go home.

And so it became only Charlie and me. I would wake up alert and eager every weekend, already smelling boiled hot dogs, damp earth, and old wood. I would find another patient girl with whom to play jacks or marbles while waiting for Charlie's best lot to come up, and if it was a good day there would be ice cream on the way home.

"So it is your contention, Agent Hoopes, that . . ."

Agent Hoopes's eyes were fixed on a newcomer to the courtroom, another physically fit, suited individual much like himself. Even in my reverie I had noted that he carelessly let the hall door slam shut behind him. Now he waited impatiently in the aisle at the end of the first empty pew.

"I'm sorry. What was the question?" Agent Hoopes asked the Assistant U.S. Attorney.

Prosecutor Lloyd repeated something, and I suppose the FBI man answered; but my attention, as that of most everyone in the room, belonged to the suited intruder who kept shifting his weight and twisting the button of his suitcoat.

Eventually the jury's turning heads forced the prosecutor to wonder what the distraction was. Immediately he announced, "I have no further questions for this witness," then excused himself. "Pardon me, Your Honor. May I have a moment with Agent Figurelli?"

"Really, Counselor. Are you sure this interruption is necessary?"

"Yes, sir. I believe it is."

"Very well," Judge Bjorn intoned with a heavy sigh. "The jury is dismissed. Mr. Hoopes, you may step down."

Everyone stood impatiently while the jury filed out. When at last they were gone, the judge reminded Lloyd to make it quick, and we all settled down to observe the exchange between the prosecutor and the newly arrived FBI agent.

Jack leaned toward me and whispered loudly, "Bjorn's as curious as anybody. Look at his face."

I preferred to watch Samuel Lloyd's expressions, which

were closer to me and more easily readable. Agent Hoopes, who had jointed his interviewer in the aisle, also faced my direction. The messenger spoke too quietly for anyone at our distance to hear, but I did catch both his listeners recoiling with shock, then exchanging a concurring glance.

"Would you care to share anything with the court?" Bjorn asked heavily into his microphone.

Lloyd did a couple goldfish gulps before walking back toward the open space in front of his table. He wasn't near his microphone, but the room wasn't so vast that Jack and I, sitting in the middle pew, couldn't hear perfectly well.

"Knowing how Your Honor feels about delays," the spokesman began, "the prosecution was very concerned about the absence of one of our first witnesses, a textile expert named Dr. Edward Stewart."

"Yes?" Bjorn goaded the obviously rattled prosecutor.

"My secretary phoned Stewart's home, uh, repeatedly, as well as the Philadelphia Museum of Art, where Dr. Stewart worked."

"Go on."

Lloyd was red-faced and sweating now, wiping his hands on his trousers. "So, so Agent Hoopes suggested we send Agent Figurelli to Stewart's apartment to see what was wrong. He, he wasn't there, sir."

Bjorn's sigh was amplified electronically. "And where *was* he, Counselor? I'm not overly fond of suspense."

"Yessir. He's in the morgue, sir. Stewart's landlord told Agent Figurelli that Dr. Stewart died suddenly last night after leaving a restaurant where he'd just had dinner."

"He died on the street?" the judge inquired with no effort to hide the distaste he had for that idea.

"No, sir. The police found him in his parked car."

Judge Bjorn took a moment to breathe. He was a square-faced Scandinavian, losing both flesh and hair to time, but still formidable looking and handsome for his age.

"He was your next witness, Mr. Lloyd?"

"Yes." Lloyd held perfectly still now, but for the clenching and unclenching of his hands.

"So you'll need some time to find a new expert and prepare him, I presume?"

"Yes, Your Honor."

"How long do you think you'll need?"

The Assistant U.S. Attorney stared at the carpet for a few moments while his fists found each other. "Three days should be enough, sir."

Bjorn's jaw was rolling from the stress on his teeth, but he lifted his gavel and replied, "Very well, Counselor. Court is adjourned until nine-thirty Monday morning. No later."

"Yessir."

Beside me Jack was gleeful. "I knew this was going to be a good one," he said.

I leaned away and gave him a scolding stare, and he had the grace to blush. Then he grabbed his jacket from under his seat, stood, and inquired, "See you Monday?"

"I don't know," I answered truthfully, but I would be there just the same.

Chapter 4

Like an old address book, twenty-five-year-old memories must be updated from time to time.

To me, my old baby-sitter was still perfectly round chocolate-chip cookies, which were to be nibbled rather than dunked and never consumed in quantities that ruined your dinner. Our former neighbor two doors down had gardened in a denim skirt, always drove a spotless, if inexpensive, car; never ate beef and disapproved of anyone who did. She was also fanatical about playing bridge, primarily because it was orderly and just. I remembered this because my mother refused to join the neighborhood club for exactly the same reasons, claiming that poker and hearts better reflected real life and anyway were much more fun.

The Finnemeyer family's pet had been a parakeet, blue. It singsonged "Birdie, Birdie, Birdie" all day; and Birdie—the woman—dutifully warbled back. At age eight this eerie echoing so disconcerted me that I scrupulously avoided the room that housed the bird's cage.

So naturally, as Birdie the Senior Citizen hurried toward me in the hallway outside Courtroom 6-A of the Philadelphia Federal Court, my mind warbled "Birdie, Birdie, Birdie." It was all I could do to plaster an appropriately concerned smile on my face.

The woman in question glanced around and said, "Where's Cynthia?"

To my amazement I now had six inches and twenty pounds on Birdie Finnemeyer, which made me feel like that cartoon character, Baby Huey, diaper and all.

However, I possessed the ability to form sentences. If I tried. What had she asked me? Oh—where my mother was. Birdie Finnemeyer assumed that Cynthia Struve and I had come to Charlie's trial together—on purpose.

"I, um, she . . . My mother isn't here. I came by myself." If you didn't count Ryan Cooperman.

Birdie's powder-blue eyes blinked behind rimless glasses. She wore no makeup, which was probably best. Makeup tends to collect in crevasses.

"Charlie is innocent, of course," she said pugnaciously.

"Of course," I agreed.

Up close Mrs. Finnemeyer's scalp was even pinker, her hair a fine gauze scarcely masking her skull. I flinched to see this because I'd rather not visualize anyone as skin over a skeleton. Nobody should look quite that defenseless, not even with good reason.

However, Birdie's most vulnerable spot stood seven feet away, a heavy-looking large canvas bag tilting him to the left. His gaze refracted off me but was drawn mothlike to his wife. Charlie Finnemeyer simply wanted to go home—preferably forever.

Part of me longed to gush "Uncle Wunk, it's me, your little Ginger Snap!" because clearly he had no clue. After all, I did have six inches and twenty pounds on his wife, which certainly had not been the case twenty-five years ago. I refrained. The canvas bag seemed to be the least of the man's burdens just now.

Responding instinctively to Charlie's needs, Birdie touched my arm with a heavily ringed hand. "Thanks for coming, Ginny," she said. "Not many from the old neighborhood would have bothered."

No one from there or anywhere else, as near as I could tell, although I had no intention of pointing that out.

My name was another matter, a self-image issue similar to Birdie's perfectly round cookies.

"How about calling me Gin?" I suggested, and when my former baby-sitter's eyes popped, I added, "All grown up now" with a little shrug.

What happened next was your classic gut-wrench. Birdie Finnemeyer looked me squarely in the eye, allowing for a penetrating, one-hundred-percent woman-to-woman connection. For an instant I was privy to her terror, the onerous demands Charlie's situation put on her, and all the pressure and self-doubt their role reversals had engendered. Back when my mother and I knew this small, superfeminine woman best, she had always been the pampered one. Now those days were gone, and the Birdie Finnemeyer of today could scarcely cope. Plus I thought I detected something that hadn't been there the moment before. A sadness, perhaps.

"Gin, of course." The fragile old woman ran a hand down my cheek and blinked to forestall the spillover of tears. "Please give my regards to your mother."

That was it. She knew. Cynthia's absence meant I wasn't there for them, and the realization had rendered Birdie and her husband even more alone, isolated, and friendless than they had been before I showed up. Even worse, there was nothing I could possibly say to repair the damage.

Huhph, my breath squooshed off my tightened diaphragm.

"Gin?" another voice inquired. "Gin Barnes?"

Eric Allen approached as I watched Charlie and Birdie take the last two spots in the down elevator.

"Do you know my client?" Rip's estranged prep school friend wanted to know. Beside us, only a few people who seemed to work in the building remained, and they were farther down the hall.

"Uh, um, yes," I answered. "How've you been, Eric? Long time."

"Yes, right," he agreed. "Rip okay? The kids?"

"All fine. And you?"

He sighed and relaxed against the wall, accepting what wasn't really an oblique criticism of his manners at all. My first order of business every evening was to unclench the fist

Rip had become during his workday, so instinctively I had done the same for Eric.

"Can't complain," he said to end the subject, but his attention was wholly on me now and his muscles at ease.

"So who's Charlie Finnemeyer to you?" my inquisitor asked again.

I laughed, knowing how silly my connection to the defendant would sound to his lawyer. "He and Birdie used to baby-sit for me."

"For your kids?"

"No. For *me*."

Eric's crooked smile transformed his face into something almost kissable—to somebody else, of course. I was immune. Or maybe I was just rabidly loyal to my husband, which amounted to the same thing.

However, that didn't mean I didn't enjoy the warm humor emanating from Eric's beautifully lashed sun-on-the-sea green eyes, which, by the way, did match his suit. The tie lacked the expected texture, however; it was a blah taupe and green stripe.

"But you must have kept up. I mean, you're here."

"My mother may have," if only via Christmas cards. In the grand tapestry of Cynthia Struve's life, anyone she ever met remained a securely connected thread waiting to be woven back in.

I explained why I was in the courthouse and how I happened to observe Charlie's case.

"Figures, I guess," Eric remarked. "We're the most interesting trial in the building right now."

"Has it been in the paper?"

The lawyer shook his head. "It's a relatively small case. They'll probably pick it up when there's more to say." Thank goodness for small favors.

"You here often?" I wondered.

"Not very. You don't stumble across that many federal crimes in Ludwig, so I was delighted to get Charlie's case. Makes a change from burglary and murder, which I guess you know are tried locally."

I winced because I did know. A famous friend of mine had recently been murdered in Ludwig—in my best friend's guest room, to be exact.

"Rough world out there," I commented.

Eric tilted his head and shrugged his eyebrows. "Pays my bills."

Our conversation reminded me of the textile expert whose death had delayed Charlie's trial, so I asked whether the change in witnesses would inconvenience him very much.

"It could," the lawyer admitted. "I had something on Dr. Stewart that would have helped Charlie, an old gripe that suggested Stewart might have wanted to bring him down for personal reasons."

"Oh?"

"When Ned Stewart had his first job at a museum out in Pittsburgh, Charlie exposed an item Ned wanted very badly as a fake. They had a huge disagreement over it and have been professional rivals ever since." He wagged his head with chagrin. "I doubt we'll get that lucky with the next expert."

"Too bad," I sympathized.

"These things happen." Allen dismissed his disappointment with a sigh, then looked me in the eye. "I don't suppose you know what was behind Charlie's early retirement."

"Not really. Why do you need to know?"

The defense attorney stared down the length of the hall. "Instinct," he said. "Plus a couple of the prosecution's witnesses are from his last year's graduating class."

Evidently, that was all the explanation I was going to get, yet I found myself trusting Eric's judicial sixth sense. Experience usually promoted a built-in warning system, and successful people invariably learned to heed it.

"Charlie won't tell you?"

Eric shook his head. "He's got emphysema, you know. Conserves his breath." At least that explained the bag; it must have contained an emergency oxygen rig.

"But you're his lawyer," I complained. "Are you saying he doesn't talk to you?"

"Oh, I got the basics before I took the case. Not guilty,

yada, yada, yada. But since then . . . He likes to joke that he's paying me to speak for both of us."

"But that's . . ."

"Foolish?"

"I was thinking scary; but yes, it seems stupid, too." Then I began to wonder. "Are you planning to put Charlie on the stand?"

Eric wagged his head. "The day I asked, he got so pissed that he actually looked dangerous."

"Pride?" I speculated, thinking how self-conscious many older people become over their infirmities.

"That's a little simplistic." The lawyer's gaze told me not to press it, that I was wandering into privileged territory.

"What about Birdie?" I asked instead. "Did you ask her about the retirement?"

"Of course. She claimed it had no relevance to the trial; but if Charlie didn't want to talk about it, she wouldn't either. A regular pair of bookends, those two."

"I guess I could ask my mother."

Eric handed me a card from the leather case in his pocket. It had embossed gold lettering on thick white stock and included his business address in Ludwig and two office numbers.

"What if the retirement information is detrimental to the case?" I wondered aloud.

"Better to know and be prepared with a defense. Never good to get ambushed."

I accepted the logic of that. Anyway, a brief conversation with my mother was the least I could do to help the Finnemeyers, who had done far more for me. Also, Mom and I were attending an art class together on Tuesday evenings, so I could take care of the chore tonight.

"Oh, wait a minute." Eric forestalled me. "Maybe you can help with one more thing." He rummaged around in his briefcase until he came up with a sheet of paper.

"See if you recognize that eighth name, the circled one. The Finnemeyers can't remember him."

Ignoring my skeptical glance, he handed me a photocopy of a typed list that had apparently originated in his opponent's

office. I hastily perused the page, looking for a hint to the
identity of the circled "Oscar Tribordella."

"No, sorry," I had to admit. "I think I would recognize that
name if I'd heard it before."

Disappointment aged Eric's face. "Would you mind running that by your mother, too? I'm having a hell of a time
finding out who he is."

"These are all government witnesses?" I surmised, and my
companion nodded glumly.

Why, I wondered, would the Finnemeyers handicap Charlie's primary advocate by withholding facts he obviously
needed? They had to realize that their silence made Charlie
look guilty. Eric's discouraged expression seemed to concur.

A glance at my watch prompted me to summon the elevator. I needed to go collect my date for the afternoon, but
first I hoped to coax a smile out of Eric Allen.

"We used to have fun, didn't we?" I remarked, alluding to
our not-yet-forgotten salad years.

The resulting laugh was short and the smile halfhearted.

"You had fun," he said. "I had Carol."

Judge Rolfe was eager to see the back of Ryan Cooperman.
The door opened immediately after my knock, and the large
man himself stared down at me. I thought I saw dismay hastily
obscured by anger, but maybe I misinterpreted the wide-eyed
blink just before the scowl. No ambiguity, however, in that
scowl.

"Mrs. Barnes," Gerry intoned formally.

"Judge Rolfe," I greeted him back.

"Ryan all set to go?" I inquired politely.

"Quite."

"Ryan?" I stuck my head into the room and crooked my
finger at the teenager, who was lounging against the arm of a
striped, overstuffed chair. "Got a train to catch," I added just
to soften the atmosphere. I'm a headmaster's wife; I know all
sorts of social stuff like that.

"Thank you," I told Gerry after Ryan stepped into the hall.

The judge made a noise low in his throat. He seemed irked

that he couldn't put Ryan Cooperman away for a few years—
at least not yet. But then Gerry always has been a little impatient. I thought it best to escort Ryan out of the building
without delay.

Only 4:30 P.M., but headlights and streetlights illuminated
Market Street, and falling dew chilled the city. As Ryan and
I threaded our way through the early escapees back toward
the train station, the kid stuffed his hands in his jacket pockets
and actually bounced along the sidewalk, an overt manifesta-
tion of resilience if ever I saw one.

Of course, my asking him anything about his meeting
would have been improper; but it was also unnecessary. The
teenager's sneering smile told me (a) he still considered himself superior to adults, so (b) everything Judge Rolfe threatened had rolled off him like water off a duck.

Ryan pretended the curb was a balancing beam. "Did you
know it's wrong to lie?" he remarked as if this was fascinating
news.

I said nothing.

"Stealing's not so good, either," he added as he slapped the
side of a red, white, and blue mailbox.

I frowned to indicate that I was not amused.

"Actually, you were better," Ryan remarked.

I cast him a surprised look, and his eyebrows raised to
emphasize his sincerity.

Could I possibly have stuck this boy with so many unfa-
vorable labels that I obviated any possibility of rapport? I did
honestly believe that in certain circumstances advice emanating from the parental trenches just might equal or even exceed
that of a man who spent most of his time sitting on a pedestal;
and Ryan's acknowledgment of this sentiment had been so
perceptive, so in tune with my own thinking, that I couldn't
help but view him from a fresh angle. For the first time I
smiled as if I liked him, and in response his eyes twinkled and
his lips twitched.

And then I felt the tug on my leg, so to speak. Ryan's face
continued spreading into a large "Gotcha" grin that sent my
embarrassment indicator into the danger zone. Rushing blood

sounded sirens in my ears. Flames licked my neck and cheeks. My palms became slick, and my heart hammered.

With me less than an hour and not only had this kid found where I kept my pride, he successfully exposed my hideout. Having him in class for a year would be the Chinese water torture, being responsible for his discipline the headache of the century. I could scarcely suppress a Gerry Rolfe growl.

Phoning Ryan's mother from one of the stainless-steel cubbyholes in the train station accomplished much more than alerting Krystal Cooperman to our E.T.A.; it helped to save my sanity.

Checking in with my own kids completed the process. They were squabbling over the remote control; they were fine. I asked Chelsea to start heating a casserole I'd frozen a month ago. Then, as I hung up, I blessed my offsprings' apparent normalcy and my husband's professional contribution toward that elusive goal.

Centered again, I rejoined the delinquent of the day. Seven minutes later we boarded our westbound train.

Bored by my silence, or by the disinterest of the wool-clad commuters reading their vertically folded newspapers, or by life in general, Ryan Cooperman decided to speak to the first fellow train passenger foolish enough to meet his eyes. She was an Asian college student, riding in the opposite aisle seat one row back from us, and she accidentally looked up as she turned the page of her calculus textbook.

Ryan jerked his thumb in my direction and loudly announced, "Her old baby-sitter's on trial for fraud."

I'm not proud of it, but I folded my arms and snapped, "Shut up," into Ryan's laughing face.

The Asian woman and a few others eyed me with dismay.

Chapter 5

When I arrived home, the porch light was shining. The dog danced for his ear scratch, my husband came out of the kitchen and gave me a kiss, and all my body parts hummed with pleasure.

"How'd it go?" Rip inquired with a worried expression. He had loosened his tie and tucked the end safely between two of his shirt buttons. Salad tongs dangled from his right thumb.

I made a face because words failed me.

"That bad?" Dismay made my husband's eyebrows meet the hunk of dark hair that hung over his forehead. "You better tell me the worst."

"Gerry grunted," I said.

Rip thought about that. "Usually he winks."

"No wink. Only a grunt."

"What about Ryan?"

"Oh, I'd say he really enjoyed himself."

"How so?"

I consulted the ceiling. "He smiled. He bounced. He gave me a hard time."

Rip looked ready to rip the kid's head off, so I assured him I had already dealt with Ryan's disrespect.

Not yet ready to be mollified, Rip scowled as he carried the salad around from our narrow kitchen into the eating end of our living room.

I washed my hands and got out the bread and butter. The

casserole waited patiently in the oven, which was the reason I used the recipe so often. Four people, four schedules.

"Dinner!" I called toward the kids' bedrooms and the added-on family room. The TV immediately went silent and sneakers hammered down the hallway. Garry, our eleven-year-old, hadn't yet grown into his feet. I had hopes of him carrying off his dad's dark-haired good looks, if he ever outgrew this elbows-and-knees stage.

Chelsea, our thirteen-year-old, arrived with catlike silence and grace. Today she managed to make a Norfolk Tomcats sweatshirt my quarterback cousin-in-law had sent look like high fashion. As always I marveled at our few similarities—the nutmeg-red hair, skin that mercifully tanned, very dark brown eyes. Yet my daughter wasn't really like me at all. Her time slot was far more sophisticated—and better informed—than mine would ever be.

I kissed each of my children as if they were younger and accepted their sneers as my due. Rip retrieved the casserole, and the evening meeting of the Barnes clan was officially in session.

This being only the second day back to school after New Year's, the kids still had lots of gossip about what their friends did over Christmas vacation.

"Corbett Owens's mom and dad let him have an overnight New Year's party—with girls!" Garry told us with astonishment bordering on awe. "Jenny Hinkle said they let them taste champagne, too."

Rip and I exchanged a concurring glance over that. I knew he objected most to the message; I objected most to the risk. Should any of those eleven-year-olds happen to be hereditary alcoholics, suddenly what was meant to be a sneak peek into adulthood became a lifelong battle with a horrifying disease. And if the stupidity of taking that risk wasn't deterrent enough, the drinking laws in Pennsylvania should have been. Rip often dealt with the fallout from those expensive escapades.

Chelsea clinked a fingernail against Rip's glass of red wine. "How do you explain this?" she asked, after I had expressed my opinion of the Owenses' folly.

I answered her earnestly. "He's over twenty-one, and he's not driving anywhere. You'll notice I'm not having any wine because I am going out."

Rip pointed with his fork. "When you're an adult, you're expected to make responsible decisions. Before that, rules are supposed to keep you from ending up like Ryan Cooperman." He eyed me with meaning and shook his head.

Both kids perked up, anticipating another fascinating installment of the Ryan Cooperman saga. Ordinarily Rip figured the more our kids knew about the trouble Ryan brought onto himself, the less likely they would be to emulate it.

Chelsea had actually met Rip's nemesis at a Bryn Derwyn basketball game and wrote him off as the current equivalent of a "nerd." Garry, our gangster-movie aficionado, followed our favorite delinquent's escapades with another sort of interest. What sort was still in need of clarification.

All things considered, I preferred talking about something else. "Any idea why Geraldine Trelawny was crying this afternoon?" I asked Rip.

"No. Was she?"

I nodded. "Sobbing."

Rip filed that one away for future reference.

"What happened with Ryan today?" Garry pressed. All he knew about women crying was that ignorance was bliss.

"I took him downtown to see Judge Rolfe, but I didn't stay in the room with them," I told my son honestly, "so I really don't know how it went.

"But one interesting thing did happen," I said, simultaneously changing the subject and aiming my remarks at Rip. "We were early, so we sat in on part of a trial." I cut another bite of chicken before I decided I didn't want it. "Turns out I know the defendant and we both know his attorney."

"Oh? Who?"

"Eric Allen's representing Charlie Finnemeyer, the professor from my old neighborhood."

My husband stared at me wide-eyed. "Eric! Wow, it's been what, eight, ten years? How is the old boy?"

"Fine, I think. A little bitter over Carol."

Rip snorted.

"Can I go do homework?" Chelsea asked, an obvious ploy to escape our boring reminiscences.

"Me, too?" Garry echoed.

"Sure," I replied before I remembered there were dishes to do.

Yet as soon as the kids were gone, I realized I had been given the exclusive attention of an attractive man and a degree of privacy. The dishes could wait.

"So what else did Eric say?" Rip inquired.

I rested my chin on my hand and admired my mate. "He asked me to ask my mom what went on when Charlie retired from Textile."

Rip made a chucking noise in his cheek. "Poor chump."

So much for my mellow mood. "What do you mean?"

"Just that Eric probably didn't know he was asking Amelia Earhart whether she'd ever been up in a plane."

"What?"

". . . inviting Ginger Rogers to a dance?"

"Excuse me?"

"How about offering little Dale Evans a pony ride?"

"Robert Ripley Barnes, what the hell are you talking about?"

"You love that stuff."

"What *stuff*?"

"Helping people out of jams, Gin. Admit it. You can't keep your hands off a problem."

"Well . . ." I was stuck for a reply. Was my husband complimenting me or pointing out a character flaw?

"Don't look so worried. I'm actually learning to trust your judgment."

"You are?"

"Sure. I can't remember the last time you hid in the bushes with a camera."

"I've never done that."

"Right. And I trust you never will."

"Um . . ."

Rip was on a roll. "Also, I haven't seen your ratty old trench coat in years."

"It was worn out. I gave it to Goodwill."

Rip threw up his hands. "I rest my case."

I sorely needed a hint about how to react to this conversation. A smile, a twitch, a concerned frown would do. But my husband the headmaster remained inscrutable.

"By any chance are you mocking me?" I finally asked.

Rip's face expressed innocent surprise before settling into a more honest grin. "Teasing you a little, that's all," he admitted.

My own expression softened. "Seriously. Do you mind my getting involved?" And if he did, where would he like me to draw the line? Should I only help relatives? Immediate family? Extended family? Would Charlie and Birdie Finnemeyer make it onto his list?

Rip sipped some coffee before answering no. "If you took stupid risks, that would be different. But get involved? Have you ever stopped to think what I do all day?"

My eyes widened to accommodate this new insight. I was suddenly viewing my mate from another perspective, this one a little more evenly eye to eye.

"So what mire have you waded into this time?" Rip asked. "Nothing that requires a SWAT team, I hope."

I stood up and began to clear the table. "I'm just supposed to ask Cynthia that one question."

"Um-hmm," Rip murmured. "Famous last words."

After we finished clearing the table, Rip gave me a pathetic look and pleaded, "Weather Channel?"

"Go on," I said. "Git."

As tonight was cloudy and near freezing, I understood why he was anxious for the forecast. Any possibility of overnight snow meant he had to get up at five A.M. to determine whether to close school. Several hundred people would be affected by his decision.

I waved him off to his color-blotched maps and new age music, and continued to scrape and load dishes while my mind wandered. Rip's allusions to my participation in a few police investigations had set my thoughts on a cynical course.

What if Charlie's rival, the textile expert whose death had delayed the trial, really had had the goods on him? *Somebody* must have artificially aged that rug, and Charlie, who was an expert himself, certainly knew it. If the prosecution could produce a witness to swear that he misrepresented the rug to his buyer, that was fraud plain and simple. And if that was the case, what would a decades-old spat with the testifying expert matter to the jury?

After art class, I would listen to the late news, maybe check the obituary page in the morning. Knowing a little more about how Dr. Stewart died might be useful, especially since Charlie and Birdie left the courthouse this afternoon just as freely as anyone else. Obviously the judge trusted a seventy-one-year-old man with emphysema not to skip town, but unfortunately that also meant Charlie was out and about when Ned Stewart, his rival and opponent, conveniently died of a heart attack. Sooner or later someone in an official capacity would think of that.

I scowled at the clock. The death happened last night about this time. I shook my head, sorry I couldn't bring myself to be as trusting as that judge. If he could do it . . .

The clock! Oil painting class. It was held in the high school just around the corner from my mother's apartment, but I needed twenty-five minutes to get there, and I had fifteen.

Still, getting there would be easy compared to the challenges that remained: telling Cynthia Struve that one of her flock was in trouble, then trying to keep her out of it.

Chapter 6

"Vee ur vury late!" Mme. Mimi remarked as I set my canvas on the easel next to Mother's and shrugged my coat onto the pile beside us.

"Sorry," I apologized. "Long story."

Setting up for our oil painting class involved two trips in from my car: one carrying Mother's and my paint kits while she delicately carried her wet painting, another to bring in my own sixteen-by-twenty work-in-progress.

To keep them clean, I had left my gloves in my pocket, so now my fingers were frozen carrots and my nose a dripping radish. Mme. Mimi glanced at me as if she wanted to swipe at me with a tissue. I hastily saved her the temptation.

Since each of us had written "Mary Gothwald" on our checks to pay for class, we all recognized the "madame" as a kooky affectation. Our "Mimi's" fluffy, dark-blond hair floated around in independent clumps like dandelion tufts about to take off. She wore voluminous tops over peggy tights in outlandish colors, suggestive of a spinning top. Also, she was short, four eleven maybe, so making me feel childish with my wet nose had been a stretch.

The easels were a village of tipis sandwiched between two long, scarred tables. The eleven more punctual students leaned forward on their stools to smile at Mother and me while our instructor pinched her forehead and scowled at the floor.

"Where was I?" she inquired of a nearby student in ordinary South Jersey English.

Standing at the far end of the cluster, she resumed her ten-minute lecture on painting, tonight something about visual movement. I had difficulty catching on, since she had been eight minutes into the subject when Mother and I arrived.

Disappointing. Mary's brief lectures were spoonfuls of wisdom and possibly the most lasting aspect of the class. Certainly neither Mother nor I would become proficient artists, nor did a weekly glance around the room suggest that we were alone.

Mimi concluded with a clap. "Ookay," she told us. "Proceed weeve your verk." By day, I supposed that the phony accent helped her high school students focus on a subject few of them took to naturally. By night, her poses merely added to the fun.

I brought out my tablet of paper palettes and reached for my tube of white. No matter what, you always needed white.

Mother was smoothing a page from a magazine onto the table behind her. "Got something to tell you," I remarked to secure her attention.

"Umph?" she grunted encouragingly. For her class project she was taking liberties with a cigarette ad depicting clean air and open spaces. I was copying a Monet out of a library book. Mme. Mimi not only endorsed this approach, she had suggested it, claiming that anything we attempted would teach us something, so why not emulate a master?

I scrubbed a blob of cerulean blue into some of the white. "Remember Birdie and Charlie Finnemeyer?" I asked the sweetly eccentric woman who raised me.

"Of course, dear."

My prototype was a smaller, softer woman with sugar-cookie hair and sparrow eyes behind rose-colored glasses. Presently her chin jutted out the better to focus her bifocals. "What made you think of them?"

"I saw them today."

"Oh? Where?" She dabbed a brush at her canvas, then tilted her head to reconsider.

"Federal court." Mother was too preoccupied scraping off the dab to react.

"What are they doing now?" she inquired mildly.

"Waiting for the outcome of Charlie's trial, I guess." That wasn't how I had planned to reveal the Finnemeyers' predicament, but that was how it came out.

"What!"

I stopped mushing blue and white together long enough to explain about the rug and the irate buyer, about Eric Allen and the FBI. To forestall my mother's hopping onto a train first thing in the morning, I took pains to mention that the trial had been recessed until Monday; however, I did not say why. Cynthia reads my mind a little too often, and I didn't want her picking up on that imaginary scenario I'd devised less than an hour ago, the one in which an elderly, far-from-robust Charlie Finnemeyer wandered about committing murder.

Neither did I tell her the reason I happened to be in federal court in the first place. With Mother you only dared talk about one thing at a time.

Her nose lifted in a wrinkle of concentration as she squirted two different greens onto her own palette. Then she set everything down and folded her hands on her lap.

"The Finnemeyers always were a little different," she mused.

"How so?" To forward the impression of casual interest, I continued fussing with my paints.

"Charlie was all energy and sunshine while Birdie was sooo uptight. He was wildly creative, and she was his perfect little pet rock. Their daughter favored the mother, unfortunately. Boring kid."

"Karen hated me."

"I'm not surprised."

"Do you think Charlie could be guilty?"

Mother held her paintbrush ear height between two fingers. "Of faking an antique? Sure. He was very passionate about teaching. He'd do anything to help his students learn, whether the administration liked it or not."

I amended my question. "But can you see him passing off a fake as real? For money?"

Cynthia scowled until her glasses slipped down her nose. She pushed them back and repositioned her bottom and thought some more.

"No," she said finally. "Positively not."

I wasn't satisfied. "But what if the customer was some arrogant Philistine he didn't like? Is there any chance that Charlie would sit back and quietly let the jerk defraud himself?"

"Oh, I see what you mean." Mother nodded. "Not black or white, but gray." Mme. Mimi had wandered past but returned at the mention of a pertinent word.

"What's gray?" she asked.

Mom chuckled. "Not what you think, dear. *Gray area*. A friend of ours is on trial for antique fraud."

Mary Gothwald dropped all pretence and gawped.

Cynthia waved away our teacher's shock. "Don't worry. Eric is going to get him off." Obviously "gray" was a difficult concept for my mother.

Mme. Mimi moved along the line, even stared briefly at one of her student's works; but I caught her glancing back at Cynthia and me.

Temporarily, Mother's paintbrush had become a mustache supported by her pout. Now she twirled it like Groucho Marx's cigar. "You're asking if the buyer wanted to be fooled, would Charlie set him straight?" Mom thoughtfully poked the brush into a blob of brown.

"I don't know," she answered. "Charlie never cared much for fools. I like to think that's why you two got along. Shame he didn't get on that well with his own daughter." She wiggled some paint across an inch of canvas while I thought about Karen Finnemeyer Smith.

Married, four kids. Living in New Jersey. I wondered why she hadn't been at the trial. Then it occurred to me to wonder why I hadn't wondered before. Freudian probably.

Mother and I turned our concentration to painting and Freud. I had read somewhere that the father of psychiatry admitted that he could never figure out what women really wanted. "And he never asked his wife," I added with a tsk.

"I could have told him," the sage of Ludwig, Pennsylvania, remarked. She was squinting through the bottom of her glasses again.

I pretended to misunderstand. "Are you saying you know what women wanted in 1880?"

"Certainly, dear," Mother replied.

I had to ask.

"Why, comfortable undergarments and help with the dishes, of course."

Ah, my mother. The woman who can't cook, balance a checkbook, or, from the looks of it, paint. She did have her moments.

"What about now?" I prodded, lusting for more wisdom.

"You tell me."

"Okay," I said, accepting the challenge. "Comfortable undergarments, stock options, and—all together now—*help with the dishes.*"

We shared a giggle and went back to work. Mme. Mimi didn't return to comment on our progress in faux French or any other language. And I didn't remember to ask about the circumstances of Charlie Finnemeyer's early retirement until it was time to pack up.

Cynthia clicked her paint box shut. "Charlie refused to tell Eric himself?"

"Yes," I admitted. "That's one of the reasons Eric wants to know what happened."

"Humph," Mother mused. "Charlie's about seventy-one now. Retired eight years ago. At least two years early—that's all I know. Maybe they'll tell us tomorrow when we visit."

Visit? Had I agreed to that?

More to the point, did I want to waste time protesting, knowing what the outcome would be?

"You make the call," I capitulated. "And say we'd like to come early, please. I've got things to do tomorrow." My intention was to save my mother some taxi fare, of course; but since I was going to be there, maybe I could try to mend the hole I'd torn in Birdie's pride.

Mother waited in the car with the engine running while I went back to collect my painting.

Mme. Mimi must have felt guilty that she hadn't offered much personal instruction to either Mother or me, because when I returned to the classroom she stood in front of my canvas like a 4-H judge intensely evaluating a cow.

My selection depicted early morning on the Seine, one of several scenes Claude Monet had painted sitting in a rowboat. The shores were thick with shadowy trees dipping down to the water, and pale-yellow sunrise reflected off the river's ripples. My library book's photograph of the museum piece made it look as romantically appealing as most of the Impressionist paintings I've seen, but that wasn't why I chose it for a classroom project. I thought the blurry green and yellow blobs might be easy to copy.

"It's really getting there, Gin," she remarked. "I'm starting to see the edges of the shore."

"Really?" I hadn't noticed that myself.

"Oh, yes. Right here." She traced a crooked line in the air in front of my canvas. Then she beamed at me proudly, as if I actually might have learned something under her tutelage.

But what was this? Stern creases suddenly marred her brow. A manicured finger wagged.

"Just make sure you don't sign it 'Monet,' " she teased, "or we'll *both* be in trouble."

Chapter 7

An unfamiliar Jaguar was parked in our driveway when I got home, making me instantly wary. I shoved my driver's door shut with a satisfying *thunk* and forgot all about my art gear in the back. Nine-thirty on a Tuesday night! What could anybody possibly want with us?

My bootheels hammered on our slate walkway as I marched toward the front door yanking off my gloves. Rip had mentioned nothing about an evening appointment, making this visit either an emergency or an imposition.

When I opened the front door, my husband and another man faced each other across our living room. Trying not to interrupt, I silently hung up my coat and stood still to listen.

"You sent my son to get lectured by a federal judge for no good reason," boomed the visitor, the back of his black-and-white herringbone overcoat starched with anger. "I think that's excessive, and I want your apology. *Right now!* Not tomorrow morning."

Our family room lay down the long hallway to my right, and I could have, should have, gone there to afford the men a semblance of privacy; yet I remained rooted to the oval rag rug under my feet.

Rip stuffed his hands deep into his sweater pockets and waved his head. "You won't be getting an apology for that, Mr. Cooperman. Certainly not now. Probably not ever." Rip stepped out from behind the coffee table in front of the walk-in fireplace. He had on slippers and a tweed cardigan over worn corduroy trousers. Comfort clothes. The clothes you put on after a bad day.

"Why, you . . ." Cooperman blustered pugnaciously.

Rip regarded the man, his pity edged with impatience. "You seem to have forgotten. I have proof that your son intended to start a highly questionable business on the Internet. If anything, you should probably thank me for preventing him from causing you potential legal problems."

" '*Intended to start*,' you say. You 'prevented' him from causing '*potential*' legal problems. So he hadn't really done anything, had he? Doesn't that make sending him all the fucking way downtown to be grilled by a goddamn federal judge a bit premature?"

Cooperman poked the air in Rip's direction. "I hold you personally responsible," he bellowed loud enough for our kids to hear. "You had no right to humiliate my son like that. I have half a mind to speak to my lawyer about this, this *punishment* you chose to prescribe. Ryan was devastated by it, just devastated."

Not true. Ryan Cooperman had been delighted that he managed to annoy Judge Rolfe. If anything, he was proud of himself. Judge Rolfe could attest to that. I could attest to that.

However, now didn't seem like the time to point that out. I nodded to Rip that I was there in the vestibule, prepared to jump in if necessary.

He briefly met my eyes before his flicked across the spreadsheets littering our coffee table, apparently the work Lawrence W. I'm-such-a-big-shot Cooperman had interrupted.

"Judge Rolfe will tell your lawyer just how traumatized your son was by their meeting," Rip calmly informed the boy's father. "I spoke to him earlier this evening, and believe me, we'll be lucky if Ryan absorbed one word the judge said."

"My son doesn't like to reveal his feelings," Cooperman announced with misplaced pride. "He expressed himself later to his mother." That would be Krystal, the simpering woman devoted to spoiling Ryan rotten.

"Not like you, eh?" Rip observed.

"What's that supposed to mean?"

"It means, Mr. Cooperman, that I think the only reason you choose to invade my privacy, my home, was to selfishly vent your anger, and I resent that. I resent it very much, and I would very much like you to leave."

"I'm so sorry to—to have *inconvenienced* you and your lovely family at this hour," Cooperman snarl, "but I happen to have responsibilities that require me to work late."

"I'm not exactly reading magazines myself, *Larry*," Rip rejoined, waving a hand across the spreadsheets. "But this is neither the time or the place for this discussion."

An old bulldog still salivating for the postman's ankle, Ryan's father stood his ground.

Rip exhaled, relaxed one hand on his hip, offered the other palm out in his favorite lecture pose.

"Mr. Cooperman," he said. "I've already explained this to your wife." When he waved his head, another clump of dark hair tumbled forward. "Neither of you should be angry with me or any of the committee at Bryn Derwyn who devised this course of action for Ryan's benefit.

"You should be angry that Ryan finds it necessary to engage in antisocial, borderline illegal behavior for the sole purpose of getting your attention. If you worked less and spent more time with him, neither of us would be standing here tonight."

"Your wife told my son to shut up. What do you have to say to that?" The remark represented the last feeble effort to save a lost cause, but since it involved me, it stung.

Rip sighed. "Perhaps she wanted Ryan to stop talking and leave her alone. I feel the same myself right now, and I really think you should go quietly so I don't have to bother the police."

Lawrence Cooperman whirled around and flounced past me. His left arm swept me out of his way, and his right yanked open our front door and sent it bouncing against the wall.

In a moment the Jaguar's distinctive growl reverberated off our garage door and the driveway. A moment later its tires whined as they were wrenched around to point toward the mouth of our cul-de-sac.

" 'Shut up'?" Rip marveled after the static the man left behind had dissipated. "You don't even say that to the dog!"

Chapter 8

Tuesday evening's eleven o'clock news reported nothing about Charlie's trial or the reason behind its adjournment. I clicked off the bedroom TV with the remote, and Rip and I were unconscious within seconds. Another wipeout kind of day.

In the morning I checked the *Philadelphia Inquirer*'s obituary on Dr. Edward J. "Ned" Stewart. It included a short list of surviving relatives and kudos from the chairman of the board of the Philadelphia Museum of Art.

The stated cause of death was "heart failure," putting forth the impression that another old guy just happened to die in his car right after having a big restaurant meal.

Personally, I wasn't convinced that fatty foods worked quite that fast. Also, "heart failure" described almost any death, so the phrase amounted to no information at all. The real question was why did the guy's heart stop, but we certainly didn't get that answer from the *Inquirer* this morning, and most likely we never would.

Since the odds still favored the unlucky accident, I told myself to forget Dr. Ned Stewart for now. Charlie was already in enough trouble.

Mother Cynthia had a pinochle luncheon (she still refused to learn bridge), so our visit to the Finnemeyers' Chalfont home had been loosely scheduled for between eight-thirty and nine. This caused me to gulp down some decaf and hurry out the door just behind our kids' school bus. I ate a thawed bagel dry as I drove to pick up my mother. With twenty minutes more preparation time than me she looked composed and even perky in her black felt hat and plaid overcoat.

I brushed crumbs off my mouth and chest before I kissed her hello.

"Know where we're going?" she inquired, shielding her eyes from the sun's gláre. She had already forwarded Birdie's detailed directions to me over the phone, quick before they became jumbled beyond recognition. What she really wanted to know was whether I had brought them along.

"Yes, Mom."

Satisfied, Cynthia Struve climbed into the passenger seat of my Subaru and placed a distrustful hand on the seat-belt strap she knew would snare her automatically as soon as I started the ignition. Then she pointed her nose into the wind and said, "Off we go!" the same phrase that had started most of my childhood adventures.

Chalfont lay on the near side of Doylestown beyond Mont-gomeryville, about a thirty-minute drive from Mother's. The town retains some of that Pennsylvania white-picket charm with church spires and porches and tiny graveyards on rocky hills, but everyday reality showed that some of the houses needed paint. Judging by the number of vehicles vying for curb space, several of the more spacious homes had been sub-divided; and of course unsightly telephone and electric cables connected everything.

A brief stop along Route 202, the town never had what you might consider a commercial center, and it still didn't. What it possessed in abundance were developed farms that offered larger than usual yards backed up by the remaining cultivated fields.

Across the two-lane road from the Finnemeyers eight such houses huddled together like naked bodies shivering in skimpy underwear. Around their perimeter the lumpy furrows of wintered-over corn fields sparkled with frost.

Only Charlie and Birdie's house looked snug and inviting. Nestled in among the leafless trees of a small forest, it set back from the road to the right of a hundred-fifty-foot granite drive. Three different rooflines sloped front, left, and back from the wrap-around porch edged with crisscrossed stripped logs. Wood siding stained driftwood gray promoted a sleepy backwoods feeling. Barrels with the remains of frozen flower stems dotted the entrance and various spots around the yard. A fieldstone chimney wafted a clear heat exhaust, perhaps from the home's main heating system. I couldn't imagine anyone with emphysema burning wood.

I parked behind an ancient robin's-egg-blue station wagon speckled with rust, and Mother and I stepped out into the damp winter morning. A light shone inside the kitchen, so we knocked on that door rather than proceeding around to the front. The smell of coffee and cinnamon rolls greeted us as soon as Birdie opened the door.

Our former neighbor wore a bibbed calico apron and a concerned expression. Her black polyester slacks were a first according to my memory, and she was drying her hands on a noticeably dirty dishtowel.

"It's lovely of you to come," she told Cynthia. The glance she threw me seemed forgiving, even grateful. "I guess adversity shows you who your real friends are."

Mother laughed. "Must be good for something."

Birdie's wrinkles relaxed into an arrangement short of the hoped-for smile. She dropped the towel on the counter then and waved us toward padded pine captain's chairs edging a thick oval table.

The coffee and fresh rolls were then offered and accepted, all according to Hoyle. Yet Birdie's attention frequently strayed toward the closed door at the far end of the adjacent living room. Charlie had yet to appear, and this seemed to be a source of anxiety.

While I doctored my brew with cream and sugar, I took in my surroundings. The kitchen L gave way to a sizable great room populated with overstuffed furniture. Exposed posts and beams supported the highly sloped ceilings. Except for a loft across the back, the house amounted to one story. Either the retirees had prudently planned ahead, or stairs had already overtaxed Charlie's constricted lungs at the time of purchase.

The carpets—worn Orientals. The wall decorations—quilts and hand-woven pieces hanging from crooked tree branches. Throw pillows on the two angled sofas seemed to be antique lace-edged napkins sewn together and stuffed. And although the day was already bright with winter sun, little made it past the porch roofs to fade the fancy fabrics within.

Mother attempted to put our hostess at ease with old anecdotes, an effort that met with only moderate success.

"Remember when Gin picked Mrs. Fry's tulips?" Cynthia reminisced with a wicked gleam in her eye. The incident had prompted my first—and final—spanking. Thereafter Donald and Cynthia Struve favored a community-service sort of punishment for their only child. Pick tulips and you paint Mrs. Fry's fence, that sort of thing.

"Ginny did get herself into trouble," Birdie agreed. "Oh, sorry. That's Gin now, isn't it? But you did. And that Didi, too. I always wondered what you were up to out there in our chicken coop, but Charlie trusted you girls completely. Of course, he wasn't much past being a kid himself. Still isn't."

Not the first or last wife who wished her husband behaved with more maturity. Yet sometimes it seemed that the more responsibilities a man had, the sillier he acted when he was off duty.

At that moment Charlie shuffled into the living room. He wore a gray and brown plaid flannel shirt and brown corduroys and walked across the room touching furniture as he went. Tubes ran from his nose over his ears and met under his chin. From there they trailed back into the living room where they were connected to a barrel-size oxygen tank. When he arrived at the kitchen table, he rubbed his short white beard and glanced from Cynthia to me and back again at Birdie.

"This is Cynthia Struve and her daughter Gin, honey," Birdie explained. "You remember baby-sitting for little Ginny? She's the one who loved going to your auctions."

Charlie did not yet remember.

"Have some coffee, hon," Birdie instructed the man. I wondered how much caffeine would be required to bring him up to speed.

Charlie Finnemeyer had withered since I saw him in the courthouse. Depression pressed on his shoulders and tugged on his fleshy gray features. He might have stood at the edge of the kitchen until lunch, if his wife hadn't guided him into the captain's chair at the head of the table.

"I apologize for not recognizing you," he told Mother and me.

"It's been a long time," Cynthia suggested. "Twenty-five years probably."

"At least," I agreed. Trying to prod his reluctant memory, I said, "I was with you when you found the damask tablecloth and the double wedding-ring quilt." Those days had been indelible because of Charlie's irrepressible anticipation. While he waited for his special finds to reach the auction block, he had led me on an animated tour of the rest of the offered goods, impatiently poking through boxes, gossiping about the objects inside as if they had personalities. "Look at this, Ginger Snap. A skirt lifter, for lifting your petticoats up out of the mud. Be a lovely thing to have if you went in for that sort of thing."

"Which?" I had asked. "Mud or petticoats?"

Charlie had laughed like Santa Claus and moved on to the next box. "German camera." He sniffed as if offended by the mold on the leather case. "You won't get film for that now. Useless. Can't think why anybody would collect them."

I remember nearly holding my breath when the desired items were finally brought up. My eyes darted from opponent to opponent willing them to quit bidding, begging the auctioneer to hurry. My joy when Charlie outlasted the others was exceeded only by his own.

"We did ice cream on the way home," I reminisced, mentioning the part I had liked best.

"Strawberry," Charlie proclaimed. "You liked strawberry back then." He was smiling now, running his eyes all over me.

"Still do," I said, inordinately cheered that he finally re-

membered. Our friendship had been special, and his acknowledging smile meant more than I had ever expected it to. He
knew it, too, judging by his expression.

"Charlie Finnemeyer," my mother addressed him. "How the
hell did you get yourself into such a mess?"

The man blushed behind his beard and rapidly blinked, but
his chin remained level. "Jealousy, my dear," he answered.
"What other explanation could there possibly be?"

Mother grunted.

"Is it very difficult to age a new carpet?" I asked mildly,
hoping Charlie's memories of me as an inquisitive little girl
would last long enough for him to humor my curiosity.

With wisdom in his pale-blue eyes he scanned my face and
said nothing. "Aren't you all growed up?" he observed instead.
"You have a family?"

I told him briefly about Rip and our kids, and Charlie listened attentively, his smile framed by the thin white tubes.

"Did you have a bad morning?" I inquired after I'd said
enough.

Uncle Wunk shrugged and turned toward Birdie, but not
before sending a grateful glance in my direction.

Birdie was occupied straightening the fringe on her placemat.

"So what's Didi Martin doing these days?" she asked, referring to my best and oldest friend.

"She owns the Beverage Barn over on the pike. Does quite
well with it," I boasted.

"Husband?" Charlie asked with interest.

"Ex," I replied. "She's a much better judge of beer than
she is of men."

Charlie actually chuckled at that. As he well knew, Didi
was far more adventurous than I. As a result, all finger-
wagging lectures had been addressed specifically to her with
me listening intently in the background. "Don't you dare climb
that ladder, young lady," that sort of thing. Without the warning Didi was already up there with me clinging to the bottom
rungs and praying that she wouldn't break her neck.

Suddenly Charlie patted my hand, nodded affectionately at

my mother, and rose from the table. His coffee and cinnamon
roll remained untouched.

Birdie half rose with him. "But . . . "

Charlie's back was already toward us, and he lifted a flat
hand to stop any further protest. With his left hand he collected
a quantity of the plastic tube leading back to the oxygen tank.
Then he proceeded to shuffle across the great room back to
where he began.

Birdie's eyes were moist and her lip trembled as she looked
imploringly at Mother and me. "He's tired today," she told us.
"The trial . . ."

"No need to explain," said my mother. "We just wanted to
give you our support." She rose to leave.

"Oh, please stay," Birdie begged. "We've felt so, so friendless in these last few months."

Mother's face softened and she leaned toward her former
neighbor to embrace her frail form. I got up from the table
with the intention of leaving them alone. They were murmuring quietly between themselves as I wandered into the living
room.

The wall previously out of sight possessed a length of low
bookshelves below the window level. I occupied myself for a
few minutes perusing the titles, which mostly pertained to fibers and weaving.

Yet toward the far end was a row of tall thin yearbooks
dating back to the beginning of Charlie's teaching career at
Textile. Eric had mentioned that some of the government's
witnesses had been students of Charlie's during his last year
of teaching, so I searched until I found the most recently dated
volume. Dusty now and slightly sticky from several damp
summers spent on a shelf, the yearbook felt important in my
hand.

I carried it back to the kitchen.

"May I borrow this?" I asked Charlie's wife, leaving off
the part about it being for Eric. "I'll return it as soon as I can."

"I . . . " Birdie faltered, casting a worried glance toward my
mother's stern visage. As a rule, it was best not to deny me
in front of my mother.

"I suppose so," Birdie gave in, and Mother's expression relaxed.

"Well, now." Cynthia opened a new avenue. "How about telling us about Charlie's retirement?"

Birdie's chair slid backward noisily as its user stiffened and recoiled. "No," the small woman said, looking directly at me. "I saw our lawyer cozying up to Gin here." Her eyes sliced the air between us. "So I'll tell you the same thing I told him. If Charlie doesn't think Mr. Allen needs to know about his retirement, then I'm not talking about it either."

"Eric is just trying to provide Charlie with the best possible defense," I argued. "Even if his retirement has nothing to do with the case, it might be helpful for Eric to know what happened."

"No, it won't help," Birdie insisted, "so you can tell your Mr. Allen to mind his own business." Lips pressed thin and arms folded, Birdie Finnemeyer looked like the poster girl for Protesters International.

Mother stood up and addressed her friend. "Are you sure, Birdie? Gin's really very good at this sort of thing."

Birdie's expression softened into a sort of skeptical tolerance. "No, really. Sorry."

She knew me best as an inquisitive ten-year-old, playmate to her young-hearted husband. Over time the man she loved had been redefined by an illness and an indictment, and she couldn't help but be vastly different, as well.

And during that time I, too, had become what I had become—the sort of person who wanted to help Birdie and her husband because they were doing nothing to help themselves.

With that in mind I refused to let go of the yearbook while I put on my coat, switching it from hand to hand rather than taking the risk of setting it down.

Consequently Mother was ready to leave first. "Everything will work out all right, Birdie," she said. "Please forgive us for trying to help. We always mean well. You know that."

Birdie's nod seemed grudging, her folded arms a fortress.

I was tempted to tell her she and Charlie weren't quite as

alone as she thought, not with Eric Allen, Cynthia Struve, and me on their side; but I realized the woman deserved better than an illusory comfort.

I kissed her cheek instead.

Chapter 9

Mother felt like pouting all the way home, so I left her to it. It's tough caring about people sometimes, especially when they build thick walls to keep you out.

For my part, I was torn. Charlie's behavior suggested he was guilty as charged, but what I thought I knew of him made me believe otherwise. I struggled to dredge up an incident to support this, and finally I remembered the funnels.

At one of our household auction outings Karen had borrowed two pink plastic funnels from one of the kitchen lots. She was probably six at the time, making me about eight. When Charlie finished poking through some boxes of stuff lined up around a tree, he waved for Karen and me to follow him to another viewing area set in the middle of the lawn. Karen adopted a grassless patch of dust and started daintily scooping dirt into each funnel and letting it spill out again. This activity absorbed her for quite a while.

The kitchen lots came up and were systematically sold. Charlie bid on a few items but purchased nothing. The morning eventually petered out, and Charlie collected us girls to go home. Karen, now quite attached to her borrowed toys, held them behind her back.

"What have you got there?" her father inquired.

Shyly, Karen showed him the two plastic funnels.

Uncle Wunk's face immediately went red. His hair was still mostly dark, his short beard just beginning to gray. To me he looked like a bear getting ready to maul something.

"Karen, Karen, Karen," he chanted in frustration. "Don't you understand that it isn't right to take things that aren't yours? Now somebody who thought they were buying these has been disappointed."

I absorbed about half of the ensuing lecture and Karen probably less, but the gist of it was that civilization would disintegrate into oblivion if everybody stole, but life would be sweet and beautiful if nobody ever touched anything that didn't belong to them.

Subsequently, bearlike Uncle Wunk took his daughter by the hand, led her into the kitchen of the just-sold house, and made his six-year-old turn in two nearly worthless pink funnels and apologize to the dumbstruck cashier.

"Thank you," said the woman with a what-now? glance up at Charlie. "I'll see that they go to their rightful owner," she added under the large man's intense gaze. I remember copious tears coursing through the dust on Karen's face, and I might even have been crying myself.

So naturally I expected Charlie Finnemeyer to be completely honest forever and ever, amen.

Yet circumstances change and so do people. Birdie could no longer afford to be obsessively perfect, and her husband's ebullience had been cowed by emphysema and age. It was quite possible that I didn't know either of them at all anymore.

I kissed my mother good-bye at her doorstep and promised to call soon.

Then I sat in my car and thought about what I should do next. On the surface, the chore Eric had given me seemed so easy—find out about his client's early retirement. The information would probably prove to be irrelevant, but if Eric's work ethic required that degree of thoroughness, how could I possibly quit after only two tries?

Unfortunately, I dreaded the next obvious step, fearing the sort of reception I would get.

Karen Finnemeyer Smith lived in Audubon, New Jersey. A Christmas epistle devotee, she annually boasted in red and green about whatever her family had accomplished that year.

Unfortunately, Rip and I remained on her mailing list, so I felt compelled to send a return card. For that reason alone, I possessed her address in my nifty battery-driven electronic address gadget. Information provided her phone number, and I called it on my cell phone.

"Smith residence," a woman chirped into my ear.

"Er, Karen?" I asked.

"Yes, this is Karen Smith."

"Hi, Karen. This is Ginger Struve Barnes." I don't know why I said it that way, maybe in response to her cultivated airs, maybe because I wasn't sure she would recognize my married name.

"Ginny!" she effused while I cringed. "What a surprise! My goodness, it's been years. What can I do for you?"

I gulped. "Actually, there's something you can do for your parents, but it would be easier for me to explain in person. Would you mind if I stopped over for a few minutes?"

During the ensuring silence I formulated her possible questions in my mind. "Why you?" was among them with a choice of inflections.

"Sure, come ahead," she finally agreed.

I imposed upon her for directions, which I wrote on a blue and white drugstore bag.

Then I set off for the Walt Whitman Bridge.

The Smiths' house was as plain as their name—brick topped with white siding, a small porch, and a black front door with a dusty brass knocker. Street parking was the only choice, unless there was an alley in back I couldn't see. The neighboring homes stood shoulder to shoulder with two twenty-inch cement sidewalks delineating the property lines in between. The block's few pampered ginkgo and maple trees were confined to a strip of earth between the curb and a wider sidewalk parallel to the street. This left small squares of grass to mow in summer and brown hairy patches now.

Karen opened the door with a grubby girl on her hip. Aged about four, the child eyed me with bland disinterest, then, a decision made, stuck out her tongue.

"Hi, come on in," Karen told me while hefting the girl back

up to her hip. "We've got four girls under the age of seven," she remarked. "It gets a bit nutsy around here." In the background an infant cried.

"Oh, excuse me," she apologized. "Dierdre needs a diaper change. I could set a watch by that kid." She left me and the petulant four-year-old staring at each other.

"What's your name?" I asked, and the girl ran away.

The living room was temporarily mine, so I scanned it bottom to top. Brown shag carpet showing the lint of years or just this morning; it was impossible to tell. Brown and orange tweed sofa of the sort that became a queen-size bed for guests. Twenty-inch TV—tuned to a show featuring an adult in a costume singing about how "it hurts to hit." Cheaply framed photographs of Karen's children doing childish things littered every available surface. A woven wall hanging of exceptionally high quality hung out of reach behind the sofa. A couple of struggling houseplants, an indestructible coffee table, a rocking chair, and a padded chair, and that was about it except for a thousand strewn toy parts.

Suddenly the first steps and the shore vacations and the husband's promotions all had a real live context, and the Christmas letters became not only understandable but forgivable.

"All done," Karen told me with a sigh from the kitchen doorway. "How about we sit in here. I've got some coffee on."

"Suits me," I agreed, and soon I was sitting behind a mug of brew no cream in the world could dilute.

"Keeps me going," Karen explained. "You don't have to drink it if you don't like it."

I thanked her and said I would remember that.

"So what's this all about?" she asked. The infant Dierdre now dozed in a well-worn playpen to the side of the kitchen table. The four-year-old and another slightly older girl stood on a bench and splashed dolls in the kitchen sink. The missing girl must have been in school, but I'd seen her in the pictures. They all looked like Karen once had, and Karen looked like her father now—sturdy bones, flat cheeks, rounded nose, dark hair, and pale-blue eyes.

"Let's catch up first," I suggested. "It must seem strange for me to be here. To say the least."

"Rather," she admitted. "I even felt a little pissed that my parents were in touch with you instead of me. How'd that happen, if you don't mind my asking?"

I explained about Ryan Cooperman and why I had been killing time in Courtroom 6-A. I told how Rip had gone to high school with Eric Allen and that I only recognized her parents after putting two and two together. Even though I worded my narrative carefully—pushing for sympathy over being stuck with Ryan, minimizing the importance of Rip's job, emphasizing the coincidental nature of it all—the jealous expression I remembered from Karen's youth still seemed readily accessible as an adult. She might try to be polite about it, but Karen Smith still resented my past relationship with her father.

"So I'm really doing a favor for Eric that just happens to involve your parents."

"Oh?" Skepticism and distrust.

Might as well get it over with. "Do you have any idea what was behind your father's early retirement?"

"Early?"

Apparently she hadn't paid much attention to the timing.

"Yes. He retired two years early. Do you have any idea why?"

"I suppose he was tired of working." Now she was peeved that I had revealed how little she knew of her father's business. Of course. In less than five minutes I had already found out that she had never managed to bridge the chasm separating their two personalities.

So obviously she had long ago chosen to ignore him rather than suffer any further rebuffs. And that explained why she still resented me.

However, this visit was not about me.

"Are you sure that was all there was to it?" I asked, hoping for any tidbit I could get.

"Sure. What else could there be?"

That was the whole point, but I held my temper. If she didn't know, she didn't know. Instead I angled for the answer to something that had been bothering me.

"I was kind of surprised not to see you at the trial."

Karen lowered her eyes and waved a hand to indicate her outdated kitchen. "I'd like to go," she confessed, "but Mom didn't seem to want me there."

"Your folks are acting a little weird about this whole thing," I remarked. "Eric can't understand why they aren't more cooperative."

"Maybe they're embarrassed."

"Maybe," I conceded, although I suspected there was much more to it than that. Best not to delve into those implications with Karen, however.

"Your dad seems awfully worn down," I said instead, sticking to my agenda. "I bet it would mean a lot to him to see you there."

"You really think so?"

I genuinely believed what I said was true, so it wasn't difficult to convince Karen. Her face even softened toward me, revealing some of her innate beauty.

"But I don't know any daytime baby-sitters," she lamented.

I smiled mysteriously. Cynthia Struve had been feeling useless not an hour before, pouting over it, in fact. Four kids would probably wear her to a frazzle, but I knew she would fall into a sound sleep every night wearing a grin.

"That a sofabed in your living room?" I inquired.

"Yes. . . ."

I outlined my plan, and after a minimum of fuss Karen allowed me to place the call.

I was scolded for interrupting a winning hand of pinochle, but Mother quickly came around, promising to begin her pro bono employment Monday when the trial was scheduled to resume. She figured to get a ride over to Audubon with her current beau and stay nights with her girlfriend Maryjane, who had a guest room and lived less than twenty minutes from Karen. I could hear the contentment growing as she worked it all out in her head.

Apparently, Karen sensed some of this. "You're quite proud of yourself, aren't you?" she accused me after I hung up the phone. I suppose her viewpoint was understandable, but I preferred my own spin.

"What goes around comes around," I said. "Your parents used to baby-sit for me. My mother is happy for the chance to reciprocate."

Karen grunted, either with acquiescence or derision.

Abandoning the battery acid she called coffee, I got as far as the front door before remembering my other assignment.

"By the way," I said, "ever heard of a guy named Oscar Tribordella?"

"You never quit, do you?"

"Well, did you?" I pressed.

"No, I never heard of Oscar Tribordella," Karen taunted in babylike singsong. "You happy now?"

"Not really."

Karen just snickered and shoved me the rest of the way out the door.

Chapter 10

Driving back across the Walt Whitman Bridge, flowing along with the business traffic of a sunny winter Wednesday, I evaluated my visit with Karen Finnemeyer Smith. Naturally I was pleased she had agreed to attend the trial, but her presence in the courtroom would only help in an intangible way.

My main motivation for meeting with Karen in person, for driving through Philadelphia, across the Delaware, and back into the inner recesses of Audubon, New Jersey, had been a bust. She hadn't known a thing about her father's retirement.

So, with all the easier avenues exhausted, I decided to go directly to the source. This involved exiting the Schuylkill Expressway at Lincoln Drive, winding around until I was on crooked, narrow Wissahickon Drive, turning right at the police station, and left at the dead end onto School House Lane. The steepness of the latter two streets caused me to send silent thanks to the weather goddess for today's sun, since even a hint of ice would have rendered my route impossible.

Now that the former Ravenhill Academy was owned by Philadelphia College of Textiles and Science, its buildings didn't look nearly as sinister. Passing them during their empty years had always summoned visions of a long-haired maiden in a cape running away from some guy with a knife scar.

Houses, including the university president's imposing home, lined the few remaining blocks up to the traffic light at Henry Avenue. I continued straight across that wide busy thoroughfare on slower, safer School House Lane, aiming to turn into one of the college's parking lots and read a few signs without getting buzzed by traffic.

The students were obviously still on winter break, because the Main Campus lot was nearly empty. I abandoned the Subaru and ambled over to a colorful map showing which building was where.

Nearby Archer Hall, which housed Human Resources, proved to be a welcoming former residence of off-white stucco. The single-door entrance faced a driveway circle foreshortened by a parking lot on its right and an internal campus road to the left. Most likely the decorative cabbages, struggling now with the January climate, had been planted soon after the fall chrysanthemums froze.

Inside I was directed upstairs and around to the right by a mildly curious adult. The stair carpeting, an innocuous green edged in tweed, muffled my steps and permitted me the delusion that I wasn't bothering a soul.

The second-floor landing offered rose-colored walls, a water cooler, and a broad bulletin board littered with announcements. Stalling, I drank a cup of water and braced myself for imposing upon a stranger. How salespeople made cold calls for fun and profit seemed unimaginable to me. If Charlie's future welfare hadn't motivated my visit, I'd have tiptoed down the stairs and run for my car.

Human Resources was the first room to the right of the stairs with a desk facing the door. An elderly air conditioner filled the right-hand window, and a hanging fern owned the one across from the door. I tapped on the doorjamb and the woman manning the desk, so to speak, looked up from whatever she was reading.

"Yes?" she asked. "May I help you?" She had short-cropped black hair and granny glasses, the better to peer at you, my dear.

I gave her my name, told her I was there on behalf of Charlie Finnemeyer's lawyer, Eric Allen. The woman listened sympathetically until I inquired, "Can you possibly tell me the circumstances surrounding Professor Finnemeyer's retirement?"

"Are you Mr. Finnemeyer's attorney?" the Human Resource asked.

"No," I said hesitantly. Hadn't I just told her who I was?

"Then that information is confidential." End of interview.

"But Mr. Finnemeyer's attorney specifically asked me to get that information." I tried one more time. "I figured this was the best place to come."

"Why didn't he just ask Mr. Finnemeyer?"

Good point. I couldn't very well say "Because Mr. Finnemeyer doesn't want to tell him," but that probably showed all over my face.

The visage behind the granny glasses puckered with sour victory. Then the personnel lady folded her hands on the desk in front of her and peered as hard as she could.

I must admit she had every right to peer at me like that, but I wasn't quite ready to give up.

"Can you please direct me to the president's office?" I said.

A little smile appeared, suggesting that if I thought she was a brick wall, wait until I got to the president's secretary.

"Certainly," she replied, and soon I was on my way.

Moving my car to a lot off Henry Avenue seemed prudent, so I did that. A kindly campus cop in an enclosed scooter recommended that I put a sign on my dashboard stating that I was a visitor, ". . . then you can park here all day."

Worried that the college president might have run off to an early lunch, I hurried up steps and between buildings along a cement path dotted with gaslight-style lamps. With my collar held tight around my ears, only my eyes searched left and right for the chief administrator's office building.

Appropriately named the "White House," it possessed a couple of decorative columns set irregularly to the left of the centered front door. A glassed-in solarium on the right balanced the effect. I visualized the latter as a bar or buffet and, on a balmy day in May, the wide slate patio crowded with board members, or big donors, or both, nibbling catered foodstuffs and yakking about how well things were going.

And why not? According to the newspapers, the place was growing, building on a solid reputation in textile design and technology, business administration, architecture, various medical fields . . .

Inside, the White House retained the feel of a grand old Philadelphia mansion, not as huge as those of the South, but up here we have heating considerations. Philadelphians are perennially frugal about such things, if not downright cheap. There was a wide-open first floor with warm walnut wood and Oriental rugs, two dark winged-back chairs bracketing a usable fireplace, a broad stairway leading upward from the center of the back wall, and a receptionist immediately on my right raising her eyebrow.

"It's okay," I said, since I had no other words at hand. Then I brightened my face and crossed her territory, heading straight for the alcove containing the president's secretary, except she probably wasn't called that anymore, and anyway she was a he.

As I approached, *he* rose from behind his wide desk. I had an impression of elegant cream-colored decor and sun, but of necessity my attention was preoccupied by the young man. His brow had puckered as he noted my age, which was post-student but pre–college parent, apparently a curiosity to him.

I examined him in return. Buttoned-down mauve shirt with maroon and mauve tie, black slacks with knife-edge crease. Gaunt face and olive/gray eyes under neat eyebrows. Also medium-thick lips that might have been his best feature if only he'd allow them to smile. The haircut was short and gelled to a wet-looking sheen. His watch had a luminous black face and was so thickly embedded in gold the timepiece could have doubled as a blunt instrument. This Executive Assistant, for surely that was his title, opened with "Yes?" and concluded with "May I help you?"

"I certainly hope so," I said. "Is Dr. Davidoff in?" Charlie had mentioned his former boss's name once or twice, and a nameplate over the doorway had confirmed my memory.

"He's with someone."

"Yes, of course. I know how little time he must have—"

better than you can imagine, judging by your face. "But I need his help with something important, and it will only take a minute."

I was hoping to persuade Davidoff to tell his Human Resources lady to open up, which would involve two minutes of background from me, then, if I got lucky, a thirty-second phone call from the college president to his employee.

But first I had to get past Robot Boy, who was in the process of performing what I viewed as secretarial triage. "Perhaps you can tell me what this is about, and I can see whether Dr. Davidoff will allow me to make an appointment for you."

I sighed, weary of the age-old routine. "It's a sensitive matter regarding a former professor," I told Davidoff's minion, hoping that would be enough but not too much.

Oops, too much. The executive assistant's demeanor galvanized before my eyes. Apparently he guessed that this was about Charlie's trial, which he probably viewed as a potential smudge on the reputation of the college. I didn't see it that way since Charlie was eight years removed from active employment here; but if I had been less biased myself, I might have expected this protective reaction. Colleges are structured quite a lot like private schools, and both institutions stay afloat only as long as the public retains a good opinion of them. Bad press can be quite costly.

Come to think of it, that might have been the HR lady's mind-set, too.

Just then the interior door to the left opened and a woman emerged. I now noticed that white curtains backed an entire wall of clear, leaded glass rectangles, affording privacy for what could only be the president's office.

Perhaps in her early fifties, his ex-visitor had just begun the battle with middle age. Her russet-brown hairdo glinted with too much artificial red. Her shoulders had rounded slightly, and so had everything else.

She wore a richly woven multicolor tweed suit and a blue silk blouse the same hue as her eyes. Medium black heels hinted at her identity—they were the same comfortable style

I favored for school-related functions. However, the way she
closed the president's office door was the dead giveaway.

Employees always leave their boss's private domain in a
state of animation. For them, the meeting has been emotionally
charged and quite probably difficult in one way or another.
They've been asking for something, making a pitch. Or
they've been called in to hear the results of a decision that
affects their work or their income. Sometimes they've been
warned or chastised or even fired. Their bodies invariably re-
flect tension on the wane, their faces residual stress. Same with
supplicants of any sort—salesmen, job applicants, contractors.
"Phew" is written all over them.

In contrast, this woman shut the door in a decidedly do-
mestic manner, the way a mother might leave the room of a
sleeping child. Also, her smile was private and self-satisfied,
as if she had just broken off a pleasant conversation with
someone she loved. She was Dr. Davidoff's wife, or my name
wasn't Ginger Struve Barnes.

For further proof, when she began to shrug into the black
overcoat she had been carrying, Robot Boy scurried around
the end of his desk to help.

"Promise me that he'll eat some lunch today, Barry," she
begged with twinkling eyes.

"Of course, Mrs. Davidoff. I remind him every day, but
you know how busy he gets." I read into that that the man
didn't give a damn about eating but there was some sort of
medical reason why he shouldn't skip a meal.

"Bring him something if he doesn't go out. Please?"

"I will."

The older woman beamed apologetically toward me, and I
injected my returning smile with as much rapport as I could
manage. Just let me finish with Boychick, here, and I'll be all
over you like a rash.

"Bye now." She waved over her shoulder.

"Maybe I'll come back when Dr. Davidoff isn't so busy,"
I suggested as soon as Barry-boy and I had his work area to
ourselves.

"Why don't you do that?" he agreed.

To my surprise, Mrs. Davidoff was quicker on those low heels than I expected, because I didn't catch up to her until the parking lot.

Chapter 11

The college president's wife was already tugging on the door of a dark-green sedan when I caught up with her. Noon sun glinted off the car's chrome, and the red highlights in her dyed hair lit up as if electrified.

I feared she might have her car started and moving before she noticed me, so I shouted, "Wait!" and finally she turned her head.

"Yes?" she asked. Her expression was open and pleasant, as if the idea of danger within the campus's sheltered environment never occurred to her.

"Mrs. Davidoff," I began, "my name is Ginger Barnes, and I'm a friend of Charles Finnemeyer. He used to teach here. Do you happen to remember him?"

Davidoff's wife shaded her eyes in order to appraise me. A brisk breeze ruffled a nearby hemlock before threading through our hair.

"Let's get into the car," she suggested. "I'm freezing, and you must be, too."

The passenger door closed with that solid *thunk* peculiar to heavy, airtight automobiles. I inhaled an intriguing combination of Lauren perfume and leather while I made myself comfortable on the cool seat cushion.

Mrs. Davidoff's vivid blue eyes examined me with cautious intelligence. I would have to bet everything on the truth; there was no other option.

"You remember Charlie," I stated.

"Yes."

"Are you aware that he's in trouble?"

"Yes."

Holding my coat collar closed for warmth, I began my explanation. "The Finnemeyers used to baby-sit for me when I was a kid," I said, "and I became very attached to Charlie. Uncle Wunk, I called him. He . . . I can't believe he's done anything wrong. He made such a point of teaching his daughter Karen and me to be honest . . ."

Mrs. Davidoff held her back very erect, giving no indication of either interest or sympathy. "So why are you here?" she prompted.

"As it happens, I'm also friends with Charlie's attorney, Eric Allen. He and my husband went to school together." I briefly described how I stumbled upon the trial.

"When Eric realized I knew his client, he asked me to find out whether there was anything behind Charlie's early retirement. He knows it may not be relevant; but if it is, he doesn't want to be 'ambushed by the opposition'—his description. Already there's a prosecution witness he can't get a line on, a man named Oscar Tribordella . . ." I paused to see whether the name had registered.

My car-mate blinked; but it may just have been time for a blink. "I can see how that would make an attorney nervous," she remarked.

"Yes," I agreed. "Eric's really only trying to do his job, but for some reason the Finnemeyers refuse to cooperate."

A couple more slow blinks and a promising inhale, so I continued.

"I started by asking my mother and Charlie's daughter about his retirement, but neither of them were any help. Then I decided to try your personnel department, but they told me the information was confidential."

"So I suppose you were outside my husband's office hoping to get him to tell you."

I smiled slyly in response to her observation. "My husband runs a private school," I was forced to confide.

The woman smiled back, acknowledging mutual membership in our peculiar club. Vicariously, both of us knew privileged information about what was happening at our respective institutions. No one but our husbands knew more. Based on his experience as a headmaster, I sometimes teased Rip that he might consider a second career as either an actor or a poker player—so much of his job revolved around knowing what information to release and what to withhold.

"Which school?" Davidoff's wife inquired, probably to permit me my pride. I told her Bryn Derwyn Academy and watched for any sign of recognition.

"We've taken students from there," she responded.

A long minute expired while our breath fogged the sedan's windshield.

"Wait here," Mrs. Davidoff told me finally. Then she climbed out into the cold and shut the door with another resounding *thunk*.

The prospects of shivering inside what amounted to an unheated metal chamber for any length of time forced me to hop out of the car after her.

"How about if I wait inside that door?" I suggested, pointing to the entrance to Hayward Hall directly in front of us.

"Fine," Mrs. Davidoff agreed without slowing her stride.

Only the center door of the rectangular brick building was unlocked, and the hallway inside wasn't exactly toasty. Yet it was an improvement over being outdoors.

Figuring I had at least ten or fifteen minutes to kill, I allowed myself the fun of a little exploring. This seemed to be the building where Charlie once worked, judging by the fabrics artistically arranged inside a flat display case.

A peek into the first open room showed what I remembered from visits with Uncle Wunk, a classroom crowded with elementary looms—relatively narrow boxy wooden frames operated by hand as looms had been by our ancestors' ancestors.

If memory served, the more complex of these simpler looms had ten treadles under eight harnesses, which allowed for about 256 lifting combinations. I had thought that sufficiently complicated until Charlie, ever the teacher, showed me the dobbies, the next step up.

On those the patterns were programmed using a chain of joined wooden slats with assorted holes. The chains dictated which lift combination came next, almost like a crude flip-flop computer. Thirty-two harnesses offered lots more pattern possibilities; however, the possibilities were limited by the length of the chain.

Acutely feeling Charlie's presence, I wandered through the first classroom and into the second. Here a young woman looked up from a book she was reading and said hello in a musical dialect I supposed to be Jamaican.

"Hi," I told her back. "Mind if I look around?"

"Ooh, no, ma'am. Are you interested in signin' up den?"

Noticing my age, she probably thought I was considering a career change, so I hastened to set her straight.

"I'm just waiting for someone, and thought I'd peek in and see how different everything is. A retired professor used to bring me here—about twenty, twenty-five years ago."

"Ooh, den come wid me." She led the way through racks of spools and huge empty creels into the third and larger room. "Have ya seen our Jacquards?" she asked, waving a graceful hand toward a gray metal contraption with gears and handles on the right and a box high on the left. The V of tightly stretched warp threads in alternating blue and white lay horizontally, almost like a tabletop, and the finished cloth dropped off the front and hung down toward the floor.

My guide tapped the gray box. "Takes its commands from here," she said. "Off a computa disk. CADs, we call 'em." Computer aided designs, she further explained. "This uns best for organic shapes—flowers 'n leaves and such. Dis, too." She tapped another loom as she walked around it. With tall tight threads like a harp rising nearly to the ceiling, this loom looked quite a lot like the inside of an upright piano and was set up to produce a design involving suns and moons on a dark red background.

The girl's objective was another even wider machine painted neutral green with SULZER RUTI front and center in block letters. She poked at a command box on its left; and in about three clattering minutes six inches of a beautiful, richly textured design was woven before my eyes.

The student watched as the machine's mesmerizing action stretched a grin across my face.

"Buy yourself a couple hundred of these and you can corner the market," said a deep male voice at my elbow.

I turned toward a man much like Charlie—white beard, kind face. Yet this instructor was merely in his fifties, and healthy, as near as I could tell.

"Corner the market?" I asked stupidly.

"Sure," he said with a smile. "It's an electronic dobby, best for textures and blocks—and speed. A couple hundred of these babies will produce thousands of yards a shift."

"Fantastic," I exclaimed, for I had not seen such a loom before.

The man warmed to my enthusiasm. "Did you know we can scan an antique masterpiece into a computer and program one of the Jacquards to reproduce it exactly?"

The nature of Charlie's trial dimmed my enthusiasm for that somewhat, but I answered "No, I didn't" cheerfully enough to keep my new companion from noticing.

"Sure," he confirmed. "We can tell those things what to do down to the last thread.

"You with Polly?" he asked, nodding toward the student who had returned to her book.

"No, just waiting a couple minutes for Mrs. Davidoff to come back. Thought I'd see what's new in here."

"New since when?"

"Since about twenty-five years ago."

"Ah, yes." Now his expression saddened. "Soon after Philadelphia's textile industry died."

"Oh?"

"Philly used to have lots of very productive family-owned companies. But about thirty years ago the overseas markets wiped them out."

"Totally?" I asked, and the man shrugged.

"Don't worry. Technology's making it interesting again."

"How so?"

"We're making fabric arteries now, roadbeds, car bodies, even spaceships. All NASA's reentry modules are made of woven carbon fibers—won't burn. Same thing with our stealth bombers. The whole damn plane's a woven structure molded into a composite."

"I had no idea."

"Most people don't."

"Well, thanks," I said, offering my hand. "Gotta go, but it's been an education."

"Any time." Now that he was satisfied I wasn't a thief or some sort of nutcase, he was eager to turn his attention to the bored Jamaican, who was probably stuck on campus over the holidays.

I hurried back to my semi-cozy doorway to watch for Mrs. Davidoff, a wait of about five minutes. As soon as she appeared, I trotted out to her car; and we slammed our doors and faced each other almost simultaneously.

Yet the woman's gaze wouldn't hold. It slid back toward the brick classroom building and stayed there for a minute or two. Then she abruptly swiveled back toward me and rested her left arm on the steering wheel.

"Your friend Eric isn't going to like this," she opened with a sympathetic sigh, "but you're right in thinking that he needs to know."

She shook her head. "My name's Leslie, by the way." Then she fixed me with a serious stare and spoke with almost threatening gravity, "What I'm going to tell you is highly confidential."

"I understand."

"J. D. retired Charlie to minimize the damage to the college, and he certainly doesn't want the whole mess exhumed again."

"All right."

J. D. could only be her husband, James D. Davidoff. If the incident actually had threatened the reputation of the college, the top man would have—and should have—dealt with its containment himself.

"If it reflects badly on Charlie," I reminded the president's wife, "Eric certainly won't be the one to make it public. Of course, I can't say what the prosecution plans to do." I was thinking of those ex-students of Charlie's scheduled to testify to who knew what, plus that unaccounted-for witness, Oscar Tribordella.

Leslie Davidoff seemed to accept the ramifications of that. If the government chose to raise the issue, at least it would be for the sole purpose of making Charlie look bad, not necessarily his former employer.

"So what happened?" I finally asked while my racing pulse heated my hands and ears.

Leslie Davidoff looked past the rearview mirror at something internal. "Do you have any idea who John Hewson was?"

"Not a clue."

"He was an early American fabric print artist. The best in the colonies. Apparently Benjamin Franklin talked him into coming to Philadelphia from England around 1773."

"That sounds like our Ben," I remarked.

Leslie's quick smile indicated that she shared at least some of my amusement over the famous Philadelphian's pragmatic modus operandi. When Franklin had run out of reading material, he dreamed up the lending library. To cure the mud problem for pedestrians (such as himself), he initiated sidewalks. To save fuel, he invented the Franklin stove. Streetlights, the militia—all for the greater good, but suspiciously self-serving, as well. Enticing an excellent fabric artist to come to the States sounded just like him, especially if his wife had expressed a desire for new drapes.

"As late as 1782, England still prohibited the export of any of the tools or equipment used in printing calico cotton, muslin, or linen," Mrs. Davidoff elaborated. "The sheep bred in America didn't yet produce the long, high-quality fibers for worsted, and we didn't have any skilled woolcombers anyway. Even into the early 1800s the colonies were still sending linen to Ireland and cotton to England for processing. Our textile industry just plain couldn't compete.

"So yes, it was very astute of Benjamin Franklin to convince John Hewson to come to Philadelphia. His craftsmanship was equal to Paul Revere's work in silver."

I had to admit my confusion. "What does this have to do with Charlie's retirement?"

"Everything," Leslie replied. "Charlie loved to introduce his students to fabric printing by way of John Hewson. He even had them duplicate Hewson's methods—applewood or maple print blocks, penciling in the blue portions—"

"Penciling?" I interrupted to ask.

"Hand painting. Back then blue dye was indigo mixed with arsenic, and it had to be brushed on very quickly. Evidently Hewson's wife and daughters did this part of the work. In fact, if you look at the underside of a genuine Hewson print, the blues will have soaked through, but none of the rest."

Her demeanor emphasized the importance of all this, so I tried to pay close attention. "How else can you tell a piece was his?" I asked.

Leslie rewarded my interest with a smile. "He favored urns and birds and butterflies. One of his products was a handkerchief with a pineapple print and a fan border. Because only seven colors were available to him, he often did roses and carnations in madden shades or pinks, honeysuckle, lilies, and wheat ears using brown, black, and yellow. He overprinted yellow with blue to get green. Lots of colonial reproductions emulated his style, but J. D. says only about ten genuine pieces of his work remain in existence."

I guess I breathed a little heavily, and Leslie Davidoff picked up on my impatience.

"Charlie allowed one of his students to appliqué her Hewson imitations onto an old whitework quilt he found somewhere. That was how Hewson's work was often used, you see—housewives cut sections of his designs from a large grouping, then sewed the smaller pieces all over their quilts. Winterthur—you know Winterthur, the du Pont estate that's a decorative-arts museum now?"

I nodded and said, "Outside Wilmington, Delaware," to confirm that I was familiar with the place.

"Well, this particular student took her class project down there to try to put one over on the Textile Conservator. Apparently she even had a note—forged, of course—suggesting that the quilt had been a gift from Betsy Ross to Benjamin Franklin."

I nodded encouragingly.

"J. D. thinks the girl might have tried to sell the fake elsewhere, too, but the only complaint he received came from the Textile Conservator at Winterthur."

Now I was sitting upright in my seat, clinging to the dashboard. I had vowed to contain myself until Leslie Davidoff was through speaking, but too many questions clamored to get out. "What was the student's name?" just happened to be the first.

The woman shook her head. "Charlie told J. D. that, unlike him, the girl had her whole future ahead of her, and he didn't want to ruin a promising career before it even started."

"He never told?"

"Nope."

I made no effort to hide my astonishment. What an amazing sacrifice! It seemed almost unbelievable—unless you knew Charlie way back when. Unless you realized he was doing the exact same thing all over again.

Leslie Davidoff sighed and became expansive. "Charlie Finnemeyer cared very much about his students," she said. "Nobody ever questioned that. But once in a while he went way overboard on their behalf. J. D. tolerated those occasional excesses as best he could, but this quilt thing got way too far out of hand. Somebody had to take the fall, and Charlie quite arbitrarily decided it should be him."

"Exactly what transpired?" I asked. "I still don't understand."

Leslie relaxed into her comfy driver's seat and spoke as if relating the story to the world in general.

"The fake quilt disappeared from a hallway display of student work," she said. "It was gone about a week. Charlie was busy with midterms and didn't bother to report it, and nobody else who noticed thought to mention it until later.

"Apparently the morning after the quilt was returned, J. D. received a call from Winterthur tipping him off that one of our female students had tried to sell the museum a fake Hewson. The conservator thought J. D. might want to discipline the girl so she wouldn't attempt anything like that again. When the name the girl used turned out to be false, naturally J. D. went straight to Charlie.

"Charlie refused to cooperate, preferring, as I said, to take all the blame himself. Of course J. D. could have interviewed other students and gotten to the bottom of it, but in return for a discreet early retirement, Charlie got my husband to promise to drop the investigation. Winterthur accepted that. Problem solved." She waved a gloved hand toward the sky.

"Except the student got away with attempted fraud."

"I believe there was an unspoken understanding between Charlie and J. D. that Charlie would deal with the student directly. And to be fair, the quilt disappeared again and hasn't been seen or heard of since."

Something bothered me, a little detail that didn't add up.

"How did the Winterthur person know the student came from here?"

"Somebody saw a Textile parking sticker on the girl's car." Her eyes fluttered up at that. "Believe me," she said, "it was extremely embarrassing—to J. D. and potentially to the college."

I said, "I'm sure," although it had always seemed to me that if the poor behavior of one individual could affect his or her workplace all that much, churches, schools, businesses, sports teams, governments—just about every institution in the world—would die of embarrassment.

Leslie Davidoff glanced at her watch, and I reached for my door handle.

"I do hope this helps your lawyer friend," my confidante told me. "I liked Charlie—and so did my husband. Still, it wasn't easy convincing him to let me talk to you. I hope you appreciate that."

I assured her I thoroughly understood. "Not only do I appreciate your help very much, sooner or later I'm sure Charlie will, too."

My Subaru felt flimsy as I backed out of my slot and eased my way onto Henry Avenue; but the heater kicked in nice and quick, so I didn't have to shiver while I tried not to cry.

Chapter 12

A person who is crying isn't thinking, but a person who is both crying and hungry *really* isn't thinking.

Coming out of Textile's parking lot I turned right, the path of least resistance. Going west, Henry Avenue offered miles of hilly four-lane traffic punctuated by lights—not ideal, but in my state of agitation I preferred not to face the squirrelly route back to the Schuylkill Expressway and the dangerous shunt onto its westbound speed lane.

In less than a mile I encountered three lunch choices, two of them cheesesteak shops, one a neighborhood bar called The Nineteenth Hole. I opted for D'alessandros because there was a parking space right beside the door. Before I went in I fixed my face and even combed my hair to give my teary blush a chance to recede.

The place wasn't big, but its business was. There were Formica tables brightened by a long low window and waitress service, but clearly take-out was preferred by the natives. I ordered a steak sandwich with fried onions and a Coke, well aware that skipping the cheese made me eccentric or possibly even foreign. When it came, my sandwich was the perfect fluffy, easy-to-chew concoction Philadelphians brag about. I downed half of it with ketchup before my brain agreed to reengage.

Charlie—involved in another fraud. Eric would have a duck. Who cared if the guy's intentions were chivalrous? In a way that only made it look worse. What could this student have been to Charlie that he shortened his teaching career by two years to protect her? Was anybody that selfless or idealistic anymore?

Well, yes, I realized, some people were precisely that idealistic. The education field boasted an overwhelming percentage of responsible, optimistic souls who believed that what they passed along to the next generation mattered more than anything else in the world. A quick inventory of my many teaching acquaintances yielded about four or five individuals who might even blame themselves for a student's transgressions. Probably only one or two might be foolish enough to act on that guilt, but apparently Charlie was among their number.

I tried to review the Charlie Finnemeyer of my youth through adult eyes, not mine since that was virtually impossible, but Birdie's. Adjectives like *childish*, *spontaneous*, *kind*, *fun*, *funny*, and *frivolous* came to mind, which from Birdie's perspective became words such as *irresponsible* and *immature*. My darling Uncle Wunk suddenly began to sound like the male half of many a divorce, the guy who refused to grow up unwisely partnered to a woman who once thought she could change him.

Then, of course, you had the apparent mismatches that were in reality a perfect pair. In their younger years Birdie's home management competence may have been exactly what Charlie needed, while his lighter, more creative personality probably balanced out her rigidity. Yet adversity had altered the balance of their lives, and what should have been a comfortable stroll into old age had become an obstacle course.

While I chewed the last bite of sandwich and erased ketchup with my napkin, I realized I was doing it again—privately suspecting that Charlie was guilty while fervently wishing he were not. One fraud, two, three, forty—it really didn't matter. My hopes had no real relationship to his guilt or innocence.

"Let the jury decide," I advised myself as I left my tip.

"Innocent until *proven* guilty," I recited while crossing the sidewalk and rounding my car.

I would let Eric make of this Hewson thing whatever he would. He was the professional; I, just a concerned volunteer.

After starting up the Subaru, I plugged my cell phone into the lighter socket and consulted the card Eric had passed me in the courthouse hallway. A well-trained receptionist lamented that Mr. Allen was still at lunch. "Would I care to leave a message?"

No thanks, not this message. I told her I would call again later.

From habit, I also checked our home machine. I'm not an inveterate worrier, but sometimes kids forgot their lunch money, or turned up sick during school, maybe even broke an arm.

Rip's taped voice simultaneously sat me upright and sank my heart.

"Gin, I hope you get this in time. The Coopermans are coming in at two-thirty to talk about Ryan's so-called *trauma*. I hate to ask, but could you possibly sit in? It probably won't help, but . . . would you mind?"

What story had Brat Boy invented this time? And why on earth were his parents buying it? I let my temper boil while I phoned Joanne Henry, Rip's administrative assistant, to tell her I would be there.

By my calculations I had an hour and a quarter free before I had to head back to Bryn Derwyn for the meeting with the Coopermans.

It bothered me that when I told Eric about the Hewson quilt, I would be unable to say which student had been involved, largely because the original probe had been discontinued as a condition of Charlie's early retirement. I thought if I could cross-reference the most likely culprits with the prosecution's witness list, maybe I would have something useful to offer Eric.

Back at Textile I reparked in the same lot and consulted another campus map. To my dismay the Alumni/Development office appeared to be in the White House, and without Leslie

Davidoff for a buffer I feared my reception would be less than cordial. Still, the worst thing that could happen was that someone even more formidable than Wonder Boy might show me the door before I got my information. That, I figured, I could survive.

Overhead the sky had clouded up a bit, causing me to walk between buildings under a shadow. Even the breeze seemed to suggest that I be off and out of the way. But my mind was made up.

And no one was at the Executive Assistant's desk. Lunch, probably. I treated myself to a deep breath, smiled, then asked the receptionist for directions to the Alumni office.

With only a slight pucker between her eyebrows, she told me first door on the left at the top of the stairs.

I managed to climb the center staircase without sustaining any arrows in my back. Along the way I even admired the row of stained glass windows above my head. At the woven wall hanging of red, blue, and green leaves I paused briefly for courage, then gamely entered the domain of the professional glad-handers.

"May I help you?" an Asian woman with long, impossibly straight black hair and perfect skin inquired as she turned away from her computer. Her desk faced another in the middle of the room. Behind her and below the stained glass sat a row of black file cabinets. Angled across the far exterior corner was a small fireplace I wouldn't have used on a bet, and above that hung a small, framed patchwork quilt.

Since the woman was alone, I deduced that today was her turn to mind the phones while her coworkers ate lunch. You never knew. Somebody fogged by the euphoria of their second martini just might ring up their alma mater and offer a library or two—right in the middle of the day. It paid to be there for the call—*about once every other decade.*

"My name is Ginger Barnes," I explained as disarmingly as possible, "and I'm here on behalf of Professor Finnemeyer's attorney, Eric Allen."

Detecting no negative change of expression, I continued. "Mr. Allen was wondering whether you might be able to provide him with a list of the professor's former students. Just the last year would be fine. He's thinking of using a few of them as character witnesses."

"Oh!" the woman exclaimed. "You mean like the list we gave the Assistant U.S. Attorney?"

My tongue suddenly thickened in my mouth. "Yes," I think I mumbled along with something vague. Such a list in the hands of the prosecution—very revealing, very worrisome. Eric would probably father a whole flock of ducks.

"Would that include current addresses and phone numbers?" I inquired without much hope.

"Address, phone number, current occupation, courses taken, their major—whatever you need."

I breathed in a hearty whiff of her flowery perfume and exhaled my tension. "Whatever you gave the prosecution will be just fine," I replied.

The woman spent a few moments entering commands into her computer, and within minutes I had a printout worth its weight in gold.

Chapter 13

Before I left Textile's parking lot I tried to reach Eric Allen again. He was in a meeting. Car phones, faxes, answering machines—they're all supposed to help us communicate better, but I honestly think we're spending more time and money to speak less.

At least Henry Avenue worked out. I was door to door between Textile and Bryn Derwyn in just over half an hour, making me early for the meeting with the Coopermans. Rather than obsess about my not-insignificant role in what they were calling "Ryan's trauma," I grabbed my valuable new list and the yearbook I had borrowed from the Finnemeyers. Maybe I could match a few names and faces before I faced the firing squad.

The time of day was almost the same as when I was there yesterday, second-to-last period, and I had to resist the impulse to sit in the same spot on the worn lobby sofa. I nodded to the receptionist, who was on the phone giving directions to an away basketball game. At her station outside Rip's office Joanne Henry took a break from wiggling her fingers over her computer to wiggle them at me. Rip's door was closed, which meant he was with somebody.

Social customs served, I casually strolled around the corner and into the mail room to hide. The copy machine gave off a nice warmth, and I even found an empty hook on Joanne's coat rack. However, the only seating was a tall wooden stool circa 1908, and the coffee needed an oil change. I took a chance and turned off the pot before settling down with my reading material.

Only two or three of Charlie's last-year print design students appeared to be men and therefore exempt from suspicion. That left about ninety-five women on the list, half of whom were seniors. It was dead simple to put a face with each name since everything was in alphabetical order.

At a glance only one name stood out, and when I found her yearbook page I realized why.

Janella Piper was on television every Thursday at 7 P.M. Her half-hour cable show, *Janella Piper Presents*, was a popular potpourri of information about African American decorative art. Each show included an interview with a real live craftsperson, highlighting several pieces of their work with enticing footage of the galleries that showed them. Then a do-it-yourself segment might demonstrate elementary batik or some special weaving technique. Then finally there was everybody's favorite part, Janella's appraisal of an item owned by a viewer. Would Aunt Sadie's coverlet be worth a million, or was it a worthless rag? Each week the host cleverly teased the hopeful owner with historical information and compliments on the item's beauty before letting the second shoe drop.

The public loved the suspense, but even more they loved Janella. Her fashion sense and flirty way with the camera worked like catnip. Not gorgeous in any way that made other women jealous, she was just plain fascinating to watch. Her deep, vibrant voice summoned thoughts of cool bubbling water. When she laughed or winked or pouted over a chip in a homely looking plate, viewers' hearts went along for the ride.

Studying her yearbook photo—flashing black eyes and soft natural hair, the notice-me uplifted chin, the straight back and confident smile—I decided she could easily be the one. A charismatic minority student who needed a clean beginning? Why not? Making such a grand gesture just might have struck Charlie as the perfect finale for a long career in self-sacrifice. And maybe, just maybe, he was sick of teaching anyway, something he might not have cared to admit.

The stool was beginning to bruise my backside, so I hopped down briefly to readjust, steadying myself with the copy machine. The yearbook remained opened in my left hand with my thumb marking Janella's page, but the whole book tilted and flapped around a bit while I tried to get comfortable. As a result, a newspaper clipping dropped out onto the floor.

Flat and yellowed, it was merely a photo and a brief caption stating the names of five female participants in an international fabric design competition sponsored by a French manufacturer. Representing Textile, Charlie's team had come in third. In the picture Janella Piper, Pamela Zenzinger, Sally Schultz, Amy Quilleran, and Maxine Devon all held the edges of a length of fabric that had been wound once around Charlie as he sat on a chair. A good time was being had by all.

"Gin!" Joanne Henry called to me from her adjacent office. "The Coopermans are here."

"Rats," I muttered to myself. I replaced the clipping and alumni list in the yearbook for safekeeping, rubbed my backside, fluffed my hair, and prepared to be shot.

The mahogany office furniture Rip inherited from his predecessor had dictated the rest of the decor, and Rip couldn't justify the cost of replacing it. So he lived with the red drapes, the black-shaded brass lamps, a threadbare Oriental carpet, and the stilted Ivy League impression all of it forwarded. Since he had actually attended the University of Pennsylvania, which was still Ivy League the last I heard, Joanne once teased that he probably got what he deserved. Of course she may not have realized how sensitive Penn graduates can be about such jokes. Rip's revenge was to never let her in to tidy up.

Now, fingers tented in front of him, my husband faced his guests from the brass-studded power chair behind his desk. His blue blazer was spending its day in the closet again, but a nice silk tie protruded front and center of his blue, buttoned-down collar. Rip's expression was serious, just short of stern, the headmaster hard at work. He nodded me into a slender wooden chair along the wall to his right.

Naturally, the red leather visitor chairs went to the Coopermans, but Mr. Lawrence W. opted to stand behind his. He also chose to ignore me altogether. His vested brown tweed suit probably cost as much as Rip's desk and at the moment looked almost as pliable.

"I suppose it's a given that you'll defend your wife," Cooperman snapped snidely. From her position adjacent to my knee, his own wife shot me a nervous glance.

"Yes," Rip agreed from his seat. "As you would yours."

Krystal wasn't so sure about that, judging by her worried grimace. She wore dove gray today, which flatters only certain porcelain-skinned blondes, and Krystal Cooperman was not that sort of blonde. She appeared to be either in mourning or ill.

"Your wife pinched our son's ear and told him to shut up," the irate father challenged bluntly.

Talk about getting right to the point. Breath whooshed from my lungs. My fight-or-flight response filled my veins so full of adrenaline my ears buzzed, and my cheeks bloomed like the month of May.

Rip, however, listened with the same bland attention he gave to my redecorating ideas.

"With provocation, Mr. Cooperman," he responded, his right hand shooting up in a don't-dare-interrupt-me stop signal.

"I realize now that I should not have allowed my wife to accompany your son downtown. She is not, after all, an employee of the school. However, no one else happened to be available, and I preferred not to delay Ryan's meeting with Judge Rolfe. It was a mistake. She had no leverage over the boy, and he took advantage of that."

"But . . . " Cooperman tried to interject, and Rip simply said, "No.

"No, we are not going to discuss how my wife behaved yesterday. That is not the issue here. Your son arrived home safely, and that, Mr. Cooperman, is all there is to that."

Rip was also on his feet, resting his hands on his hips. His tie had stuck on a fold of his shirt and was canted into a J position. The usual disobedient shock of dark hair drooped boyishly over his left eyebrow; but his eyes, ordinarily a hazel green, looked like the Great Plains just before a tornado. Robert Ripley Barnes, my husband, was as fiercely angry as I'd ever seen him, and I was delighted down to my toes.

He had stood up for me. Literally and figuratively stood up. This was new. This was *major*.

Wow. To different degrees the two of us have always felt connected. Like two magnets, being together has always felt right—it was that simple and that complex. You came home, you flipped through the mail, you kissed or touched or merely smiled at each other—anything that plugged you back into your power source—then you hung up your coat and said hi to the kids. As natural as breathing, and almost as taken for granted.

Yet every once in a while a surge of high-voltage electricity lights up your marquee big time. I was having such a moment. If Rip had spared me one little glance right about then, a two-ton truck could have driven across the bridge, no problem.

Instead, Rip was concentrating on Ryan Cooperman's future, which was as it should be.

"Let's go over your son's record again, folks. See if maybe you can understand what I'm up against here." Rip sat down and very patiently began to reiterate the list of transgressions Ryan had accumulated between September sixth and January second. It took some time. Locker room intimidation, throwing spitballs, insults, physical scuffles, a chronic attitude of belligerence, smoking cigarettes on the school grounds, and several "boyish" pranks that he alone had found funny.

Arms folded, Daddy listened from his standing position while Mommy shrank into her blouse and sucked in her eyes and lips. Once in a while she sighed.

Regarding their children, parents are the least objective people in the world, even when they're trying hard to be realistic. I couldn't help but notice that Krystal and Larry Cooperman were not at all interested in trying, even if it meant that sooner or later their son might end up in serious legal trouble. Each for his own skewed ego reasons, they needed Ryan to be misunderstood, falsely accused, persecuted, and above all— perfect.

Larry, being influenced by testosterone, had no qualms

about retaliating viciously to all charges, especially when the attempts to contain his son's behavior escaped the confines of the school proper.

"This is bull," he contended. "Ryan doesn't deserve this," which coming from his mouth sounded suspiciously like *I don't deserve this*, but perhaps I wasn't hearing properly. "Ryan happens to be wealthy and bright. Teachers are threatened by that. Other students, too. We've had this problem before—school personnel maligning our son out of jealousy." The superior way the man eyed the head of his son's school put forth the impression that Rip was just one more envious flunky.

Absorbing that, my husband squinted slightly. Then he pursed his lips and tented his fingers again. No doubt he was remembering what the head of Ryan's last school had told him in confidence when he asked for advice about accepting Ryan to Bryn Derwyn. "A subversive little shit," I believe were the words. "And that's putting it mildly." Obviously other kinder references had persuaded Rip to take the chance.

Eyebrows raised, Larry announced, "I want you to know that I have a call in to our lawyer. You invaded our family's privacy and defamed our son's character, and I'm sure we have a case against you and against the school."

"I see. And how is what we did different from your invading my house and maligning my integrity?" my husband inquired.

Lawrence Cooperman huffed. "There's quite a difference, dammit. My son didn't do one thing to warrant the treatment this school's given him, or any other school, for that matter."

"Let me see whether I've got your position right," Rip said, scrunching his eyebrows together in thought. "To your knowledge Ryan's never done anything wrong?"

"Never," Lawrence Cooperman emphatically replied.

Amazing. Nobody else in the room or perhaps even the world could believe that of anybody. Especially not of Ryan Cooperman. Not even his mother bought into her husband's stance, according to the sheepish look that escaped the corner of her eye.

Extremes can be extremely revealing. What was becoming eminently clear was that Ryan's dad hated to have a prominent member of the Philadelphia community, a judge no less, in possession of information that reflected badly on him, Lawrence W. Cooperman, Business Big Shot and Egotist Extraordinaire.

His lawsuit trump card centered squarely on the table, Cooperman jutted out his chin and looked down upon Rip from all his height. High noon at two-thirty in the afternoon. I caught myself leaning forward, noticed Cooperman's wife subtly doing the same.

Wrinkles across his forehead, Rip let his hands rest flat on his desk. He stared up at his opponent.

"I see," he said with none of the malice that was being aimed at him.

Then Rip joined his hands on the desk and bounced them a little while he appeared to think.

Finally he leaned back against his chair and linked his hands behind his head. He looked up at Lawrence W. Cooperman again and said, "You ever visited one of those X-rated Web sites, Larry?"

"What?"

"You're in the Internet business. You know the ones I mean."

"I'm afraid not." Larry grabbed the back of his red leather chair and shot a chivalrous look at his wife and me to indicate that he was at least as pure as he alleged his son to be.

"Sure you do, Larry. They usually start out XXX. Blue background. Something titillating in the heading like HOT HOT HOT."

Cooperman didn't seem to be breathing, and Krystal squirmed in her seat, a full left/right back-and-forth squirm. After she finished doing that, she fixed her eyes on Rip's face and left them there.

Rip dismissed his opponent's unuttered reply with a wave of his hand, but Krystal cut in before he could continue.

"Larry," she said. "I think we should leave now."

"Not yet, dear," her husband shot back. "I'd like to see

where Mr. Barnes is going with this." The glint of litigation gleamed ever brighter in his eyes.

"Larry . . ." Krystal begged, but the man refused to listen.

"What's your point?" Cooperman pressed.

Rip seemed to be enjoying himself, and I was eager to find out why.

"It's just that our kindergarten teacher, Mrs. Beggs, has been getting invitations to those sites for a month now. On the average of about three a day," he explained. "She's very . . . how shall I say it . . . prudish, our Mrs. Beggs. She finds the lurid suggestions quite offensive. And of course she's terrified that one of her students will accidentally see something they shouldn't."

"So?"

"So I've been trying to help her block the ads, but it isn't very easy to do. Among other things, they usually give false return addresses, plus our provider is so backed up with similar requests that they haven't been able to stop the problem, either."

"Larry?" Mrs. Cooperman was standing now, tugging on her husband's expensive tweed sleeve.

"What's this got to do with us?" Mr. Lawrence W. asked.

"Ah, that's the point, isn't it?" Rip agreed. "Your son, Ryan, is a very distinctive-looking boy, wouldn't you say?"

No answer.

"So if, for example, he was seen coming out of Mrs. Beggs's office one day back in December, even a kindergarten-age child would probably be able to identify him."

"Larry!" Krystal's demand for her husband's attention finally succeeded.

"What do you want?" the man snapped.

"I think we should leave now," Krystal said aloud. The rest of the message was in her eyes.

Cooperman and his wife stared at each other until Rip finally supplied the information the businessman wanted so desperately to reject.

"Ryan did the same thing to your home computer, didn't

he?" He addressed his remark to Krystal, the one who obviously used the corrupted computer.

"Yes," she admitted, still staring into her husband's eyes, tears filling her own.

"Can we go now?" she asked him.

Larry didn't respond, just grabbed his coat and stalked out.

His wife had to retrieve a purse from the floor and gather her own coat from the rack. She took her time, perhaps because she wanted her husband out of earshot before she told Rip and me she was sorry.

"I'm sorry, too," Rip assured her. Then before the woman disappeared through the door he told her, "Something will get through to him. We just haven't found it yet."

Rip could only mean Ryan, and the boy's mother knew it. Not even an act of Congress would change her husband, and she knew that, too.

As soon as Krystal Cooperman closed the door behind her, I asked Rip, "How did you know?"

He shrugged.

"Lucky guess?" I was astounded.

Rip grinned, and someone tapped politely on his door.

"Yes?"

Joanne Henry's pudgy, apologetic face peeked through an eight-inch gap. Her pale hair remained rigidly arched and flipped over her forehead, and her two-piece knit dress encased her rounded middle-age frame as smoothly as it had the day she bought it, back when brass-buttoned double knits were in style.

"Sorry to interrupt," she almost whispered.

"No you're not," Rip pointed out. Joanne tended to be a bit officious, and her efforts at tact usually fell flat.

She opened the door the rest of the way and straightened up.

"Okay, Mr. Smarty Pants. I'm delighted to tell you that somebody wedged a pan of poster paint above the doorway to the art room, and a poor little eighth-grade girl is presently trying to shower green out of her hair. Perhaps you'd like to investigate before the last bell rings and everybody runs out of here."

Rip squeezed my arm on the way by but didn't bother to speak. He left Joanne and me to stand there and blink at each other.

"Damn," I said. "Where's the Chardonnay when you need it?"

Rip's inherited assistant and I had achieved detente over a jug of cheap white wine after my first faculty party fiasco. For quite a while after that, "Chardonnay" served as our all-purpose buzzword, our club slogan, so to speak, alluding to our similar but different loyalties toward Rip. Now that we were far enough past that, "Chardonnay" substituted for a string of four-letter words.

"You said it," Joanne agreed. Then she withdrew back to her territory and her job, leaving me alone in the dead air of the office.

The borrowed Textile yearbook leaned against my purse on the floor where I had left it, reminding me how much there was to tell Eric Allen. Six of the eight lines on Rip's phone were open. The door was closed, nobody near enough to listen. I dialed the lawyer's office, and this time I got him.

"Boy, have I got news for you," I began. "Are you sitting down?"

"Yes," Eric answered, but I could hear him walk around his desk to close his own door. "Go ahead."

So I did. I told him about the Hewson imitation, throwing in every detail I could remember—Charlie's assigning the block prints to teach his students the way it was once done, the penciling of the blue, the extra-credit appliquéd whitework quilt and how it disappeared from the hallway display for a few days. I told him about the Textile Conservator at Winterthur, Betsy Ross and Benjamin Franklin, and how the school sticker on the student's car ultimately embarrassed the college and led to Charlie's early retirement.

"Tell me again why we don't we know which student did it," Eric prompted.

"She used a false name; and when Charlie agreed to retire,

he stipulated that the investigation end. The president wanted the problem to go away badly enough that he agreed."

I could almost hear the attorney nodding. "I suppose because no money changed hands, the fraud was going to be difficult to prove."

"I guess." The finer points of what constituted fraud remained a bit vague to me. All I knew was that the deception had to be intentional and that profit was involved.

"Anything else?" Eric seemed impatient to get to work on what I'd given him.

"Well, yes, now that you mention it." I proceeded to tell him about the list I'd obtained from the alumni office.

"Splendid!" he effused. "How in the world did you manage that?"

I re-created my wording as best I could, and he said, "Jeez, Gin, you should have been a lawyer."

"Thank you," I said, because it was the only thing to say.

He was distressed by the number of names on the alumni list until I told him about the newpaper clipping. "That might narrow things down a bit."

"Great, Gin. That's great. How soon can you get me this stuff?"

Rip returned just then. His hair had been raked through with his hands, probably several times, which for him was a sign of extreme frustration. He looked exhausted, too. Plus his blue oxford shirt had a swipe of green poster paint on the left sleeve.

"How about if I fax you the list? I'll circle the names from the photo." Old and yellow as it was, the newspaper photograph would probably transmit as one big black box.

Eric grumbled, but I didn't care. Rip was holding his head in his hands and staring at the wall.

I finally told our old friend, "Take it or leave it, fella. I'm going to be busy tonight."

Chapter 14

At 7:30 A.M. Thursday still seemed pretty promising. I had finished my Kellogg's Sugar Pops and coffee and stood stretching and smiling at the world outside our front door. Rip and the kids were already off to their respective schools. The sky was dotted with blue clouds on a white background, a phenomenon that would last only until the sun rose a little higher.

An hour ago a morning radio announcer had informed us that the temperature was forty-two, the wind-chill thirty, prompting my outfit of ragg wool socks and hiking boots, jeans, a navy turtleneck, and a thick blue and white Norwegian pullover. I felt cheery and comfortable. I felt like walking the dog.

Naturally, Gretsky sensed this thought and started whimpering and poking me with his nose. In his opinion it was impossible to get out the house fast enough.

So off we went past homes with all their kitchen lights shining, sniffing and squirting the long way around the neighborhood. By the time we returned home about forty-five minutes later, I'd worked up a healthy sweat underneath my thick sweater, and my heated breath fogged the air.

I opened the door to a ringing phone. Full of optimism and fresh air, I picked it up and said hello, effectively putting an end to the best part of my day.

"Is this Mrs. Barnes?" The voice was masculine and none

too cordial. Considering the hour and all that had been happening, I thought he might be Lawrence Cooperman's lawyer. Still, I was Mrs. Barnes, and at that point I foresaw no reason to deny it.

"This is Dr. James Davidoff." A dramatic pause invited me to think that through.

I gave myself points for remembering he was the president of Textile, making him the one who had confided the terms of Charlie Finnemeyer's retirement to me via his wife. Beyond that I was stuck.

I said, "Yes," again, inviting him to go on.

Davidoff's voice took on that deep, intentionally intimidating tone favored by angry fathers and the occasional professor. "I'm calling to tell you how unprincipled I think you are," he informed me, "and if you ever attempt to speak with my wife again, I've instructed her to call the police."

"Uh . . ."

"Because of the way you introduced yourself, Leslie trusted you, and I made the mistake of trusting you in turn. It goes without saying that neither of us will ever make that mistake again. In fact I would appreciate it if you would refrain from ever stepping foot on my campus again."

"I . . . um . . . I'm sorry," I said. "But I'm afraid I don't understand why you're so angry. I told your wife up front that I was helping Charlie Finnemeyer. And when you gave me the information about his retirement, I thought you understood that it would be used to help prepare his defense."

Davidoff had been making attempts to interrupt, and scarcely a millisecond separated my last word and his next. "Mrs. Barnes," he intoned, "the whole point of Mr. Finnemeyer's retirement was to protect the college from adverse publicity, and toward that end even he agreed that the terms should remain confidential. Now, thanks to you, the whole mess has suddenly become front-page news . . ." What! What was he saying? ". . . Now—eight years after the fact—a, a *prank* some misguided student tried to pull has been blown all out of proportion." My body parts had gone on strike. I had to force myself to breathe. "... How can you possibly claim this isn't your fault?"

Because I knew it wasn't, but I also appreciated why Davidoff held me responsible. Using the ethically questionable means that came to hand, I had succeeded in prying sensitive information out of him. Somehow that information had made its way into the newspapers, and the simple fact that I had opened Pandora's box made me culpable, no matter how the leak actually occurred.

I forced some words through my tightened throat. "Dr. Davidoff," I said, "I've known Charlie Finnemeyer since I was a child, and I'm very fond of him. I would never knowingly do anything to hurt him, or to hurt your college for that matter. There is no reason why I'd want to. I honestly don't know how the press got hold of the information you gave me, but I can tell you that I am profoundly sorry it happened. I hope you can believe that."

"And yet it happened."

"Yes, sir, apparently it did."

"And you say you have no idea how."

"None."

Davidoff's pause suggested an immense disappointment in the human race, me in particular. "Good-bye, Mrs. Barnes," he said. "I think this conversation is over."

I hung up the phone and sank to the kitchen floor. Gretsky's leash was wound tightly in my hand with him still attached. I unclipped his collar and he licked my face, flopping onto the linoleum beside my knee. His concerned eyes monitored my every movement.

"It's okay," I assured our sixty-five-pound pet. "I just hate to be chewed out for something I didn't do." The dog seemed to understand, even empathize.

Gratefully I stroked the sculpted bump on his red head and fingered his ears. The breath across his tongue slowed and his eyes squinted. *Learn from me,* he seemed to say. He was already beyond my distress and halfway into a nap.

In response, my own dismay diminished to a manageable ache. I hopped up and walked around to our dining end of the living room, which was where Rip had abandoned today's *Philadelphia Inquirer* along with his used coffee mug.

"NEW EVIDENCE IN FRAUD CASE," said the simple headline. "Reliable sources report that the defendant in a federal antique fraud case, Mr. Charles Finnemeyer, may have been involved in a previous incident involving a fake early American quilt. Finnemeyer chose to retire early rather than implicate a student who allegedly helped perpetrate the fraud."

The article continued to reiterate exactly what I had learned yesterday, which was that a textile expert from Winterthur had been offered the fake Hewson piece by a young female using a false name and that the item originally had been a project related to Professor Finnemeyer's fabric print class. "As validation, the student offered a note supposedly from Betsy Ross to Benjamin Franklin indicating that the quilt was a gift."

I flopped back on the living room sofa and blinked away stinging tears. Before I could work up a world-class case of self-blame and remorse, the telephone handled it for me. I didn't answer, just listened to the caller giving hell to the machine in our kitchen.

"Dammit, Gin. Where are you? Look at your paper and then get over here. We need to talk."

Eric Allen, no mistake. Angry because his ammunition had backfired in his face.

How on earth had that happened? I hadn't given the information about Charlie's retirement to anyone but his lawyer and Rip, who I had filled in right after I got off the phone with Eric. It went without saying that I trusted my husband not to repeat the confidence to anyone for any reason, just as I would never even consider betraying his trust. And fortunately our children hadn't been around to hear anything. So as far as I was concerned the Barnes family was in the clear.

Of course, I *had* called Eric on a school phone, but I had noticed no telltale clicks to indicate that someone accidentally picked up on my line. No "Oops, excuse me." No nothing.

To prevent astronomical bills, the rest of the school's eight-button phones were all located in secure places—the admissions office, the faculty room, on the desks of Rip's upper administrators. At that time of the afternoon, those units were either in use by responsible adults or locked up where students couldn't get their hands on them. Before she left each day I knew the receptionist routinely locked her telephone in her desk drawer.

Joanne Henry's unit was connected to the school's answering machine, and she handled anything that came in after the receptionist went home. Probably she was the most likely person to have overheard my recital; but Rip's office door had been closed, and I knew it to be remarkably soundproof.

Plus even if Joanne Henry had caught a word or two, which I doubted, why would she bother to involve herself in Charlie Finnemeyer's life—a man she had never met? Same argument for anybody else at Bryn Derwyn. Nobody there had any reason to hurt Charlie, or, by inference, the Philadelphia College of Textiles and Science.

Yet the facts were there in plain black and white. The story had been leaked, apparently by somebody who realized its significance.

Since the Assistant U.S. Attorney had been talking to former Textile students, as Eric feared, he probably knew the conditions of Charlie's retirement in all their damning detail. But give away his silver bullet? Never. That simply would not have happened.

And of course Charlie and Birdie had refused to tell even Eric, who at least had a legitimate reason to want to know.

The Finnemeyers' daughter? As of yesterday, Karen hadn't even realized that her father retired two years early. Although she still resented what she perceived as his indifference toward her, she didn't seem to hate her father enough to deliberately smear his name in the newspapers. Especially not when it might help send him to jail.

Davidoff and his wife were out for obvious reasons, as was anyone from the college office who may have overheard the couple's private conversation. You simply don't bite the hand that feeds you.

Also, it was too coincidental to think that anyone from Textile who knew what went on eight years ago just happened to choose last night to reveal what he or she knew. Davidoff had been justified in his cause-and-effect condemnation of me, no matter how much I hated to admit it.

And that covered everybody I could think of. If the newspaper hadn't been right on the floor beside me, I'd have talked myself out of its existence.

Like appliances colluding to break down in threes, bad thoughts attract other bad thoughts. The domino effect. Misery loves company. I couldn't help thinking about that expert witness, Dr. Ned Stewart, the man from the Philadelphia Museum of Art. Had he been approached by the duplicitous student eight years ago before she tried her spiel on the woman at Winterthur?

I sickened myself even imagining it; because if Stewart had been approached, surely he would have thrown that log on Charlie's fire. With Stewart gone, would anyone else remember one undesirable item the museum refused eight years ago?

Highly unlikely, which was why I was so concerned about the coincidence of Stewart's death. Only Charlie appeared to benefit from the lucky accident—if it was an accident at all.

Naturally, the suspicions that followed that thought truly terrified me. Murder doesn't always take great strength. All that's really required is a huge need for it to happen. Unfortunately, at Charlie's age, with his poor health, the outcome of this trial would probably affect the remainder of his life.

No. I couldn't think it. Wouldn't think it.

The phone rang again. This time it was my mother, so I grabbed the living room extension before she finished her message and hung up.

"Birdie called me," she said, and although I had a pretty good idea what they talked about, I waited for my mother to express herself in her own way.

"She thinks you told the papers about some old quilt Charlie tried to sell." Mother only reads her horoscope in the morning. For amusement purposes, not for real. She claims that if something important happens in the news that she ought to know about, she'll hear about it before the day's over whether she wants to or not.

"He didn't try to sell it," I corrected her. "One of his students did. And I didn't tell the papers. In fact, I can't for the life of me figure out who did."

"The Finnemeyers are very upset," Cynthia hinted in that worried tone an only daughter dreads—dreads because you know anxiety will creep into your mother's every conversation until the situation that's bothering her gets resolved, preferably by you. It didn't help that I was already feeling like the red dot in the middle of everybody's dart board.

"They should be upset," I said, hoping to throw off Cynthia's aim. "I'm upset, too." No need to mention Davidoff's call—or Eric's.

"Isn't there something you can do?" Mother inquired optimistically.

"Mom, you've eaten my cooking. When I tried to fix your toaster, we practically had to call the fire department. I'm really not the genius you think I am."

"Of course you are, dear. Everybody makes a mistake now and then. Even Jefferson had slaves, and wasn't he the one who insisted that everybody was created equal? By the people, for the people, and all that?"

My track record trying to straighten out Mother's historical references was abysmal, so I skipped to what I considered the bottom line.

"I was trying to help Charlie, and obviously I did something that made everything worse." Factor in the Ned Stewart thing, and I wasn't even sure Charlie could be saved. "I'm a little afraid to do anything else."

"Nonsense. You just told me you didn't give that story to the papers. Why are you being so hard on yourself?"

Because J. D. Davidoff and Eric Allen put the idea in my head; however, I'd already decided not to admit that.

"Mom," I said. "What if Charlie is actually guilty? What then?"

I could almost hear my mother stiffen with indignation. "Ginger Struve Barnes, that's preposterous, and you know it."

"Yeah, but what if his lawyer thinks he's guilty, and maybe even his wife has her doubts? What if the prosecution has lots of witnesses all set to testify to how he defrauded that man, and the jury believes them because nothing else makes any sense?"

"Ginger Barnes, I don't know what's gotten into you. But you stop that talk right now. The Charlie Finnemeyer I know wouldn't even lie about his age to get into the movies half price. He certainly didn't cheat anybody out of a lot of money. That student probably did it and blamed him. And if everybody else thinks he's as guilty as you say, then you ought to make that student go to court and tell the truth. Really, Gin, I raised you better than that."

Bull's-eye. Ouch.

I sighed with defeat. "Okay, Mom. I'll try to do something. What, I have no idea."

"That's better."

Then she asked me how to make beef barbeque. I told her to buy a foil envelope of spices and mix it with tomato sauce and hamburger, and soon after that we said good-bye.

Then I propelled myself down the hall to collect the kids' dirty sheets. Guilt seemed to have annexed a few more vital organs while I wasn't paying attention. Probably ought to find myself a hair shirt and plan on bread and water for lunch.

Or maybe I should just sit down and figure out exactly what my mother said that was nagging me. Something about "making that student go to court and tell the truth."

"Dammit, Cynthia," I complained to the bedroom walls. "I hate it when you're right."

Chapter 15

Getting the student Charlie had protected to testify on his behalf was a long shot, but if Charlie was in as much trouble as I feared, such a gesture would go a long way toward swaying the jury's sympathy. Eric still needed to disprove the current accusation, but unchallenged, the story behind his client's retirement almost guaranteed a guilty verdict.

Yet even if I knew the identity of the alleged student/cheat, which I didn't, prying the truth out of her under oath would require as much leverage as I could pull together. Toward that end I decided the Philadelphia Museum of Art was the place to start, maybe because it seemed safe and easy. Hey, you've got to start somewhere.

Before I left I dug through an envelope I keep of handouts for various Philadelphia attractions. They mostly came in handy for out-of-town friends, but once in a while I offered them to teaching applicants Rip had brought in for an interview.

My history of the Philadelphia Art Museum seemed to be a Web page printout from the time I chaperoned Chelsea's fifth-grade class outing. With the exception of the Otto Kretzschmar von Kienbusch Collection of Armor and Arms, which excited the boys no end, the trip had been a miserable succession of kids acting up, wandering off, and nagging their teacher and her minion—that would be me—for either a rest stop or food.

Scanning the material now, an interesting connection to the Philadelphia College of Textiles and Science caught my eye. Apparently when the museum was founded (to accompany the Centennial Exhibition of 1876), one of original aims had been to train artists and craftsmen, especially for the textile industries of the state. The resulting school, Charlie's longtime employer, only became independent of the museum in 1949.

I dumped my cold coffee and read the rest standing in the kitchen. Then I told Gretsky the sad words "Not this time" as I headed out the door.

After easing out of a Main Line residential area forested with taupe tree trunks and shivering evergreens, I picked up Route 76 East, joining some intense truck drivers and some even more intense businesspersons driving along the Schuylkill River's beautiful southern edge. The museum would be across the water on a rise just past Boat House Row. I didn't dare turn my head to admire the imposing edifice, which had been described as a "vast neoclassical temple with wings embracing an open court." I already knew it looked like something airlifted in from Greece.

Instead I steered off the expressway and left across the Spring Garden Street bridge, savoring what I had just read about the ingenious minds behind one of Philadelphia's proudest possessions.

In a very astute, Franklin-like move, the side wings of the museum had been erected first, so that rethinking the building's funding and stopping short of completion made no sense. A particularly wise benefactor also sped things along by stipulating that the museum couldn't have his collection if no suitable place to house it existed within a reasonable time after his death.

During the depression, when the city had more urgent bills to pay, the director launched the museum's first huge capital campaign, which fortunately succeeded. Over the years private individuals also donated several sizable personal collections, until such gifts came to comprise more than 90 percent of the museum's holdings. It seemed that both museums and private schools had something in common with the Tennessee Wil-

liams character Blanche DuBois, the one who habitually "re-
lied upon the kindness of strangers."

After circling around to the back parking lot, which I
vaguely remembered was free, I locked my car, then proceeded to enter the museum's West Entrance.

My footsteps echoed inside the solid marble lower hall
while the sheer size of it stole my breath. The oval Information
counter rising from the floor, the diminutive ticket desk, the
cloak room in an alcove to the right, adults all around—all
this conspired to make me feel younger than any of the fifth
graders I had squired around those few years ago.

Obviously I had forgotten the power of the place, but the
message returned swiftly with a worrisome new footnote. Dr.
Ned Stewart had worked at this august institution as a department head, and I realized now that that fact alone might
have sunk Charlie Finnemeyer's hopes. Even if both men had
been academic equals, which they probably were, the guy with
the title was the guy who carried the clout. The jury would
have sensed that from Ned Stewart's voice, seen it in the cut
of his clothes. "Dr. Edward J. Stewart, Curator of Textiles,
Philadelphia Museum of Art" read his business card, and listeners would have known that just as surely as they knew that
Charlie Finnemeyer had no business cards in his wallet what-
soever.

At the Information counter I told a short, jacketed woman
wearing a total of seven earrings that I hoped to speak with a
member of the textile department.

"Costume and Textile, you mean. Who do you want?"

"Ned Stewart's assistant, if that's possible."

She consulted a notebook, picked up a phone, punched in
an extension. Then she turned away and mumbled into the
instrument.

"Who shall I say is calling?" she asked. I told her, offering
nothing more.

"May I tell her what this is about? She's busy right now."

I smiled. "Of course. I'm not a reporter if that's what wor-
ries her. But tell you what. Why don't I stop back here in an

hour. Maybe she'll be able to give me five minutes then. Will that work?"

Some more mumbles.

"Sure. She'll be here."

We checked our watches, I thanked her, and the guide began to turn away, but I tapped her arm. "Name?" I asked.

"Oh, sorry. The woman you want is Patricia Cooke."

"How will I recognize her?"

The guide looked me over head to toe and chortled to herself. "Oh, I think she'll find you." The pros and cons of red hair never end.

Of course, it might have been the hiking boots.

I purchased my ticket and checked my thick sweater. Then I climbed the stairs to the Great Hall. Galleries branched off left and right like chambers in a pyramid, and a grand staircase led to more. Diana, tired of threatening New Yorkers from above Madison Square Garden, nonchalantly pointed her bow and arrow at tourists from the head of the stairs.

My first pleasure was a peek out the front entrance, and I wasn't alone. Two visitors shivering in the breeze were photographing the same thing.

As the fictional Rocky Balboa, actor/writer Sylvester Stallone popularized the fabulous view from the top of the museum's many marble stairs down the length of Philadelphia's romantic, almost European parkway toward the heart of the city. Visualize a fairy-tale foggy dawn, a wide avenue of trees lined with decorative flags, circles containing sculpted fountains—a broad expanse leading your eye toward City Hall, everything, even Stallone's sweatsuit and breath, in shades of frosty silver-gray. Now picture this studly American movie hero powered on raw eggs and ambition, boxing gloves raised, jogging in place to celebrate a sweaty run all the way from the distant Italian market to the top of those stairs.

Okay, now bronze it all, including the knit watch cap and the towel around Stallone's neck, and you've got the tacky statue somebody briefly stuck on the museum's upper doorstep—that is, until somebody with common sense moved the

thing to the Spectrum, which is where most Philadelphians,
including me, think it belongs.

Good movie, though.

Next, with my painting class and the Monet I was forging
in mind, I headed straight for the European Art 1850–1900
section to the right. Strolling among names like Manet, Cour-
bet, van Gogh, and Renoir could probably absorb me all day,
and half an hour felt like a minute.

I stood for a while in front of "Interior of a Tavern" by
Peter Severin Kroyer, 1886, and admired late-afternoon sun
coming across dark plank tables from some small side windows. There were graceful bottles here and there and men
smoking long thin pipes. Some of them clustered together
laughing while one lone man appeared to be contemplating
the meaning of life. Been doing it for years, I guessed, and
would continue for years more. I knew how he felt.

My special goal was to check out Claude Monet's screwy
brushwork, which seemed to go every which way. The paint
had been applied thicker than I supposed, too, something I
would try during my next class. Again, I felt sure the artist
had stirred some colors together right on the canvas, but now
I noticed that he must have added highlights after some of the
darker background colors dried.

Cataracts, Mme. Mimi told us, accounted for some of the
blurriness of his work, the very effect that everybody loved.
The fates certainly enjoyed playing with irony. Monet, Bee-
thoven, that little Belgian prince who wandered off so long
ago. His dad, the king, promised to place a statue wherever
they caught up with his child, but the boy was found urinating,
so now there's this cute little statue, really a fountain . . . I
sighed and moved on, shadowed by thoughts of Charlie Finnemeyer, my first artistic mentor.

In among some twentieth-century art I stared at two ce-
ramic candlesticks with blue flowers, wondering whether I
thought them special enough to be there. A footed silver goblet
seemed slightly more worthy because the handles twisted in
an original way, like strips of ribbon curling off a spool.

Upstairs I glanced in at the weaponry collection that had

so delighted the fifth-grade boys. The pewter-colored armor and spears glowed much more beautifully in the daylight than I had expected, but with concerns about untimely death already disturbing my subconscious, I preferred to wander through the ages just as Fiske Kimball, that very forward-thinking early director, had wanted me to do.

Kimball decided the second-floor galleries should display masterpieces of painting and sculpture along with furniture and other artifacts in rooms of their period set up in chronological order. So in theory, visitors could walk through the centuries viewing the best that each time span had to offer—in situ. It took a little finagling, a lawsuit actually, but today it was all ready for me and millions of tourists to make of it what we would.

Personally, I was struck by how long a period artists were preoccupied by God, death, and drinking, the latter perhaps because of the previous two. Still, I was doing fine, rising above the mood of the Dark Ages, until I confronted a bronze of "The Beheading of Saint Paul," head already rolling, and soon after a "Still Life with Hare and Birds" that depicted a fly on the rabbit's upside-down crotch. Suddenly it seemed like a great idea to spend the last minutes of my hour tour perusing the decorative arts of Pennsylvania.

After I finished eyeing the clocks and stove plates and buckles and patch boxes, I returned to the Information booth. Easily distinguishable from the crowd was a tall woman in a white silk blouse and black silk pants impatiently tapping her polished nails on the counter.

I approached, and her hand shot out. "Ginger Barnes?" she inquired.

"Yes. You must be Patricia Cooke. Thanks for giving me a minute." I shook what seemed to be a delicate assemblage of toothpicks and wire.

The way she rested her elbow on the high Information desk suggested that we would not be proceeding back to her office. "What can I do for you?" she prompted.

"I'm a friend of Professor Finnemeyer, and I'm trying to help his attorney gather some background information."

A brown eyebrow arched above one of Patricia Cooke's dove-gray eyes. Her thin lips pressed tighter and formed another even more disapproving line. She was waiting for clarification.

"Your late boss was going to testify at Charlie's trial."

"Oh, that Professor Finnemeyer."

"Yes. My question is, do you keep records of items the museum turns down?"

"What kind of records?"

"Description of the item, its background, who offered it?"

"You must be referring to the quilt that was mentioned in the paper."

I put a couple more gold stars on her chart. "Yes. Would there be any written record of its being offered to Dr. Stewart?"

"Not that I'd show you without a subpoena."

My face probably crumbled. It *felt* like it crumbled, and that elicited a tiny surge of sympathy from the textile expert. She sighed and relaxed herself against the Information oval in an almost amenable manner.

"I can tell you this," she conceded, her expression world-weary but reconciled. "If the story that was in the paper was the story the scam artist told Ned, he didn't bother to write anything down."

"Why?"

Patricia Cooke snorted delicately. "A gift from Betsy Ross to Benjamin Franklin—with a note to authenticate it?"

"What's wrong with that? Was Betsy Ross illiterate?" Women weren't always schooled back then, maybe that accounted for the instant dismissal.

"Oh, she was literate. Quakers taught girls reading and writing too. It's just that she was a businessperson, an upholsterer, which back then meant she sewed almost anything, in her case lots of flags for the navy."

"So why not a quilt to give Benjamin Franklin? Didn't she know him?"

"Probably. Her church pew was adjacent to George Washington's, and Franklin's son signed her third marriage certificate."

"But that's not it," I suggested.

Patricia Cooke tried to organize her words. "A genuine Hewson piece with that sort of provenance. Don't you kind of wonder where it was all those years?"

I shrugged. "Stuff does turn up."

Cooke's face screwed up with disdain. "Okay, so it's possible, but it's also highly improbable. You ever look at one of those appliquéd whitework quilts? Can you imagine how long it took to hand stitch one of those things?" The woman shook her head. "No, Betsy Ross couldn't have afforded to give away that much time. Plus she didn't write much of anything very often. I only ever heard of one receipt she wrote being found."

"Why?" I asked, sounding very much like a kid on a tour.

"There was a war going on, remember? My guess is the woman had better things to do."

My house of cards suddenly seemed threatened by a gust of what-ifs. What if Stewart had never been offered the quilt? Answer: He probably never met Charlie's duplicitous student. Result: My favorite suspect had no reason to fear Stewart's testimony, and the man probably died of a perfectly ordinary heart attack.

Unless, of course, just the worry that Stewart knew his connection to the fake Hewson prompted Charlie or Birdie . . . I shook away the thought.

Idly, just thinking out loud, I asked the Assistant Curator, "Do you think Dr. Stewart would have even looked at what that student was offering?"

Patricia Cooke folded her arms across her chest and scowled. "Maybe," she decided. "For about two seconds."

"That's what I thought," I said, but the woman misunderstood my satisfied nod. To her, two seconds was short shrift.

I thought of it as the difference between life and death.

Chapter 16

"John's moving his stuff out tonight. Can I come over?" Didi's phone voice sounded like the front edge of a crying jag.

"Overnight?" I suggested. My best friend didn't own even one houseplant, she was that heavily into freedom—not because of her divorce, because of her marriage. Men loved that about her, for a while.

She considered the invitation while I stirred dinner, one of those prefabricated just-add-beef stews.

"I guess he won't steal my TV. Sure, overnight." Which meant we could stay up late enough to talk through the departing John thing with time to spare for the mess I'd gotten into. Way back when, Didi's mother's preferred baby-sitter had been Nancy the Hun, so Didi might be more objective about Charlie Finnemeyer than I.

She breezed in about five-thirty, a vision in gray stretch pants and a bulky sweater designed to slip off her slender shoulder. As usual, she wore her long blond hair in a dancer's French twist.

I immediately put out our food. The kids sat at the table with their backs toward the pass-through. Rip slid into the hallway end, Didi to my right at the other end. Judging by the expressions, the stew wasn't half bad.

"Sell any pictures yet, Flash?" my buddy quizzed Garry, who lit up much like her nickname for him. In honor of his teeth (our son's mouth was elbow level to many of his peers), he had volunteered to manage the sixth-grade basketball team, which gave him ample opportunity to use his camera.

"No, but . . . " If he hadn't been trapped against the wall, our son would have fetched his latest set of prints.

"Any cute boys in the chorus?" Didi asked Chelsea.

Our daughter's face screwed up with scorn. "There are no boys in my chorus."

"Ooh, that's right, I forgot," Didi sympathized. My stage-struck friend still sang with an adult group that performed jointly with Chelsea's school singing group. Last fall the director had invited our famous high school friend, Jan Fairchild, to do a number at the end of one of their concerts, which tragically turned out to be Jan's last performance anywhere. Didi deftly suppressed such memories, but innocent details often got wiped clean along with the rest of the slate.

When the catch-up conversation dwindled, I asked Rip if he ever found out why the art teacher, Geraldine Trelawny, had been crying the other day.

Rip waved his coffee cup and nodded once. "Motorcycle guy she'd been living with drove off into the sunset. Broke her heart. Apparently he took all her Grateful Dead CDs. If the sniveling continues much longer, I'm going to have to have her in for another talk."

I checked Didi to see whether the story had touched any nerves, but she was busy winking at Garry and feeding herself salad.

Rip sipped his coffee. "Guess who we think rigged that paint pan above the art room doorway."

My jaw dropped. "Ryan Cooperman?"

"Yup."

"Got any proof?"

Rip waved his head. "Nobody actually saw him do it. But we have him for cutting last period yesterday."

I remembered that Joanne Henry had summoned Rip to the paint pan disaster immediately after our meeting with the Coopermans.

"So Ryan actually skipped class while you were conferring in with his parents?"

"Um-hmm."

"What are you going to do?"

"Three-day suspension. His parents have to come in again tomorrow. I'm going to tell them this is Ryan's last chance with us. If he so much as walks down the hall with his shirttail out, he's gone." The dress code required shirttails to be tucked in. As violations go, it ranked right up there with chewing gum.

Didi had been monitoring our conversation intently, probably because Ryan had been a source of interest before. "What will that solve?" she wanted to know.

"Ryan's a very frustrated, very unhappy kid," Rip began his serious answer to Didi's serious question, "and he's been going to great lengths to make his parents notice. We've pointed this out to them—and to Ryan—but nobody's listening. Bottom line: Ryan doesn't want to be at Bryn Derwyn, so he won't allow anything we do to get through to him."

"So you're going to kick him out?" A timely flashback reminded me that my best friend's own high school behavior had been a little sketchy.

"We're not doing him any good, Didi. And he's doing our school a lot of harm. There comes a point when you just plain have to cut your losses."

Didi, always a tenacious fighter, disliked that answer.

"We're not exactly giving up on him," Rip reminded her. "In fact, we're putting the decision of whether he stays or goes into his own hands."

Didi nodded at that. Free will. Right up her alley.

When the time came, Rip asked whether I wanted any help with the dishes; but I thanked him and shooed him and the kids off to do school work.

"That's nice," Didi remarked sadly after everyone else was gone.

I poured the remaining stew into a smaller container to refrigerate it. "What is?" I had to ask.

"That Rip offered to help in the kitchen."

"He was probably just hinting that the kids should do it."

"Still," Didi persisted, "he would have helped if you wanted him to." When she looked up from the dishwasher, I noticed tears in her eyes.

"What are we really talking about here?" I asked.

Didi's lower lip quivered, so she bit it. Then she folded her arms across her blue-gray sweater and fixed me with storm-cloud eyes.

"John," she admitted. "He's such a jerk."

"And you miss him already."

She straightened up, tucked a strand of blond hair behind her ear, squeezed her French twist to tighten the hairpins. "No," she said finally. "No, I don't. It's just . . ."

"I know," I told her. She had had hopes for this one; and the hopes had died, so she was mourning them.

"I take it that your breakup had something to do with dishes?"

"Guess they don't call you Nancy Drew for nothing."

"Not in my presence they don't."

"He seemed so considerate, you know? He did the car door bit, held my coat for me, all that old-fashioned stuff. I didn't know how I felt about any of it until he told me about a radio show he heard, a call-in. They'd been talking about husbands and wives being polite to each other."

"Yes," I said, turning off the water so I wouldn't miss a word.

"This guy, who was supposed to be an authority of some sort,"—she rolled her eyes in an aren't-they-all dismissal—"said it was only fair for the man to help his wife with the dishes."

"Why?" I asked. "Because she cooked?"

"Yeah, probably," Didi said with an expression indicative of how equal that was.

I wagged my head. Rip happened to be a better cook than I. He just didn't have any time to do it.

Didi had compressed her lips, and now she released them. "That wasn't what John and I argued about."

"Oh?"

"A woman caller said whenever her husband helped her clean up dinner, he behaved as if he thought she ought to thank him."

"Oh dear," I said.

"Exactly. The expert didn't understand what was wrong with that. He said it didn't cost anything to say thank you."

Just the woman's self-esteem. "How did John respond to that?"

"He didn't get it, so I explained it to him. I said the husband's attitude implied that doing dishes was women's work; and even though the man occasionally helped out of the goodness of his heart, he felt he was lowering himself to do it."

"So?"

"So John still thought the radio psychologist was right, that the wife should thank her husband for doing something out of the goodness of his heart."

"Did you kick him out then or later?" I asked.

Didi smiled, a crooked, laughing-at-my-pain grin that made the tears in her hazel eyes sparkle. "Actually, I did exactly what Rip is doing with that kid."

"What do you mean?"

"I put the decision about whether John should stay or go into his own hands."

"His own hands?"

"Yes, I told him that's what his love life would amount to if he didn't get the hell out of my house."

We drank strawberry milkshakes while watching a Bruce Willis movie, the second go-around for me, the fourth for Didi, but then I had never aspired to act. Didi, obviously, devoted herself to fantasies of all sorts.

Around nine the kids turned in, Friday being a school day. Rip put the computer to sleep around ten-thirty and himself shortly after that. I wanted to see the eleven o'clock news in case something further had been learned about Ned Stewart's death.

Early on I had told Didi everything I knew about Charlie's trial, but the subject kept popping up as if it had never been dropped.

"Do you really think Charlie might have killed that witness?" she asked just as the news program began.

I shrugged, unwilling to make too much of my fears.

Didi slurped the last of her milkshake. "Seriously, Gin," she assured me, "he's one of the good guys. Bank on it."

"You haven't seen him in decades," I argued. "He's changed, Dee. So has Birdie."

"So you're telling me Ozzie and Harriet have become Bonnie and Clyde? Puh." She switched channels with the remote.

"Wait, wait. Go back," I shouted. "Somebody died. I want to see that."

She clicked back to the station we just left. A female newscaster with a perfect complexion and a perky nose solemnly informed us that Mr. Roland Ignatowski had been found dead by his wife, "who came home around four P.M. from a shopping trip to find her husband asleep in his armchair. 'Except he wasn't asleep.'

"Mr. Ignatowski, an avid antique collector, had purchased an Oriental rug that an appraiser told him had been artificially aged, allegedly by Mr. Charles Finnemeyer, a former professor.

"Earlier this week a prospective witness at Mr. Finnemeyer's trial, Dr. Ned Stewart, the Curator of Textiles at the Philadelphia Museum of Art, was found in his car just outside the popular Philadelphia restaurant, Jack's Firehouse, also dead of an apparent heart attack.

"Although there was no evidence of foul play in either case, Mr. Ignatowski's death is the second sudden death connected to the fraud trial, and for that reason an autopsy will be performed."

My hands had gone clammy as I stared wide-eyed at the screen.

"You don't still think . . . ?" Didi remarked, her whole body shrunk back in denial.

I grabbed her arm. "Why couldn't it be murder?" I snapped, surprised by my own vehemence. "You've got to admit it's suspicious, Dee. Charlie doesn't need this. He really doesn't."

"It is not suspicious," my friend asserted. "Getting rid of the guy who bought the rug from the dealer makes no sense. His death won't make a bit of difference to the trial."

I scowled. "I don't like the timing, and obviously neither do the police. It just plain looks bad."

"How so?"

"The scandal over Charlie's retirement appeared in the morning paper—and Ignatowski dies the very same day? There has to be a connection."

Didi wagged her head at the TV. "I don't see any." She clicked the set off.

"Be right back," I said, sticking my feet into slippers and trotting down the hall toward the front door. I yanked Rip's overcoat off a hanger and flipped on the driveway spotlights. The Textile yearbook of Charlie's last teaching year was still in the back of the Subaru.

Didi waited cross-legged on the couch. "What's this all about?" she asked after I handed her the book.

It had been freezing outside, and I still wore Rip's overcoat. Now I wrapped the long, black wool sleeves around myself. "I want to finish matching some names and faces," I told her.

"Why?"

"Possible witnesses against Charlie," I said, and quickly explained about the list the prosecutor had solicited from Textile's alumni office.

"Okay, okay." Didi humored me. "Assuming the two deaths were murder, which I don't, but just assuming—why would any of these women murder either Stewart or Ignatowski? Who cares about an eight-year-old student prank that didn't even work?"

Not wanting to admit that she had a point, I shook my head. "Charlie took early retirement to shield somebody—somebody who *attempted* fraud at his expense—and I don't like her getting away with it. Especially when coming clean now would help him so much."

Didi waved her blond head. She had washed off her makeup and years of maturity.

I told her, "I just can't pinpoint any other villains in this story, can you?"

Didi's face said how stupid that sounded. "Listen to yourself, Gin."

"Well, Charlie, yes," I admitted. "But you just told me he's one of the good guys."

"And you just told me he's changed. Birdie, too. Make up your mind."

I worked on that a minute. "I don't think he drives anymore," I mused aloud. "But if he got a ride . . ." I shook my head at the sheer absurdity of our conversation.

Didi stared me down until I protested, "Jeez, Dee, the guy carries oxygen around with him."

"You started this," she pointed out, and of course she was right—on both counts.

After a couple minutes of chewing my lip, I said, "Guess that means it had to be poison or something easy."

"Now you're talking," Didi congratulated me. "Got to be half a dozen different drugs out there that can cause a heart attack." She seemed buoyed by the notion, and I made a face to tell her how that struck me. "Hell, they've got one to do just about everything else," she defended herself.

"I guess."

We settled into a thoughtful silence. The house breathed and groaned over the cold outside while my friend and I faced each other in the softly lighted room. Our feet tucked under us like teenagers, once again we seemed to believe that together we could figure out the world if only the world would give us a couple of hints.

"What we really need to know is which student Charlie shielded," I declared.

"Then what?" Didi wondered. "Talk her into testifying on Charlie's behalf?"

I shrugged. That had been my earlier plan, but I held out less and less hope.

"If we find her, then we go from there," I concluded. "Anyhow, I can't think of anything else to do."

"Or anybody else to do it," Didi remarked.

Which was quite true. The FBI had wrapped up its investigation prior to the trial; and if the autopsy of Roland Ignatowski indicated an ordinary heart attack, the current police investigation would also stall.

However, if the autopsy was inconclusive, or if it suggested murder, Charlie would be scrutinized within an inch of his life.

I tapped the yearbook on Didi's lap. "I'll read you a name," I told her. "You find the face."

At first we concentrated on the women from the newspaper clipping, the five participants in the international fabric design competition. Since they were probably Charlie's best students, I figured they were the most likely candidates for his protection.

Only Amy Quilleran was ruled out because of geography. She had married and moved to Texas. The other four—Janella Piper, Pamela Zenzinger, Sally Shultz, and Maxine Nash née Devon—had remained on the East Coast, and sadly all were scheduled to testify against Charlie.

We didn't stop there, though. We tried to find faces to match everyone else on the prosecutor's list (no luck); then, working with the information from the alumni office, we tried to identify the seniors who had taken classes with Charlie during his final year at Textile.

"My eyes ache," Didi complained. "Where are we anyway?"

"Nowhere," I admitted. "Let's go to bed."

Chapter 17

Friday, January 7, offered snow squalls, little eddies of soap flakes swirling earnestly around in circles only to disappear into the gloomy morning shadows. Our household went through a similar routine.

First Didi hurried off to open the Beverage Barn. Then, hunching low into their coat collars, the kids scurried down the street to their bus stop, and finally Rip trotted from the door to his car with a plaid scarf thrown across his mouth.

Abandoned in the empty front hall in the even emptier house, Gretsky and I glanced at each other with identical poor-me expressions.

"They'll be back," I comforted our dog, but he recognized a bone when he was tossed one. A very carpe diem sort of animal, he lumbered off to kill some time with a nap.

I went upstairs to make the bed and clean the bathroom, killing some time of my own until a more suitable hour for dropping into a business establishment. Eric Allen had summoned me not once but twice. I couldn't put off our meeting any longer; I bid my own farewell to the dog and drove back across the river to my hometown.

Five stories of gray stone block was as sophisticated as architecture got in Ludwig, Pennsylvania. The tinted glass double doors had plain black plastic handles that opened with a whoosh of suction and vibrated two more interior doors. The lobby extended left and right to an internal post office and small bank branch respectively. Straight ahead across the gray-threaded white marble floor were elevators and a discreet set of stairs.

The people coming and going at that morning hour wore more business suits and ties, high heels, and silk blouses than I had ever seen in town as a kid, but then the building contained mortgage and insurance companies, an appointment-only jeweler, three law firms, and a travel agency. Mom and Pop could ignore this place for most of their lifetime and make out just fine. Unless they were well off or in serious trouble like Charlie and Birdie Finnemeyer.

Up on the second floor I pushed through the door with Eric's firm name painted in white script. The whole office front was faced with tinted glass, showing me even before I entered that any visitors were already in conference with their attorneys.

The receptionist seemed intent on transcribing some dictation into a computer. That, or she was listening to Led Zepplin through little earphones while she wrote her boyfriend in the Navy. Fortunately, she didn't mind being interrupted. She lifted the right earphone and smiled.

"Eric Allen?" I asked.

"He's with clients right now. Do you mind waiting?"

"The Finnemeyers, by any chance?"

"Oh," said the fresh-faced young woman. She wore a black suit with no blouse and had spent twice as much on her haircut as I could afford. "Are you Mrs. Barnes? I think Eric is expecting you."

"He's been expecting me for a couple days," I pointed out, and the smile broadened.

"Go ahead in. Third door down." She pointed to the hall on the right.

I couldn't get the words, but Eric's voice wafted into the hall from a medium-size conference room with a round wooden table in its center. Through a wire-reinforced glass window I could see that Eric's foot rested on the seat of a chair, and I made a mental note to avoid parking my white wool slacks on that particular spot.

I tapped on the glass, and Eric's head snapped up. He immediately raised a finger to ask the Finnemeyers to hold some thought, then opened the door for me.

"Gin!" he said with vehemence. "Long time no see."

I stepped inside. "Birdie," I said, nodding my hello. "Charlie. I hope you're both well."

In return I received a brief, disappointed nod from Charlie and a cold stare from his wife, obviously more fallout from the newspaper leak that everybody believed was my fault—unfortunately, even me.

Yet, judging by their body language, the older couple had more than the retirement scandal on their minds. Finished with me, they shriveled back into their chairs, two lumps of fresh dejection. Birdie blinked rapidly behind her glasses and watched Eric as if he held the rope to her guillotine blade. Charlie furtively stroked his white beard and mustache as if the habit were a crime. No oxygen tubes so far, but if the stress level in the room skewed any higher, I suspected they came next.

"I'll get to you in a minute." Eric motioned me into a clean chair, then focused on Birdie.

"You were telling me why you went to the Ignatowskis' house yesterday," he reminded her.

I almost choked on ordinary air. Birdie Finnemeyer had been at the Ignatowskis'? Yesterday? The day Roland died? I wanted to jump up and pace, maybe glare at the woman or yell "Yikes!" Instead I just squeezed the polish off my chair arms.

Eric ignored me, waved a hand to encourage his client's wife. "Please explain."

His words held no threat, but there was a discernible edge to the attorney's voice that frightened the older woman. Her lips twitched. Her hands mangled a hankie. Her eyes wanted to look somewhere else, anywhere except Eric's face.

"Charlie had an episode yesterday," she mumbled at her lap. "A bad one." She risked a glance at Eric but her eyes quickly scurried back to her tweed skirt. "I was afraid . . . I wanted . . . I thought if I convinced Mr. Ignatowski to drop the case that, that all this would be over and Charlie would, would be okay."

Charlie seemed not to grasp her recital, because he added nothing, merely manifested his sympathy for her distress with a pained expression and a couple of pats to the back of her chair. Clearly he was the least powerful person in the room, in need of all sorts of help. And although he may have been resigned to that, it diminished him. In his actual presence last night's speculations about how he might have managed to commit murder seemed ridiculous.

Eric consulted the ceiling. A white shirt and charcoal pin-striped vest accentuated his slim waist and broad shoulders. The shoe on the chair seat was black, wing-tipped, and shiny. His trousers held a crisp press. Even his clean shave and tidy haircut screamed privilege and power. He was doing his best to relate.

"Mrs. Finnemeyer, let me try to explain this to you. The plaintiff can't drop the case at this point, only the government can."

Birdie's eyebrows, thin strips of sparse fuzz, curled with confusion.

"So your going to the Ignatowskis' was a futile thing to do, and also foolish, as it turned out." Eric's latter remark was an aside to himself, but I caught the implication even if Birdie didn't. So far, Miss Muffett remained ignorant of the spider's existence.

"Please don't forget you were this close to being indicted yourself," Eric continued, "and if you pull any more stunts like yesterday, you will probably be arrested."

Birdie glanced at her husband, hoping for comfort. He stonewalled it, but this time I sensed that he had heard and understood his attorney perfectly.

Eric addressed Birdie exclusively. "Now suppose you tell me exactly what you did and did not do when you went out to the Ignatowskis' house."

Birdie gulped and visually sought her husband's permission to speak. Charlie appeared not to care one way or the other.

Worried but willing, Birdie began. "I told you Charlie had

an episode yesterday—terrible coughing, lots of trouble getting his breath. I took him to the doctor, and afterward he was
exhausted. He fell asleep in the car.

"I . . . I was quite upset. I got to thinking about how much
of a strain this trial has been and how wonderful it would be
if it all went away. So like I said, I drove out to Gwynedd to
speak with Mr. Ignatowski, you know—to try to convince him
to, to, . . . "

"Did you go into the house?"

Birdie's chin lifted. "No. I rang the bell, but nobody answered, so I looked around a bit. The garage was open and a
car seemed to be missing, so I decided to sit on the front step
and wait as long as I could. I figured if Charlie woke up, we
would just leave."

"How did you know where the Ignatowskis lived?"

"Oh, uh, the newspaper and then the phone book. Even the
rural roads use house numbers now. We have one, too."

"Go on."

"Well, I just sat there, crying, for a while. It'd been a tough
day for me, a tough month, and then Mrs. Ignatowski came
home."

"What happened then? Did she let you in?"

"No. No, I met her halfway up the path to the front door."

"Yes?"

"She doesn't always come to court, but she knew who I
was, and she asked me why I was there. Then she told me she
was sorry, there was nothing she could do."

"Anything else?"

Birdie blushed and spoke again to her lap. "She said she
didn't think it was a good idea for us to be there, and if we
didn't leave she would have to call the police."

Eric's sudden "Good, good," exclamation startled the
woman. "So you left almost immediately after Mrs. Ignatowski came home. Is that correct?" the lawyer asked eagerly.

"Yes, of course. Charlie woke up and, yes, of course we
left. There was nothing else to do."

"That's good, Birdie."

"It is?"

"Yes. Now why don't you take Charlie home and have a nice restful weekend. The trial resumes on Monday, and you'll both need your energy."

"Okay," Birdie agreed as we all stood up, then just slightly louder she told her husband, "Come on, dear."

When the Finnemeyers were gone, Eric and I regarded each other for a stiff, silent moment. He seemed to be firing up a scorching blast, but I deflected him with an observation.

"Birdie doesn't realize that Mrs. Ignatowski went inside and found her husband dead, does she?"

My immolation was delayed while Eric answered, "Nope."

"Or that if the police decide it was murder, she and Charlie will be the number-one suspects."

Eric's eyes widened. "You really should've been a lawyer," he told me again. "I'm impressed."

I assured him I hated paperwork, which was true enough. "What did you mean when you said Birdie was almost indicted?"

Eric dusted off his chair and finally sat down, gestured for me to do the same. "You really don't know?"

"Would I have to ask if I knew?"

My husband's old friend studied me a moment before he decided to confide. "She was the one who actually sold the rug to the dealer, who then sold it to the eventual fraud victim, Roland Ignatowski."

My confusion must have shown, because Eric elaborated. "Birdie approached the dealer about the rug—a few times. When she finally managed to get him interested in it, she negotiated the price and later physically delivered it. It's only five by ten and not very thick, so it wasn't especially difficult for her to carry."

I stared out the draped window at the Ludwig horizon, the flat roof of a two-story hardware store, a church spire behind some distant trees. This new information had answered one of my biggest questions—how a man who had trouble walking across a room could manage the sale of a rug without help.

"So why wasn't Birdie indicted?" I wondered aloud.

"The government has a more provable case against Charlie—witnesses to testify that he artificially aged items a number of times in the past."

"For teaching purposes," I argued.

"That will be my stance, of course. But in Birdie's case, it would be her word against the dealer's. No corroborating witnesses. Impossible to prove anything either of them said."

"I see." Although I didn't entirely. I was just happy that one of the Finnemeyers was safe, at least for the time being.

Eric picked up on my optimism and grunted to dismiss it. "The Finnemeyers still seem to believe that Charlie's poor health will sway the jury, probably even get him off. You already know what I think of that."

"You're not as trusting as they are."

He shook his head. "Not at all," he replied. "Juries are extremely unpredictable. I'd be a fool to count on sentiment to get an acquittal. You know why the feds have such a phenomenal conviction record? Because they don't even go to trial until they're ninety-eight percent sure they can win." He waved his head glumly, apparently ruing his underdog situation. "Getting Charlie off will take all the ammunition I can muster—and a whole lot of luck."

I nodded, fully appreciating the scope of his dilemma for the first time.

Eric closed his eyes. His cheek rolled from the tension in his jaw. "Please tell me you didn't leak that retirement story to the press."

Years before, when we were closer, I might have dismissed his question with a joke, but not today.

"No," I assured him. "And no, I can't think of how it happened. It just did." Eric ran his hands through his hair and sighed.

I had to ask. "Do you think the leak triggered Ignatowski's death?"

"You mean our second highly suspicious heart attack?" The attorney's jaw was rolling again, and his eyes bored into me. "It's risky getting old," he said. "Everybody knows that."

So he didn't want to speculate about either death. Can't say I blamed him.

"Right," I said. "I guess I watch too much television."

Our discussion could have ended right there. I certainly didn't want to delve into the leak any further, but I was troubled by a detail. "Don't newspapers usually insist on two sources before they print a story?"

"Gin, you're giving me a headache."

"Don't they?"

"Yes, they do. Elementary precaution."

"So two people told them about the retirement?"

"No. One leak, one confirmation. In this case Birdie Finnemeyer provided the confirmation."

I was shocked and apparently looked it.

"A rather brazen reporter phoned Mrs. Finnemeyer and asked whether it was true that her husband retired after a scandal over a fake Hewson quilt. 'How did you find out?' our Birdie chirped. Voilà—confirmation."

"Oh, dear," I said.

"Oh dear, indeed," Eric agreed.

On the way past the receptionist's desk, I paused as if I'd forgotten something.

"Excuse me, June," for that was the name on the desk plaque. "I meant to ask Mr. Allen where the out-of-town witnesses stay during a trial. Somewhere secure, I hope."

"No, not especially," the young woman replied. "They stay at the Holiday Inn at Fourth and Arch. We've never had a problem."

"Thanks," I said. "Give my regards to your boyfriend."

She tilted her head as if I were crazy.

Chapter 18

Sitting in my car with the heater running, I phoned Didi at the Beverage Barn. She sounded as cold as one of her beers, which at this time of year could be drunk without the benefit of artificial refrigeration.

"Got any weekend plans?" I inquired.

"You know I don't." I also knew how she felt about that. John was gone but not yet forgotten.

"How'd you like to spend it at a Holiday Inn?"

"What do you mean? Hooking? I'm not quite that desperate."

"Ho, ho, ho," I replied to let her know I knew she was kidding.

"Hmph," she responded, as if I'd made my own poor joke.

"The government witnesses from out of town stay at the Fourth and Arch Holiday Inn," I finally explained.

"And you want me to find out . . . what do you want me to find out? These people are against Charlie, aren't they?"

"Mostly," I agreed. "They're probably lined up to testify about the fakes Charlie used as teaching tools. But one of them might know who appliquéd the make-believe Hewson quilt then tried to pass it off as real. Worth asking, don't you think?"

"Oh, yeah."

She sounded ready to ring off and go pack, but I held her another second. "You still remember what all the suspects

looked like?" Charlie's last students would be eight years older
than their yearbook pictures, but Didi has always been pretty
good with names and faces.

Her reply: "Does a duck quack?"

My drive-thru hamburger lunch was eaten in the car, parked
opposite the house I lived in as a child. Also in sight was the
Finnemeyers' previous home two doors down. Reluctant to
begin my chore, I persisted with the food until rigor mortis
claimed the fries and the creamer congealed across the top of
my coffee. Only then did I give myself over to the confusing
sensation of being a little girl again.

Not even out of the car yet and memories swarmed me,
almost tactile in nature. I could feel the rough sidewalk
through the soles of my roller skates, and instinctively I sent
a hand to check the scar on my knee.

Beside the car to my right a blue spruce from one of Didi's
family's Christmases had grown as high as the second-story
window. Its strong scent tainted the aftertaste of my French
fries. In fact, every tree on the block was either much bigger
or, like the Finnemeyers' red maple, missing entirely.

The tasteful white siding of the house in between theirs and
ours was now an indestructible yellow aluminum dulled by
the cold white winter sky. Along the block several other paint
colors also seemed new.

Our house, so small to my adult eyes, had been built of
brick. The roof peaked front to back, and the shape reminded
me of the attic playroom my mother once cleared for me. In
summer it became intolerably ripe with roasted dust and old
furniture, but in my memory I heard soothing rain on the roof.
Then, closing my eyes, I visualized our blooming Rose of
Sharon tree from above, the lavender and maroon flowers like
crepe-paper tufts stuck onto a houseplant. Bliss.

Next my mind traveled down to my bedroom, where char-
treuse fauns on a background of purple shyly peeked through
loops of daisies. White ruffles, white dresser, white everything
else. It had been a bold room for a girl, zany and different,
and I was proud that my father once said it suited me.

My father. The basement shop, the darkroom for his photography hobby . . .

I stepped out of the car to forestall more. I wasn't there to mourn but to follow the threads of memory for Charlie and Birdie's sakes. I was hoping for an inspiration.

Yet if I trespassed into the small yards or even lingered for long, women would emerge from their houses to pull a weed or pick up a newspaper, any excuse that would allow them to memorize my face or perhaps even learn my business. Nostalgia would not do. I needed a genuine errand the present residents could embrace.

My purse still contained a copy of the prosecution's witness list, including the name Oscar Tribordella. Lloyd's mandatory justification for calling this witness read simply "rug expert," but if Tribordella was so knowledgeable, why had the trial been adjourned until the deceased Dr. Ned Stewart could be replaced?

Like Eric, I suspected that Tribordella wasn't just another textile Ph.D. He probably knew something key, which meant he knew things about Charlie that Charlie would not want told. The retirement can of worms all over again. It seemed unlikely that I would learn much about him here, but the ruse was plausible enough to serve.

My first encounter was with an elderly lady hastily wrapped in a man's overcoat. She emerged from my old house, eyed me sternly, and lifted the lid of the mailbox attached to the porch railing.

"I used to live here," I called.

No response.

"Do you know anyone named Oscar Tribordella?"

She backed through her front door and pressed it soundly shut.

I had crossed the street by now and stood exposed on all sides roughly front and center of the yellow-sided house. The January air barked my cheeks and hands, and in my frozen mind Charlie and Birdie stubbornly remained as they as they were now—elderly and overwhelmed.

Shivering and wishing something would happen in my

head, I began to circle the block. From the fourth house clock-wise a mother carrying a toddler hurried toward her car, keys jangling in her reddened fingers.

"Hi. I'm Ginger Struve Barnes," I hastily introduced myself. "I'm looking for Oscar Tribordella. Does he live around her anymore?"

The young woman paused to look at me, decide if I was for real.

"No," she said, and that was that.

An alley separated our former backyard from the back neighbors. Rutted crushed stone caused me to watch my footing until I reached our old garage. Warmer now, I stopped to look around, drink in the changes.

Dad's patch of raspberry bushes had been cleared away, replaced by tomato plants frozen black. And in all the years nobody had bothered to fix the cement walkway leading to the back door. Its heaved-up segments were useless now even for hopscotch.

I ventured around the far side of the garage away from the view of the current owner and gazed toward the Finnemeyers' yard.

The breeze wiggled a tree branch and shocked me with an unexpected image. Sunshine stroked a dripping wet rug, which flapped and snapped in the wind. I must have possessed the imprint before but suppressed it. Now I remembered.

Once in a while, one at a time, some unusually beautiful item hung from the Finnemeyers' clothesline, strung as another line was now from porch to pole. Other items might have lain on the grass, supported just above the muddy earth by the thin green blades. Quilts, tablecloths, napkins, and occasionally an embroidered blouse. Some of Charlie's yard sale discoveries remained exposed for days, others only hours, probably the difference between preserving and ruining the piece. But at five, seven, ten I assumed that that was the way Charlie cleaned his treasures.

For some old fabric pieces, of course, that was true. But not hand-tied wool rugs. Without realizing it, I had seen Charlie aging his teaching tools, preparing samples for his students to judge. Real or fake? Notice this patch? When was it done, Sally? See this wear here? What does it tell you, Brian?

I marched up the sidewalk to the back door of the yellow-sided house, Charlie's former next-door neighbor's home.

A middle-age woman answered my knock. Her dark hair was uncombed, her sweatshirt smeared with cinnamon brown. She wore running shoes as I often did and a more trusting expression than I would have had I encountered a stranger on my back doorstep.

"Yes? Can I help you?" she inquired. Pouches under her eyes, no makeup. She was as at-home as you can get.

"I'm really sorry to bother you like this, but I'm a friend of Charlie Finnemeyer, who used to live over there." I waved a hand at the house to my left. "I lived over here as a kid." I pointed a shoulder to my right. "Anyway, Charlie needs to find somebody named Oscar Tribordella, and I'm trying to help. It's really very important. Have you ever heard of a man by that name?"

"What's your name, honey?"

"Ginger Struve Barnes." I felt childish saying it, especially since I should have said it before, but my answer was well received.

"Oh, Cindy's girl. Come on in a second," the woman said decisively. "I got cookies in."

It had been years since anyone called my mother anything but Cynthia, and the familiarity of it disconcerted me. Yet I thanked her and entered a kitchen redolent of spice.

And charred cookies. The woman put on an oven mitt, extracted a batch of what aspired to be ginger snaps, and tossed the whole sheet into the sink.

"Damn," she swore. "I gotta get a new timer."

"It's my fault," I apologized. "If I get anywhere near baking cookies they turn into hockey pucks."

The woman's face finally thawed. "I'm Gertie," she said. "My mom liked your mom a lot."

"You got married and moved away," I said, retrieving the information from my mental archives.

"Something like that."

"But you're back."

"My mother gave me the house. Never figured I'd need it, but here I am."

We had settled into her kitchen chairs and faced each other over racks of cooling goodies, baked before me and my cookie curse arrived.

"Do you know what's going on with Charlie?" I inquired. She didn't, didn't even remember Charlie, but I filled her in anyway.

". . . so Eric Allen, Charlie's lawyer, would like to know more about one of the government witnesses—Oscar Tribordella. Just to be prepared, you know?"

Gertie watched me looking dejected for a minute. Not only was I wasting her time, I was wasting my own as well. Probably this Oscar character had nothing to do with Ludwig. For all I knew he lived in Milwaukee and raised cows for a living.

"You want to ask my mom?" Gertie inquired.

I did a double-take. "I thought . . ."

"You thought I inherited the house, didn't you?"

I opened my mouth but there was nothing in it.

"It's okay. I'm lucky my mother is still alive. You want me to call her?"

"Um, sure," I mumbled.

Gertie worked on an old-fashioned red wall phone and was soon engaged in one of those lifelong conversations we all have with our mothers, the kind that gets interrupted but never really ends. Even after the grave, I'm told that women hear rebuttal after rebuttal from their female parents, advice they never want and rarely heed. "Don't marry that creep, he'll make you as miserable as your cousin Sue. Listen to me, young lady, I know what I'm talking about."

Eventually, the current topic (salt intake as it related to high blood pressure) slowed, and Gertie was able to mention me.

"Cindy's girl Ginny's here, and she wants to know did you ever hear of a guy named . . . what was the name?"

"Oscar Tribordella."

"Oscar Tribordella, Mom. Ever hear of him?"

Gertie widened her eyes and handed me the phone.

"Uh, hi, uh . . ." I shrugged, hoping to get some help with her mother's name.

"Selma," she whispered.

"Hi, Selma. This is Ginger Barnes."

The older woman had already left the starting block, a gossip greyhound way too eager for the chase. "Oh, you must remember him," Selma insisted. "Gawky boy, glasses."

"Um."

"Oh, sure you do. Mrs. Fry's son-in-law. Sold furniture or some such crap at Wanamakers before it became whatever it became. You remember, don'cha?"

"A little before my time, maybe," I offered in my own defense. The department store in question had been sold and renamed long before I got my first credit card.

"How old are you anyway?"

I told her.

"Oh, crap, honey. You're just a baby."

At times I agreed with her. Today, however, was not one of those times. "Uh, Selma, can you please tell me a little more about Oscar? He sold furniture, you said. Did that by any chance include rugs?"

"Rugs, smugs. I don't know. He was a pain in the ass, that one. If raccoons got into your trash, he'd be on the phone at dawn complaining about the mess in the alley. Never gave to the heart fund—I collected the block, you know—and he handed out dimes for Halloween. Cheap bastard. What could you get for a dime even then?"

"So he lived . . . where did he live?"

"He and the bride lived with her mother, Mrs. Fry, for a couple years, saving money the old lady always said, but squeezing a buck until it yelled ouch was more like it."

I didn't care about that. "You say Oscar was quite a complainer?" I prompted. The phone was flattening my ear by then; and after my cold, greasy lunch, the cookie smell was killing me. But I thought I almost understood where Oscar Tribordella fit into Charlie's woes, and I wanted to make sure Selma gave me everything she had before I rang off.

"One time my youngest boy handed out fliers—about mow-

ing grass or something. Oscar called me up to tell me it was
illegal to put stuff in mailboxes that hadn't been mailed. He
did that kinda crap all the time. Real pain in the ass."

"Thank you, Selma. That's actually quite helpful."

"It is?" She sounded as stunned by that as I was.

I mentally connected the dots. Oscar worked at an upscale
department store in the furniture department, which typically
included carpeting and reproductions of Oriental rugs. Presum-
ably a man with such an occupation would be more likely to
notice a beautiful rug dangling on a clothesline for a few days,
especially if he had occasion to walk to the back of his mother-
in-law's yard, for example to put out trash or get his car out
of the garage. I had no recollection of Mrs. Fry's son-in-law,
but I did remember that her property lay directly across the
alley from the Finnemeyers'.

So. If this Oscar character actually was the pedantic
whistle-blower Selma described, he very well may have volunteered to seal Charlie's fate in court. With glee.

Crap, as Selma so aptly put it.

I left Gertie's kitchen carrying the burden of two regrets.
One, I had nothing good to report to Eric, quite the opposite—
again. And two, Gertie never offered me even one cookie.

Some days you can't even steal a break.

Chapter 19

The other day in a fit of clumsiness I knocked my night table lamp to the floor, denting the shade pretty good and providing me with just the excuse I needed now. The route out of Ludwig toward a Line Lexington lamp store ran near enough to the Finnemeyers' semirural home that I could reasonably claim that I just dropped in to see whether they needed anything.

Primarily I wanted to alleviate my compounding concern. In view of their recent decisions, the elderly couple didn't appear to possess one reliable brain cell between them. Only yesterday Birdie had risked approaching Roland Ignatowski—exposing herself to potentially disastrous implications she clearly did not fathom. And, although I worried less about Charlie's reasoning ability, I doubted that withholding information from his attorney would remain his only miscalculation.

With these thoughts in mind I sped north toward Chalfont. Friday afternoon traffic had picked up, but if the travelers were aiming for the homes out here, at least they were hurrying toward a slower, saner pace, a place of open fields and broad sky, blanketed horses and apple orchards. Ice lay white in the grassy gutters, crows foraged among the remnants of cornstalks; and where developments huddled in the chilly breeze, dry late-season leaves scudded across the sidewalks.

As I reached the edge of the Finnemeyers' property, I could

see Birdie loading something into the back of their station wagon. While I slowed my car, she slammed the hatch of the rusting, robin's egg blue vehicle and brushed her hands briskly down the front of her carcoat, a person pleased by an accomplishment.

"Please don't tell me this is what it looks like," I asked whatever deity was on duty. Panic warmed me to my ears, made me oblivious to anything but Birdie, who began to march purposefully back toward her house as soon as I turned into their drive.

I left my keys dangling in the ignition and rushed to catch up with the elderly woman. "Birdie, stop. What are you doing?" I asked.

My childhood baby-sitter whirled to face me. Magnified by her glasses her powder blue eyes were hard and steady. A gust of breeze caused a tuft of her thin silver hair to quiver. Hands stuffed into her pockets, she lifted her chin and said, "Don't try to talk me out of it, girlie. You was me you'd do the same thing."

"You're going away?" I asked just to be sure.

"Yes, we are. And don't you be lecturing me about it now. I don't want to hear it."

"Okay," I said. "Fine. May I at least come in and say good-bye to Charlie."

That jostled her slightly off track. She glowered at my jacket zipper and thought for a second, long enough for me to open the kitchen door and hold it for her.

"Oh, all right," she agreed, "but only for a minute. I got things to do."

"Yes, I'm sure you're in a hurry. I'll be quick."

Luckily, that satisfied her. She bustled past me, through the kitchen and living room, and disappeared into the bedroom off to the right.

Sitting on one of the padded captain's chairs at the kitchen table, Charlie looked up from a mug of coffee and blinked at me. I thought his eyes looked teary, but perhaps I imagined that. He waved his hand at a facing chair and said, "Ginger

Snap, have a seat." Then he rubbed the back of his hand under his nose.

"Uncle Wunk," I replied, in lieu of a greeting.

We harbored our own thoughts for half a minute, then I said, "I suppose you know you can't go."

"Yes, I know. Birdie just needed something to do."

"She thinks she's packing for real."

Charlie grunted. "She isn't. How's your family?"

"Fine, thanks."

"Got any pictures of your kids?"

I showed him a couple from my wallet. He seemed wistful and pleased, so I gave him a few motherly details, proud stuff I thought he might enjoy.

He smiled in a distant sort of way, keeping much of himself private. "Girl looks like you," he decided. This was accompanied with a stroke of his mustache and a hint of irony.

"Payback time," I admitted with a nod.

Charlie waved his head, which was mercifully free of oxygen tubes today. I interpreted that as a good sign, an indication that he wasn't nearly as upset over recent developments as his wife.

Of course, he also may have become fatalistic, but as long as he wasn't going anywhere except back to court on Monday, I could live with either mind-set.

"She's not handling this too well," I remarked.

"My wife? No, but let's keep that our little secret."

I backed off and showed him the palms of my hands. Then I asked, "How about you?"

When Charlie sighed I could hear his lungs rattle. "If I'd have known I was in for this sort of shit in my old age, I'd have sucked a gas pipe ten years ago."

I flicked a crumb off a placemat. "Sorry," I said, "but I don't believe you."

"Oh?" He pretended surprise. "You're suddenly such an expert?"

"Yep," I assured him, because for some reason I felt perfectly certain of myself, of him. Our rapport was back. It had just taken a few meetings for the gap of time to close.

"I know you've been trying to help Eric . . ." Charlie raised a thick white eyebrow, lifted a hand.

"Do I hear a 'but' coming next?"

My former father figure shrugged a flannel-clad shoulder. "You don't need to bother yourself. You've got a family to worry about. I'll be fine."

"I just told you my family *is* fine. It's you I'm worried about, and to be honest, I don't see how you can stop me from trying to help."

The corner of Charlie's lip curled, and he looked me in the eye. "Never could, now that you mention it. That what you meant by payback time?"

"Yup," I agreed. "In spades. My daughter's just as bad."

"I wouldn't call it bad, exactly," the man allowed. "Irritating maybe, but not bad."

I smiled my appreciation of the distinction, then I said, "Didi's helping, too. She's scoping out a couple of the government witnesses this weekend."

"Glad you girls are enjoying yourselves."

"But you don't think it will do any good."

"Look at me, Gin. Do you really think a jury will convict me?"

So that was still the source of his equanimity, the delusion that he was too pathetic a figure to convict. Unless he was more accomplished an actor than George C. Scott, his world was truly free of Ryan Coopermans. He continued to believe that any nastiness or spite he encountered were aberrations, moments of weakness. Duplicity was a youthful mistake deserving of a second chance. Overweening self-interest and hate and even murderous rage were unfathomable to him. He preferred to view others as fair and good, worthy of his trust.

I looked into those moist, elderly eyes and I was unable to tell him otherwise. "Didi and I are just shopping for insurance, that's all," I said.

The remark must have sounded suitably harmless, because Charlie let it go.

As I prepared to leave, he asked if I would do him a small favor. "Anything."

"Put the kettle on, will you? Birdie's got a big disappointment coming, and I think she's gonna need a cup of tea."

I did as he bid. Then I ran my fingers down the side of his beard and quoted a classic Peanuts' cartoon. "You're a good man, Charlie Brown."

About then Birdie came in carrying another suitcase, so I kissed them both good-bye.

Chapter 20

Saturday afternoon Rip was watching Big Five basketball—Villanova versus LaSalle—but about one-thirty he answered the phone. A couple seconds later he appeared in the kitchen doorway and said, "Dave and Linda Hoffman are going to Bhuna Faun for dinner. They want to know if we'd like to join them."

I stopped lifting plates out of the dishwasher and wrinkled my nose. Were we such social orphans that we were likely to be free? Or did the Hoffmans consider us good enough friends that they felt we would forgive the obvious afterthought? Much to consider and no time to do it. Apparently one of the Hoffmans was waiting on the phone for an answer.

"Do you want to go?" I asked my spouse.

Rip cast me sheep eyes and replied, "I haven't seen Dave in an eon, and the restaurant sounds like fun." In other words, he wanted to go. But then he had always been fonder of Dave than I was of Linda.

I shrugged and told him, "Sure." I was curious about the restaurant myself. A Vietnamese/French motif housed in a former Dairy Queen stand. Bring your own booze. Who wouldn't be curious?

Rip lifted the kitchen extension and gave Dave the good news.

"We can't be out too late," I remarked before he rang off. Garry was overnight at a friend's, but Chelsea had an early

movie double date. The boys' parents were doing transporta-
tion duty, but I wanted to be back home before our daughter
was dropped off.

Rip nodded and raised his hand to concur.

"There goes our romantic evening," he lamented when he
was off the phone. With teenagers in the house, we both cov-
eted our time alone.

"So why did you agree?" I inquired.

My husband's interior debate made it as far as his face.
Evenings with real friends, as opposed to business friends,
were even more rare than time by ourselves.

I waved my hand to let him off the hook. "It's okay," I
said. "You don't need a reason."

Gratefully, the man kissed my forehead, and I shooed him
back to the basketball game.

As soon as I was alone with my busywork, I decided that
something was off about both the Hoffmans' invitation and
our acceptance. Rather than quiz Rip about it, I decided that
patience would reveal the answer soon enough.

Saturday evening was windy and quite black, transforming
Lancaster Pike into a strip of small illuminated galaxies connected by moving headlights.

Bhuna Faun was on our left tucked in among other enter-
prises as disparate as flooring and dentistry. At least for this
stretch zoning considerations seemed as thin as the area's di-
minishing hold on the title Main Line.

I was pleased to see that the restaurant's tall sloped front
windows and broad apron of macadam still said "Dairy
Queen" to anyone with a love of irony. But inside the reborn
facility proclaimed its aspirations with hanging plants and
royal-blue table linen topped with peaks of white. Only half
the tables were occupied, but probably only because of the
early hour.

A hostess led us through the first of two relatively small
eating areas around a waist-high room divider and into the
even smaller front section where the Hoffmans were already
seated. Rip handed over our brown-bagged red wine bottle to
a Caucasian waiter who discreetly went off to uncork our bev-

erage. Dave Hoffman rose to give Rip an enthusiastic hand-shake while Linda and I bumped cheeks and kissed air.

Knowing I would be scrutinized and suspecting my taste wouldn't measure up, I had fussed over my appearance as far as my tolerance for narcissism allowed, but as usual my best effort fell short.

Svelte as a lynx, Linda wore a creamy pants suit, probably a fine wool/silk blend, no blouse. Her earrings, large knots of gold almost identical to the suit's double row of buttons, looked perfect next to her salon-tanned, square face. Linda's hair, naturally streaked in several shades of blond, had been pulled back smoothly from her forehead and gathered into a low ponytail—probably since junior high, the age when she learned how to snare people with her hooded, golden brown eyes. I thought of her as a fashion mail carrier, true to her route through rain and hail and dead of night. My olive-green dress was Salvation Army next to her secure style; but my goal had been simply to survive, not to defeat, so I was able to view her stylish excess as amusing.

"How's it goin', old boy?" Dave asked Rip. Athletic almost to the gaunt degree, his looks were saved by a cheek dimple housed in a smile ravine, flashing dark eyes, and wavy dark hair that managed to remain unaffected. Also tanned and spill-ing over with energy, he had dressed down for us with a crisp white shirt under a blue cashmere blazer. Rip, with his tightly knotted red tie, looked like a squirming Sunday-school boy in comparison.

The waiter returned with four wine glasses, which he placed at the tip of each knife. However, when the young man aimed our brought-in bottle at Linda's glass, she hurried to cover it with her hand.

I had forgotten. Fitness snobs both, the Hoffmans didn't drink. Dave managed to wave the bottle away without so much as a glance, but Linda compressed her lips with distaste as the purple liquid filled my glass, then quickly masked her scorn when Rip looked her way.

In response, after the waiter departed, I raised my wineglass and toasted old friends, effectively forcing the Hoffmans to lift their water goblets and smile forgivingly.

"How are your children?" Linda inquired. Not Garry and Chelsea, but "your children," as if they were accessories like the Louis Vuitton bag dangling from the back of her chair. The question was the sort you asked to prompt the opening you craved.

Linda did not disappoint. After I delivered the abridged, innocuous version of our kids' progress into adulthood, I received the glossy magazine version of hers. ". . . gymnastics . . . Olympic potential" referred to their daughter, Diane, a sweet-natured girl who would be friendless if her mother didn't soon stop boasting about her. Naturally, the son, a swimmer, was "on course to break world records." Never mind that he was only eight. No pressure there.

Meanwhile, Rip and Dave traded boy banter like tennis players with no interest in keeping score. A lawyer out of Bryn Mawr, ethics prevented Dave from gossiping about his clients, so he gossiped about his partners instead. I caught a joke about a pending divorce and a riposte by Rip about Geraldine Trelawny mourning the loss of her Grateful Dead CDs. However, Rip withheld his subject's name; Dave did not.

While I read the menu, which seemed much more French than Vietnamese to me, Rip confided that he had just sent a student downtown to be scared straight by Gerry Rolfe.

Partly because I was interested and partly because David Hoffman held perfectly still during Rip's recital, I paid close attention to what came next.

Dave set aside his menu and folded his arms. "Have you ever been sued over something like that?" he asked my husband.

Rip made a dismissive noise and sipped his wine.

Very soberly, and in Dave's case that was as sober as it gets, the lawyer informed the headmaster that it was just a matter of time.

Rip's left eyebrow raised, and he said, "Oh?"

Dave nodded. "Our firm turned down a similar case quite recently."

"Oh?" Rip repeated in an encouraging, understanding tone. "Why?"

Dave breathed naturally and picked up his menu again. "Nuisance suit. Couldn't be bothered."

"Maybe the other firms will feel the same way," Rip suggested, but Dave stopped fidgeting and said straight into his face, "Oh, I wouldn't expect to be quite that lucky."

So that was it, the hidden agenda of the evening. Dave's firm had refused to represent Lawrence Cooperman in a suit against Bryn Derwyn Academy, and without actually breaking confidentiality rules, Dave had just informed Rip that the family was going forward with their threat.

I glanced at Linda, whose gloating smile slid from Rip to Dave as I watched.

And that was it in a nutshell. Maybe, despite any social, economic, or possibly even political differences, these two men respected, trusted, and even cared for each other. Maybe, when push came to shove, they would actually defend each other like friends were supposed to.

Unfortunately, Linda didn't give a damn about either Rip or me. She was the classic queen's handmaiden, surreptitiously securing her position in court with honeyed words as poisonous as a tainted dagger. Men were usually fooled; women— usually not. The question was, should I continue to curtsey in her presence, or should I quit bothering?

My decision was delayed because the waiter suddenly reappeared, a hologram of black-and-white clothing and youthful blemishes.

"Ladies?" he prompted.

I squinted at him while I tried to dope out what he expected of me.

"The shrimp special," Linda announced. "Raspberry vinaigrette on the side of my salad."

I ran my eyes down the inside of the menu, chose something involving pork, and received a nod from our server.

The men ordered. The food came and we ate it, but my mind was stuck in the twilight zone of innuendo. I remained vigilant, monitoring Dave's conversation for any of the gleeful undertones I now expected from his wife.

"Did you see Villanova's new center, that transfer . . . ?" Rip began, and the boys' talk took the predictable and unrevealing playground path.

Linda devoted herself to everybody's food, which she sampled uninvited and turned into a guessing game. Which spice had the chef used here? What flavor dominated the chicken?

"Corn?" I guessed, referring to what the chickens ate. Linda blinked and narrowed her eyes, so I amended it to "Peanut shells?" which made her eyes roll.

Sadly, there were no further catch-up-with-each-other questions from either of the Hoffmans, nothing to indicate any real interest in the everyday life of the Barnes tribe, either younger or elder. And because I remained preoccupied on Rip's behalf, listening for another hint of friendship from Dave, I never quite got around to asking Linda much about herself either.

Naturally she responded badly to this perceived indifference, as I might have expected she would. When you stop stroking them, cats bare their claws, too.

"Sorry Dave had to deliver unpleasant news," she remarked. We stood near their car and slightly apart from the men in the windy parking lot when this finally came up. Apparently Linda had no confidentiality problems, no compunction about salting a wound.

I shrugged into my coat collar, stuffed my hands deep into my pockets. "Well, Dave said it himself," I replied. "Not all lawsuits have merit."

The lawyer's wife opened the door of the Mercedes convertible and turned to put her representative part on the passenger's seat. "No," she concurred, "but that doesn't mean they're any fun."

Cold metal chips raked my insides as I replayed Charlie Finnemeyer's confidence, that if he'd have known what his old age was going to be like he'd have sucked on a gas pipe ten years ago. Damn Linda's callous indifference. Damn the world.

My throat burned. I wanted to kick the Mercedes' tire, light a match under its ragtop, run my car keys along its perfect paint.

But even more than that, I wanted to get Charlie Finnemeyer and his poor floundering wife back to the tea-and-muffins retirement they deserved, the sort of life where a spat about the TV remote was the low point of their day. I wanted Charlie's old age to be so placid, so monumentally uneventful that he would never need to haul a canvas bag full of emergency oxygen with him anywhere ever again.

I knocked my knuckles on the trunk of the Mercedes, perhaps a little harder than I meant to, and turned on my heel.

Chapter 21

On Sunday morning rain pelted the windows like BBs, so I put on jeans, a turtleneck, and a sweater. Of course, if it had been sunny, I'd have worn jeans, a turtleneck, and a sweater. This was the ninth of January, after all.

At ten A.M. Chelsea was still asleep and Rip was muttering to himself over the Bryn Derwyn budget, which he had spread around on the coffee table because something else was spread around on his desk. With his hair uncombed and his flannel shirt buttoned crooked, he appeared a bit deranged, the sort of man who puts the security guards at Kmart on alert.

I poured my darling a refill of decaf, patted down the wildest of the clumps of hair, kissed a scratchy cheek, and told him I was headed out to pick up our son.

Fearing I would miss a call from Didi, I regretted being away from the house for even a minute; but I was trying to be calm and reasonable. Nothing would happen to Didi in a bar on a Saturday night that she didn't already expect.

"Umph," Rip replied, which I took to mean "safe trip."

I zipped my hooded ski jacket in preparation for a wet trot to the Subaru and reached for the front door only to gasp in surprise. A man was standing outside in the shadow of an umbrella. Caught napping, Gretsky cantered into the hallway and barked superfluously as I opened the door.

Eric Allen.

We stood there wondering how to handle the situation for

several seconds, then simultaneously said, "Good morning," and "You're leaving."

Eric laughed self-consciously and might have blushed if his face hadn't already been red from the cold. "I should have phoned first," he admitted, "but I didn't want to wake anybody."

"Very considerate," I said, "but Rip only wishes he were still asleep, and Chelsea wears earplugs on weekends." I bought them for her—growing girls need their rest.

I stepped back to let Eric in out of the rain. "Don't you have a son, too?" he asked.

"I'm on my way to pick him up." And even though I wasn't going far, my instincts told me I needed to get moving.

My husband's former prep school friend glanced around the corner into the living room where Rip was either holding his hands over his ears or holding his head in his hands.

Eric cast me a look of such concern that I stopped obsessing about Didi and dropped my voice to explain. "You know those old math problems that took up the whole blackboard? Rip's doing one of those."

The attorney's expression switched to confusion, so I whispered a better explanation. "He has to figure out everybody's raises, estimate all the school's other expenses including possible emergencies, add it all up, guess what they'll get from fund raising, guess at enrollment, guess what tuition should be less financial aid, calculate that and subtract expenses, then do it again until he knows how much to raise tuition."

Eric took my arm and ushered me toward my own front door. "I'll say hello when we get back," he decided. "You drive."

"Yes, dear," I replied.

Eric winced. "Sorry. Carol hated that, too."

Once we got going, my voluntary companion took charge of everything *but* the driving. He punched off my radio, poked buttons and turned dials ostensibly to get more heat, dusted the dashboard with his palm, blew his nose into a monogrammed white hankie, then finally told me, "I got the autopsy report on Roland Ignatowski."

"How . . . ?"

"Don't ask. I just did, okay?"

The windshield wipers thunked out their homey punctuation, and instinctively we had begun to coordinate our conversation to its beat.

"What did it say?" I asked, deliberately ending the silliness by speaking out of sync.

Stopped for the turn the end of Beech Tree Lane, I was able to peruse Eric's face as he delivered the bad news. His sea-green eyes had darkened to suit the weather and his message, and his thick lashes appeared to be damp. Plus his aftershave or skin conditioner or whatever it was had been freshened by the rain because I detected an odor of lime.

Reluctant to squeeze out the words, he blinked twice, then squinted. "Ignatowski was tranked before he died."

"So it's murder," I remarked, "by somebody he knew."

"Quick," my traveling companion observed as I resumed driving. "But, yes, that is the consensus."

"So somebody slipped a tranquilizer into his coffee," I thought aloud as I took a right onto another residential street. Although rain gurgled freely into the gutter's grated drain, the road looked silvery so I kept my speed down.

"Then what?" I asked. Eric had not described the victim's death as an overdose, and nobody has ever died of relaxation.

"Air embolism, probably," the lawyer replied. "The medical examiner found a needle mark but no further chemicals in his system. Figures the deceased was injected with air."

"Why is that fatal?" I wondered as another car hissed by. "It sounds so harmless."

"Air bubble travels to the heart and creates an airlock," Eric explained. "The heart can't work. It's as simple as that."

"Like a swimming pool pump," I decided. Another turn and we were already approaching Georgie Campbell's house, Garry's geographically nearest friend.

Eric swiveled in his seat in order to gawp at me, a tipoff that I probably wouldn't like whatever came next.

"How do you know about . . . ?"

Please don't say swimming pools, I mentally begged. Because then I would be forced to deduct many many points from your lifetime score as a human being. And that would be because I know that you know that Rip and I don't own a pool, our parents never owned a pool, their parents never, and so on all the way back to William the Conquerer, whose boots our ancestors quite possibly polished.

". . . pool pumps?" he finished with something bordering on awe.

Only slightly relieved, I twisted my mouth and told him, "I know a little bit about lots of things. What's the big deal?"

Eric waved his head back and forth as if in disbelief. "It's just that women aren't usually mechanically inclined."

I gave him a pitying look and an only partly humorous reminder. "You're divorced, right?"

"Point taken. I am sorry."

"Me, too." We were on a stretch of straightaway, so I fixed him with a softer, kinder, less aloof expression until he decided to forgive my brief bitchiness and look at me in a new way.

Pretty soon he asked, "So what's the answer?"

"Summer job taking care of the pool at a day camp, that and archery." William the Conquerer would have been proud. "Every time I backwashed the filter and cleaned the hair basket I had to bleed air out of the system or the pump would seize up." And since I'd never been responsible for a pool before, I almost always caused the airlock before I remembered how to prevent it.

Around a gentle curve to the right the street opened up to reveal grand old houses set on modest-size yards. I wondered as I always did how so many people managed to support the Main Line lifestyle. Dual incomes probably, just like the Campbells.

"We're here," I announced, pulling over to the curb in front of a sizeable home of gray stone and white window trim. A thick naked wisteria vine snaked up and around the openings of a wide, old-fashioned porch.

I stepped out into the slackening rain but leaned back down to caution Eric. "Please try not to gross out my son," I said.

"No autopsy talk, okay?" Then I hustled up to the Campbells' front door.

Through the design in the frosted glass I noticed Garry's duffel and sleeping bag at the bottom of the steps. His ski jacket hung on the newel post also ready to go, which saddened me on Carolyn Campbell's behalf. I personally hate the sort of silence children leave behind, but as the mother of one mild boy, Carolyn found eleven-year-olds wearing in pairs, impossible in groups, which was why you didn't pick up your son any later than the agreed-upon hour.

"Oh, they were great. No trouble at all," she lied with the back of a hand to her brow.

"Our turn next," I reminded the worn-down woman, hoping for a smile. Perhaps she was a competent advertising account executive. As a parent, she was way way too uptight. I hoped her husband hugged their son a lot.

Thanks and good-byes accomplished in a blink, I had Garry in the Subaru and the car rolling homeward within five minutes.

As we exited the Campbells' street, I explained Eric Allen to my son, who had been a baby back when the Allens and Barneses hung out. "He's Mr. Finnemeyer's lawyer," I told him, "and Daddy's old high school friend." Garry shyly mumbled hi from the backseat and closed his eyes as if to doze.

Eric perceived this signal of disinterest as an opportunity to finish our conversation. "So it's looking pretty bad for Birdie and Charlie, wouldn't you say?"

His asking my opinion surprised me, made me feel that he had finally accepted our allegiance.

"Yes," I agreed in answer to the question. Both Finnemeyers were now at risk, particularly since they couldn't plausibly deny being at the Ignatowskis' house the afternoon the fraud victim died. Birdie had spoken to the man's wife just before she went inside and found her husband dead.

Wipers flapping, I mulled over what the police might purport, probably that in spite of the trial the elderly couple appeared harmless enough for Roland Ignatowski to invite inside his house, either singly or together. If the man happened to have been drinking a beverage before either Finnemeyer was admitted, it could easily have been doped when he wasn't looking. Or perhaps Roland Ignatowski had been foolish enough, or courteous enough, to offer coffee to his uninvited guest or guests. I didn't believe either scenario had actually happened, but I recognized that neither version was impossible.

And of course the police would argue that injecting a person already unconscious from tranquilizers took no strength at all.

Eric should be facing up to the worst-case scenario, like it or not. "Ned Stewart had a very similar heart problem," I reminded the lawyer, couching my words in the hope that Garry wouldn't catch on.

Eric shot me a quick glance. "What makes you say it's the same? We liked him as a witness." He obviously referred to the grudge between Charlie and the textile curator that he hoped would diminish the expert's credence. "No. I really think that was different. No motive."

"The Hewson quilt," I hinted. "I think the same student offered it to the Philadelphia Museum of Art either before or after Winterthur." Then I elaborated about my chat with Dr. Stewart's assistant, explaining why a record of the rejection seemed unlikely.

"Although there might be an old appointment book," I thought out loud. "Maybe her name would be in there."

Eric grumbled. "She gave a phony name at Winterthur—remember?"

"Yes, but if she used the same name both times, the police might be persuaded to take another look at Stewart's death."

"I still don't see . . ." Eric remarked with a stubborn shake of his head.

Garry leaned forward to complain into our passenger's ear. "Jeez," he said, rolling his eyes as if adults were hopelessly dense. "Whoever did the funny business with the quilt probably didn't want that Stewart guy talking about it. You guys don't have to talk around me, you know. I'm sitting right here."

For sure I would be hearing about this later. Garrett Ripley Barnes hates being patronized by anybody.

Meanwhile, Eric Allen's mouth had gaped open, and his eyes bulged. "Gin, didn't you just tell me to watch what I said in front of this kid?"

"Jeez," Garry complained again, this time with the disgust aimed at the back of my head. Being sheltered by his mother was the worst.

"Never mind," I warned with undertones meant to put that inevitable discussion on hold.

We were back in my driveway before I asked Eric how the Ignatowski "development" would affect Charlie's trial.

"It won't stop it, if that's what you're thinking. The police will probably take the time to nail down their case while the fraud trial runs its course."

"And then?"

"Then if they want Charlie for murder, they'll arrest him again."

"Or Birdie," I muttered miserably.

"Or Birdie," Eric agreed.

Chapter 22

While Garry ran through the chilly rain with his gear, I waited for Eric Allen to do the gentlemanly thing and come around with his umbrella. In a minute I wouldn't be able to ask my last question privately. Didi had parked her Audi behind Eric's white Lexus.

"Can you make the prosecution's witnesses hang around?" I asked as I hooked the attorney's arm and began to stroll toward the door.

"I can if I have a good reason," he admitted. His smile was courtly, in keeping with my own demeanor.

"Is suspecting one of them of murder reason enough?"

Eric contemplated the stream of rain leaking from the middle of our roof's gutter. "Which witness?" he asked.

"Right now anybody from Textile."

"You're really hung up on your quilt idea, aren't you?"

"Yes," I agreed. "I think someone's trying to keep that old embarrassment from becoming public, don't you? Stewart and Ignatowski's deaths don't make any sense otherwise."

"Murder's pretty drastic," he mused. "It would have to be somebody in an extremely precarious position."

"How long do you think Janella Piper would stay on television if the station found out she attempted fraud? She *exposes* frauds on her show."

"You make a pretty good point, Gin. I'll have to think about that."

"You don't have very long to think, Eric. Won't some of the witnesses leave town as soon as they've finished testifying?"

He scowled a moment, then threw up his hand. "Okay, okay. I'll say I may want to recall one or more of them, so legally they'll all have to stick around. Happy now?"

"Just relieved," I answered, wiping a stray raindrop off my face. "Now let's go inside and find out what my pal Didi found out."

At that moment my front door opened and the woman in question greeted us with a giant whoop—a genuine, arms-up, West Texas rodeo whoop.

"Gin, dear. Who's this?" Didi asked after she and I hugged. Eric had taken a moment to shake out his umbrella, but now that he was in under the hall light Didi could see him better.

"Eric Allen," I said. "Meet Dolores 'Didi' Martin. Eric is Charlie Finnemeyer's attorney; and yes, Didi, he is single."

My best friend pretended to kick my shin while smiling energetically at Eric. He grinned back and swayed a little, a mating move if ever I saw one.

Suppressing my disgust, I stuck my head into the living room to see whether we were interrupting my husband.

Noticing, Didi told me, "Rip moved his stuff upstairs. Something about a herd of elephants."

"Couldn't have meant you," I remarked. Having grown too tall to perform, Didi taught ballet until she discovered she hated being in the wings. As I recall, that took less than five weeks. All that had survived from her dancing phase was the hairdo (the elegant French twist) and a gracefulness that remained one of the most fascinating things about her. Without doubt Garry and I were the herd of elephants Rip hoped to avoid.

"Coffee?" I asked my two guests. From the family room came an aggressively cheery theme song from a Sunday cartoon. Garry always forgets about his sister—hence, the earplugs.

Didi narrowed her puffy eyes and said, "Black, and lots of

it. And can you possibly scare up some food? All I ate last night were buffalo wings, hundreds and hundreds of very spicy buffalo wings. Oh, and a little popcorn."

Both Eric and I grimaced at the thought. "All in the line of duty," Didi added, making an effort to look less hung over than she felt.

"Coming right up," I assured her, immediately regretting my choice of words.

"Scrambled eggs," the sleuthing foot soldier suggested, "or perhaps milk toast."

"Eggs it is." I could do them in my sleep, frequently did. I offered some to Eric, but he assured me coffee would be enough for him.

My guests selected seats in our Early American living room—Didi a wing-back chair in front of our huge stone walk-in fireplace, Eric the blue plaid sofa facing my elegantly hung-over friend. In the five minutes it took for me to put on coffee and scramble some eggs, I heard only the musical timbre of their conversation, which resembled two pigeons getting acquainted.

Didi demurely accepted the food tray containing napkin, utensils, salt, pepper, and the plate of steaming eggs. "Excuse me," she apologized to Eric since she would be eating in front of him.

"Go for it," he told her. "Keep all those buffalo company."

We all had coffee fixed to our tastes before Didi was ready to report.

"That Holiday Inn isn't especially large," she began, dabbing her lips with the paper napkin and addressing her remarks to Eric. "Outside you've got a U-shaped driveway, a sidewalk, and Fourth Street. Around the corner on Arch you've got that little cemetery with Ben Franklin's grave right inside the fence. You know where people toss pennies on his headstone for luck and the homeless reach in to pick them up?"

"Been there," I said.

"You've done that?" Eric questioned me, which gave Didi an idea of how much description was needed.

"Inside the check-in area faces the front doors with a little gift shop and some meeting rooms to the left and around the corner. You've got elevators and rest rooms to the right, then farther down the hall there's a restaurant and across from that a sports bar. You know—TVs, referee shirts, green carpet, posters—the usual macho shit."

Neither Eric nor I dared to protest.

"Anyway, if I was going to run into any of your witnesses, it was pretty much the sports bar or nothing."

Eric nodded to acknowledge her logic.

"Okay, so I'm all checked in and I've got on my city clothes, sort of the here-for-the-weekend-looking-for-something-safe-to-do clothes."

"What did that look like?" I wondered aloud.

Didi cast me a look. "Designer jeans, high-heeled boots, and a leather vest."

I mouthed an O, and she turned back to Eric.

"So about five-thirty I buy myself a beer and a plate of buffalo wings, right? To save some chairs I tell the waitress I've got friends coming, but I don't know when. Then I wait. The bar fills up and I've got a hell of a time hanging onto those extra chairs. In fact, I lose one to a fat trucker from Baltimore. Loud dude who ate three baskets of popcorn and put away a six-pack while he and his buddies watched basketball on one of the big-screen TVs. This all inside an hour.

"Well, just before seven I get lucky. In come three women. One looks like she does the bar scene every weekend. She's got blue eyes lined in black and black curls down to here, a white angora V-neck sweater. Black jeans, black leather jacket. She's goin' *out*.

"The other two?" Didi lifted a shoulder. "One never did a bar in her life and the other not in a long time. I'm pretty sure I recognize the teetotaler as one of Charlie's ex-students, but the others are just maybes.

"Still, one out of three is fine with me. I wave the women over. 'I've been saving these seats for my girlfriends,' I say, 'but I don't think they're going to show. Why don't you join me?'

"Well, the partier is all for it, knowing full well it's the only deal they're going to get in that place at that hour. The others are ready to turn around and leave, but my party girl talks them into one drink. Apparently, spending time with the others has made her very thirsty."

Didi sipped her coffee, and I relieved her of the tray.

"Thanks," she said with her mind back in the bar. "Turns out the partier is Sally Schultz, a real hell-raiser, and she's about to do your client one hell of a favor."

"Oh?" Eric said, completely into it now, grinning as if his life depended on it. "Who were the others?"

"Maxine Devon Nash and Pamela Zenzinger. Names ring a bell?"

"Government witnesses."

"Bingo. Maxine had a nose job, which explained why I didn't recognize her. And I just whiffed on Pamela, but of course that didn't matter."

Eric was literally on the edge of his seat now, and I kept crossing and uncrossing my ankles, running a finger under my turtleneck, shifting the magazines on the end table, and plinking my coffee mug. Finally Eric just reached out and swatted my bouncing leg with the sort of corrective slap a daddy ape would use.

"So what did you find out?" the lawyer prompted.

"To start out, we just made polite chitchat. I mention I'm a beer buyer in town to check out the microbreweries for my outlet. They mention they're in town for a sort of college reunion.

" 'Oh?' I say. 'Which year?'

" 'No,' Pamela tells me. She's the artsy one—long auburn braid, boots, long East Indian skirt, silver beads. The teetotaler is Maxine. Anyway, Pamela gets a little in-joke look on her face and says, 'No, just a Charlie's Angels reunion.'

" 'What's that?' I ask, all innocent.

"Maxine's the softy in the bunch—heart-shape face, light-brown hair, no makeup. She's working part time and taking care of two kids while her husband goes to medical school." Didi shook her head as if thinking what I was thinking, that that grueling routine often sucked the appeal out of the long-suffering wife. Then when hubby finally got his degree, she was no longer glamorous enough to suit his expanded lifestyle.

" 'We were teacher's pets,' Maxine told me, but not as if she was proud. 'Our professor just put us together to do a special project.'

"I glanced at the other faces and decided not to ask about them being friends. 'What kind of project?' " I asked instead.

" 'Boring stuff,' Sally volunteered. 'Fabric design. We were all textile students way back when.'

"I tried to get more out of the other two, but they were looking around the bar and squirming like they wanted to bolt. Finally Maxine said something about a dinner reservation, and I thought it was all over."

"But?" I said eagerly. This time Eric baby-punched my knee.

"But it turned out I was right about Sally. I told her my girlfriends really stiffed me by not showing up, and she'd be doing me a big favor if she'd hit a couple beer joints with me. She liked that idea much better than the prospects of sipping tea with Maxine and Pamela, so she sent the other two off to their Chinese restaurant and we grabbed a taxi."

"What did you find out?" Eric this time, but I kept my hands to myself.

Didi had paused to rub her temples and then her eyes. Finally she flopped back in her chair. "I've told you about everything on Maxine. She's one of those high-standards poor people who would rather starve than tell a lie."

"So if Lloyd asks her did Charlie ever use fakes as teaching tools . . ."

"She would say, 'Yessir, Mr. Prosecutor. He sure did.' "

Eric grunted and wrung his hands. "What about Pamela Zenzinger?"

"Now mind you, this took work," Didi emphasized to wring as much appreciation out of us as possible.

Eric spread his hands and said, "I'm sure," fortunately without a trace of irony, because, let's face it, he knew as well as I did that sending a beer distributor on a pub-crawl was probably like tossing Br'er Rabbit into the briar patch.

Satisfied with Eric's sincerity, my best friend continued. "Pamela Zenzinger is single. She works for an antique dealer south of Wilmington, and Charlie had higher hopes for her. *She* had higher hopes for her."

"But it didn't work out?" the attorney asked.

"Not yet."

"Did you find out why she's testifying against Charlie?"

Didi waved her head, and I spoke up. "Maybe she resents him for putting those big ideas into her head."

"Big ideas that didn't work out?"

"Exactly."

The lawyer shrugged that off. "Could be. It also could be that we'll never know her reasons."

If he could live with that, I supposed I would have to.

"Anything else?" he asked Didi.

"Oh, yeah," she hinted lewdly, and Eric puffed up with interest.

"Turns out Sally Schultz owns her own antique shop right in Philadelphia—on Pine Street. Sort of finagled it in her divorce settlement. She had just stopped by the Holiday Inn to have a drink with Pamela and Maxine. According to her, joining them for dinner had been optional all along. Said she didn't mind a little reminiscing but wasn't sure she could take a whole night of it, then she gave me a little wink."

"Entirely different people."

"Correct. So we're checking out the fourth beer establishment—don't ask me where it was, Sally was navigating—and she starts telling me more about why they were called Charlie's angels. Or I might have asked—whatever. But she starts hinting that one of the original five was more than just a favorite student Charlie wanted to get off to a splashy start."

Slightly aggravated, Eric asked, "Exactly what does that mean?"

Didi rolled her eyes. "It means—*Counselor*—there were rumors that Charlie was having an affair with one of his so-called angels."

"Which one?"

"You really like to spoil a girl's fun, don't you?"

"Sorry. Which one?"

"Janella Piper."

"The black woman?" Eric was a little too incredulous.

"What's the big deal? I've seen her on TV. She's one hot tomato."

"But . . ."

"But what?" Didi pressed. "Haven't you been to the mall lately? We've got bi-racial couples all over the place."

"But not then. Not a young woman and somebody as old as Charlie."

"Why not?"

Eric's disspirited silence admitted that he didn't know why not, he just couldn't believe that of his client.

For my own reasons, I tended to agree with him. "So that was it?" I quizzed Didi. "That was Sally's big favor—to accuse him of having an affair?"

"Well, sure," Didi said defensively. "Won't that discredit Janella as a witness?"

Eric and I just looked at each other and groaned.

Chapter 23

Monday gave us ice crystals on the lawn, thick and breakable as glass, so I sent my kids off with money to buy hot lunches instead of the usual packed sandwiches and fruit. Squinting into the slanting sunshine, I watched them scurry toward their bus stop, heads bowed into the wind.

Winter being the least demanding season for a homemaker, I quickly nailed the house down—dog fed, wash in, dinner out. Then I felt free to bundle myself up for a train ride into town. Charlie's trial resumed today, and I wanted to be there.

The local railway platform exposed us midmorning travelers to a wind chill of five, and the wiser of us stood in the dilapidated barn of a waiting strip enclosed by thin planks and grimy glass. We scrunched our ears down into our collars and blinked to acknowledge each other's misery.

The lead car of three smelled strongly of metal and stale breath. It was also overheated and painfully dry, and it rocked and rolled through the famous-named towns—Villanova, Bryn Mawr, Haverford—as if it were eager to reach the shelter of its shed. The half-hour ride seemed scarcely enough time to calm my fears about the day.

Still breathless from hurrying through the cold, I slid into the courtroom pew beside the roving juror, Jack Armstrong.

"Morning," he greeted me, then dropped a bite-size chocolate-covered toffee bar into my hand. Jack's professional spectator's white shirt and red suspenders were in place; his companion was not.

"Thank you and good morning," I said.

"You're welcome. Pay attention. We're introducing Exhibit A."

Out in the open space in front of his right-hand table, the prosecutor, Samuel Lloyd, unrolled a relatively narrow Oriental rug. About five and a half feet wide and just over ten feet long, he had to back up to allow the jury to see its entire length. After they had had a good look, he briefly shifted the item toward the judge, coincidentally giving us a view of his balding pate. Then he lowered the long rug to the floor, walked around it, and lifted the far end so the rest of us in the audience could see.

The rug's design was stunning, full of stylized flowers and pointy leaves, zigzags and angles. There were dragons and fighting animals and a narrow border of squiggles, all of which inspired me to imagine a meeting between some artistic American Indians and their Chinese counterparts with this rug as the creative result. But that was just my personal impression.

Judging by the vibrant, intensely cheery design, I supposed that the soft brick red of the background had once been much brighter. The other colors of the rug's abundant designs ranged from pale yellow to orange with bluish green leaves and outlines and curliques of black and brown. Even though the pattern's contrasts had been mitigated by time, it was still difficult to imagine such a piece in a northeastern American home, and indeed I felt certain I had never noticed it on display at the Finnemeyers'.

Lloyd supported the end of the rug with his arm in order to face his microphone. "This is what it's all about, folks," he told the fifteen people sitting in the raised seats with a Mona Lisa smile. "And Dr. Muir here is going to tell us all about it. Aren't you, Dr. Muir?"

Edwin Muir, a large ponderous person and obviously the replacement expert, leaned toward the microphone attached to the corner of the witness stand. "I'm going to try," he replied.

The judge cleared his throat. "Are we ready to ask a question now, Mr. Lloyd?"

"Yes, sir. Just a moment, sir."

While the prosecutor rolled up the rug and set it across the front of the court stenographer's table, I opened the candy Jack gave me as quietly as possible and glanced around the room.

Charlie—oxygen tubes in place today—was slumped sullenly beside his energetic, upbeat lawyer. Positioned close behind them in newsprint blacks and whites, Birdie twitched like a miscreant waiting for Mother Superior, which made me think of Karen, the daughter who should have been there but was not. I wondered why. Was my mother having trouble coping with the four children after all, or had Karen changed her mind about coming? For the time being I would put my fears on hold, but pretty soon I would begin to worry in earnest.

Perhaps fifteen additional strangers of various descriptions augmented last week's regulars; yet in spite of the crowd, no one had chosen to occupy the back-row seat preferred by the fraud victim Roland Ignatowski. For a second I had the creepy notion that the murdered man's ghost chilled the air and repelled living flesh, but more likely the regulars had shooed the interlopers away. Spooky enough, I decided as I faced front once again.

Lloyd asked his expert to outline his credentials for the record. "I'm a textile professor at UCLA," the man replied.

"Yeesh." Jack Armstrong hissed chocolate breath into my ear. "Where'd they get him on short notice?"

"And can you please relate how you came to be here in Philadelphia to testify at this trial?"

"When your local expert became unavailable, I believe your office contacted IFAR, the International Federation for Art Research. I'm one of the authenticators they recommend when an Oriental carpet comes into question."

The prosecutor paused to let that weight disseminate around the room.

"Thank you, Dr. Muir. The court greatly appreciates your help. I hope we haven't disturbed your teaching schedule too much."

"Not at all," Edwin Muir replied. "I'm on sabbatical to write a book, and I happen to have family in Philadelphia."

Lloyd nodded, then pinched his lip as if organizing his thoughts. "Dr. Muir, could you please tell us something about fraudulent antique Oriental rugs?"

"Really, Mr. Lloyd, is this generalization necessary?" the judge scolded the prosecutor.

"A brief bit of background, Your Honor. That's all."

"Keep it brief."

Muir breathed deeply before launching into his mini-lecture. "Market considerations have always been part of the weaving trade," he told us. "Styles come and go. Smart weavers produce what their customers want and stop producing what they don't. Forgers do the same. It was only a matter of time before the highly talented craftsmen employed to repair rugs for the Turkish bazaars turned their skills to better profit by producing very convincing fake antiques. They were merely answering a demand."

"Interesting," Lloyd remarked while contemplating the floor. "Very interesting. Would you say that fraudulent antique Oriental rugs are prevalent?"

"Not prevalent, no."

"Commonplace?"

"I'd say they are a problem."

"Enough of a problem to cause a buyer to beware?"

"Certainly that. The difference in value can be enormous."

"How enormous, Dr. Muir?"

The visiting expert exuded caution and competence, never so much as when he paused to think. His thick black eyebrows straightened and his lips shrunk. His hands interwove over his gray-flannel paunch with thumbs up and wiggling. He tilted his chin as if seeking the truth from above. "I'd say the range could be anywhere from a few thousand dollars to over a hundred thousand dollars."

"In one rug? In a rug like this?" Exhibit A hung down perhaps a foot from the table, allowing Lloyd to gesture toward it with his hand.

"Oh, yes. Even in a relatively small specimen. Some of

them were woven by nomadic tribes and can be quite, quite valuable, depending on—"

"Yes, Dr. Muir. As you know, we have to keep our answers brief. Now, in spite of your being called from California on short notice, I assume you've had sufficient opportunity to examine Exhibit A?"

"Visually, yes. I examined it at length on three separate occasions over the weekend."

"And that was enough time for you to reach some conclusions regarding its authenticity?"

"Oh, yes."

"Can you give us your opinion, please?"

"First of all, it was handmade—you can tell by looking at the base of the pile and the backing. If you look closely, it becomes obvious that individual lengths of yarn were looped around the weft. Then the two ends of the yarn were pulled through each loop to form a knot. If you look closely, you can make out which two ends are connected, but it's even easier to check the back. Hand-knotted rugs have curved bumps that look like purling."

"Purling?"

"The reverse of knitting."

"Go on."

"Your specimen would be described as having about two hundred forty knots per square inch, which is exceptionally fine for a rug of this type. Plus the colors are slightly inconsistent horizontally, as if different dye lots were used. We call that abrash, and although it can be simulated by machine, its presence is commonly expected—perhaps even desired—in a handmade rug." The room waited while Muir cleared his throat and sipped a glass of water, while he linked his fingers and drew in breath.

"Also, the quality of the wool is excellent."

"And how did you determine that?"

"I looked at it and ran my hand across it several times. The threads were supple and scarcely shed at all. The pile was springy, in other words it didn't move back and forth the way garment wool would; nor was it dry and brittle the way dead wool would be."

"Dead wool, Dr. Muir?"

"Wool that has been chemically separated from the hide of a, a dead sheep. Such wool is most often found in very poor-quality rugs made in Iran or Pakistan."

"Now you say you looked at the rug and touched it. That doesn't sound especially scientific."

Muir smiled and spread his hands. "This isn't archeology, Mr. Lloyd. We don't have eighteen different laboratory tests to help us determine the age of an item. No, when it comes to textiles, I'm afraid the human machine is still the most scientific instrument we have at our disposal. I refer, of course, to subjective instinct backed by experience."

"What about radiocarbon dating?"

The witness laughed. "Expensive. And only useful for dating organic material more than four hundred years old."

"Why is that?"

"Do you wish the academic answer or the simple one?"

"Simple, by all means," Lloyd replied.

"Carbon concentrations in the environment varied widely during the most recent few centuries, making some of the radio carbonation results look the same. To be more specific, the test results for wool produced in 1930 might look the same as a rug known to be woven in 1780. We call it the Stradivarius gap. There was an instance—"

"Thank you, Dr. Muir. How about amino acid dating?"

"Also not as exact as we would wish. The wool protein consists of about twenty different amino acids, and the composition varies according to breed, that is, whether the wool came from a camel, a goat, or a sheep. Composition is also influenced by the animal's diet, and I'm sorry to say we don't have all those regional calibration curves nailed down. Then there's the further problem of temperature change. Where a rug was stored affects the amino acid content."

"I see. So we're back to subjective instinct backed by experience."

"So it seems."

"All right. When would your knowledge and experience suggest that this rug was woven?"

The expert filled his lungs the better to pontificate. "In my opinion it was most likely produced at the end of the nineteenth century or very early in the twentieth." Despite Muir's revelation that the rug was roughly a hundred years old, the prosecutor's confidence seemed to swell. The whole courtroom was eager to learn why. "However," Muir added with a weighty inflection, "it has been aged to simulate a rug woven in the seventeenth century."

A few eyes widened and mouths gaped. Birdie glanced at Charlie, and Eric's body stiffened like a cat zeroing in on a bird.

Samuel Lloyd pretended to be as surprised as everyone else, but his pleasure was unmistakable. "You're saying this rug is still a fake?"

"Exactly. An old fake."

"What makes you say that?"

Muir shifted his weight and rewove his fingers. "The wear is too even, as I already mentioned. Would you mind unrolling more of the rug so everybody can see?"

While Lloyd was doing that, someone slid in beside me and touched my leg—Karen Finnemeyer Smith with chapped cheeks and a brown wool overcoat that smelled of Similac. The joy of being away from her kids obviously overrode any fears about her father's precarious situation. She might have been settling in to watch a Broadway show.

I acknowledged her with a wilted smile.

"What'd I miss?" she whispered loudly.

"Just that it's an old rug, but still a fake."

"That's my dad."

I glared to warn my old playmate/rival, adding a stern "I think maybe we should keep quiet" for emphasis.

Jack, sucking at his false teeth, concurred. "You got that right." His eyes slid from Karen's hair to her knees without finding much to like.

I patted one of the knees to soften the reprimand, but I stopped short of negating it. Then I put my finger to my lips and told Karen, "Later," because Muir had just moved onto new material.

The witness gestured toward the half-opened rug. "You can see that the original fringe has been replaced and the selvages repaired. There is also a patch—the brighter spot to the left. Since repairs would be expected in a three-hundred-year-old rug, naturally a good forger would incorporate such details into his fake."

"Doctor, you seem certain this carpet is no newer than the earlier twentieth century. Can you please tell us why?"

"Certainly." Muir waved a hand toward the specimen. "Can you see how the blacks and browns are somewhat shorter than the rest of the fibers?"

"Yes," Lloyd admitted.

"Historically blacks and browns were fixed with iron-based mordants—metallic salts—to keep the colors from rinsing out. Iron oxidizes, degrading the yarn over time, which means that on a three-hundred-year-old rug the darkest colors should be much further gone than the reds and whites, not just a bit shorter as we see here.

"Another clue is the amount of dirt embedded in the fibers, which I checked with a magnifying glass."

"Kindly explain."

"A person attempting to artificially age a rug can manage certain deceptions, but he cannot simulate the way dirt becomes embedded in fibers over many years. Old dirt can effectively be cleaned out, you see, but it cannot effectively be put in."

"Go on."

"The pattern of your piece is similar to those produced in the northern Caucasus area of Russia, and the style was especially popular in Europe in the early twentieth century. For the American market reproductions were often bleached to subdue the colors.

"A certain skilled weaver named Tuduc, born in Transylvania I believe, knew the market well and reproduced many such pieces. He frequently used wool gleaned from old rugs worn beyond repair, which he then redyed in the older, traditional fashion."

Samuel Lloyd spread his hands. "Hasn't there been a recent initiative to rekindle the Turkish carpet industry doing just that? And haven't many jobs been created as a result?"

Muir nodded. "You refer to the so-called DOBAG project begun by Istanbul's Marmara University in 1980. And yes, many jobs have been created. However, it is my belief that some of the resulting rugs will eventually be mistaken for antiques—with the help of persons following Mr. Tuduc's questionable example."

"You seem convinced that your Mr. Tuduc deliberately set out to commit fraud. How can you be certain he wasn't merely honoring the past with his reproductions just as the DOBAG weavers are doing today?"

"Because my Mr. Tuduc, as you have chosen to call him, devised a mechanical box full of river stones to artificially wear down the nap of his rugs. A similar trick was obviously used on Exhibit A.

"Also, whoever wove this carpet used natural dyes, as you can tell by the colors' resonance and undertone. Yet as early as 1870, legitimate Caucasian weavers had begun to use some synthetic color, in particular a garish bright orange that has proven surprisingly resistant to sun fade. Since your rug's oranges have mellowed with age, the weaver must have achieved his oranges the traditional way, by overdying red with yellow. This means, of course, that your weaver intended to replicate traditional methods for profit, otherwise he would have used the synthetic orange of the period on this rug."

"Just one more question before I turn you over to my colleague, Mr. Allen," Lloyd told his witness. "Can you suggest how anyone—knowing what you've just told us about this rug—might justify paying $110,000 or even $65,000 for it?"

"Objection!"

"I'll allow it."

Muir pursed his lips and twiddled his thumbs and sent his gaze toward Charlie. "Both purchasers must have believed the rug to be seventeenth century," he said. "Nothing else would have justified those prices."

"Thank you, Dr. Muir. No further questions."

The judge then called for the midmorning break, and the courtroom noisily emptied.

Out in the hallway I drew Karen Finnemeyer Smith away from the clog of foot traffic. "I'd like to ask you something," I told her hastily before her parents emerged and spoiled my opportunity. "Do you recognize any of these names?"

I held out my list of the prosecution's witnesses and one by one pointed to my preferred murder suspects.

The names Maxine Devon Nash, Sally Schultz, and Pamela Zenzinger drew negative responses from Karen.

"Janella Piper," she remarked thoughtfully. "Do I know her?"

"You tell me."

"Oh, sure. Television. The kids watch something else during her time slot, but I know about her show. Mom once asked me whether I ever saw it. Wasn't she a student of Dad's?"

Almost too dejected to answer, I mumbled yes.

Then the Finnemeyers shuffled through the courtroom door, probably the last ones out, and I relinquished Karen to their outstretched arms. Birdie's eyes smiled almost closed while Charlie's swam with tears. "Dolly," he called his daughter, an ancient pet name. "Dolly, Dolly, Dolly. How on earth did you manage to come?"

"I just did, Daddy," Karen replied. "Don't worry about it."

The family had forgotten me, which I took as a good sign. For my part I was still lamenting the expert's testimony. How nice it would have been if he had proclaimed the rug to be authentic, or at the very least worth sixty or seventy grand. Of course, that would have made him a witness for the defense, and until it was Eric's turn to shoot off his guns his challenge would be to minimize what we had all just heard.

My own immediate concern was how little we knew about Charlie's so-called angels, the nearby ones at least. Didi had gleaned just enough information to suggest that we needed to know more.

Leaning against the hallway wall, I contemplated what amounted to a pile of ifs.

If the trial had precipitated the deaths of Roland Ignatowski and Dr. Ned Stewart, most likely the murders had been committed by someone closely involved with the trial. I still believed the only credible motive for the murders was self-preservation, of either the killer's reputation, lifestyle, or income. Didn't matter. It just meant that I still desperately needed to find out who faked that Hewson quilt.

But why does the murderer have to be the same person who faked the quilt? asked the nudge who resided in my head.

Hmph. Good point. For some reason I had automatically assumed that the quilt's owner had borrowed it from the display, but if that wasn't true I might find myself accusing an innocent person of murder.

So why *had* I formed that conclusion?

Because, I realized, during the week the quilt had been missing from the display not one person had complained that it had been stolen.

Although Charlie later admitted noticing the item had been missing, he had never considered it necessary to notify security. In fact, he apparently forgot about the quilt's absence until after its return.

There was only one way that could that have happened— if he thought the owner took it herself. Perhaps she had even borrowed the display keys from him, offering a plausible explanation for the request. The bottom line: Charlie hadn't worried about the quilt's disappearance—and neither had anyone else.

Fine. The owner borrowed it. But why didn't she just wait until the exhibit was finished?

Maybe Charlie's protégée ran out of money, as college students regularly do. And maybe, rather than phoning home, our devious girl decided to make a call or two to test the market for the quilt. The woman at Winterthur confirmed that her assistant had agreed to look at the item, which probably accounted for its removal from the display case. Mystery solved.

All except for the name of the perpetrator.

My most approachable sources had come up empty, so it was time to dig deeper. I found a pay phone in the courthouse lobby and let Information complete my call to Winterthur—better than defacing government property by writing on the wall.

Chapter 24

The Textile Conservator at Winterthur, a Ms. Nancy Hunt, couldn't figure out who I was even after I explained that I was helping Charlie Finnemeyer's attorney with his trial.

"Can you meet with me a few minutes this afternoon?" I almost begged. "I'll tell you anything you want to know."

"Meet with me about what?"

"The fake Hewson quilt a student from Textile offered you eight years ago."

"I scarcely remember—"

"Please. It's very important." I might have asked my questions over the phone and been done with it, but I was a woman trying to relate to another woman, and not being able to read her expressions would have been like watching TV with the sound off.

"I don't see how I can help Mr. Finnemeyer. Really—"

"Maybe you can. Maybe you can't. I just need to know one way or the other."

A reluctant moment passed. "I suppose I can spare a couple minutes after three," she admitted without enthusiasm.

"Thank you," I gushed. "I'm very very grateful."

I would be leaving the trial, driving miles and miles out of my way possibly for nothing, but I hadn't lied; I returned to the courtroom feeling considerably lighter.

The returning jurors were students on the second day of class: familiar with their seats, but still unsure of what to expect. Yet they seemed a more compatible group, relaxed and alert.

A bond was also forming among the spectators, with the possible exception of Karen Smith, who now sat in the first row holding her mother's hand. She glowed as if coffee with her parents had been a hot dog on the beach or maybe a birthday brunch.

Of course, maybe their reunion actually had been a celebration. And as inappropriate as it seemed to me, maybe that was exactly what the Finnemeyer family needed. Who was I to judge? That was the job of the man who had just swung his floppy sleeves off the edge of the desk to free his hands.

Dr. Muir, exhibiting the patience of a well-paid expert, slouched against the back of the witness chair. Taking his turn at looking bored, Samuel Lloyd propped his chin on his fist while Eric Allen tidied a pile of papers. In a second the defense attorney straightened to his full height, buttoned his suitcoat, and strode toward his personal microphone.

"Good morning, Dr. Muir," Charlie's lawyer opened. "I have only a few questions."

Muir shrugged as if he didn't care one way or the other.

"You're an expert on Oriental rugs. I think everyone will concede that." Eric gestured around himself and smiled kindly. A few of the jurors nodded and breathed easier, seemingly relieved that the cross-examination would not be confrontational.

"But tell me something," Eric suggested. "Haven't some rather embarrassing mistakes been made by your colleagues?"

"What do you mean?"

"I'm referring to a very esteemed university in Boston. Haven't many of the rugs in their collection been found to be fakes?"

Muir squirmed. "Yes, I believe that's so."

"Your point, Counselor?" the judge inquired.

"Get there in a minute, Your Honor.

"And the famous auction house, you know the one I mean, weren't they fooled once or twice by a reproduction?"

"Yes, but they made restitution immediately."

"Yes, yes, of course. I think we all respect their integrity."

"Counselor?" warned the judge.

"No problem, Your Honor. I was just wondering. If world-famous institutions such as Harvard University have occasionally been taken in by fakes, why couldn't the reverse also occur?"

"I beg your pardon?" Muir blinked with genuine confusion.

Eric wiggled a hand in the air. "You don't understand? Sorry. I'm simply suggesting that if some of the most world's most respected experts can occasionally be taken in by a fake, why can't the reverse also be true?"

Muir got it this time and broadcast his indignation with a particularly virulent how-dare-you? expression.

Raised to abhor arrogance, I'm afraid my own incipient distaste for the man found purchase, prompting me to reconsider every fact he had offered so convincingly not half an hour ago. Now, even if reason forced me to reinstate my trust in Muir's information, it would be with reluctance.

Slumped in his chair, Samuel Lloyd had to know that the jury felt exactly the same as I did. They fidgeted. Neutral expressions had sagged into frowns. With a single petulant scowl Samuel Lloyd's expert had become an adult brat, an insufferable know-it-all who believed himself to be above challenge.

"In other words," Eric continued, "if the experts sometimes erroneously judge a fake to be real—which we know occasionally happens—wouldn't you say it's equally possible that they might incorrectly determine that a real antique is a fake?"

Muir sputtered. "That's proposterous."

"Why?" Eric asked.

"Because . . . because it just doesn't happen."

"Why not?"

"Objection. Asked and answered."

"Sustained."

Eric's hands were stuffed into his trouser pockets, his tongue stuck firmly in his cheek. "Okay, Dr. Muir," Eric began again. "This time I'll ask you an easier question. Do you have any proof for your favorite theory regarding Exhibit A—that is, proof that the weaver you mentioned, Tuduc, produced this particular piece?"

Muir's face flushed, and he mumbled his answer through a sour pout. "Just my years of experience and the fact that I've handled at least two of Tuduc's forgeries in the past."

"You say 'at least two.' Could that possibly be one or three?"

Muir refused to respond. The jurors exchanged quick glances among themselves. The judge lifted his eyebrows. Samuel Lloyd slumped until his fist was nearly in his left eye.

"All right. Let's say two. With either of those carpets, did you find any physical evidence—a signature perhaps or a certain kind of thread that told you definitively that the weaver Tuduc produced those rugs?"

"No."

"In other words, you were guessing."

"Objection!"

"Oh, I beg the court's pardon. Dr. Muir was employing subjective intuition backed by experience. Experience doing what? Guessing?"

"Objection, badgering."

"Sustained."

"No further questions. Thank you, Dr. Muir. Thank you very much."

The expert's hot glare singed even the judge who dismissed him.

I glanced at my watch—plenty of time left for Samuel Lloyd to regain the jury's sympathy before sending them off to their sandwiches. In anticipation I sat up and paid attention, as did most everyone else.

"The prosecution calls Oscar Tribordella."

I strained to get a good look as the man walked from the back door past me and on toward the witness stand.

Aged about forty-five, the department store furniture salesman had short, vigorously unruly dark hair. His deep-cheeked, narrow face was adorned by black-rimmed glasses hooked over widespread ears, and he wore a short-sleeved white shirt, black slacks, and a black tie knotted tightly below his Adam's apple. He reminded me of the tunnel-visioned cultists who knock on your door and push pamphlets into your hands ostensibly for your own good but primarily for their own. When he was sworn in, the courtroom deputy flinched as if under God's gaze.

"Can you please tell the court your relationship to the defendant?" Samuel Lloyd inquired after the preliminaries were completed.

"I used to live in the house behind his."

"For what time period?"

"Approximately four and a half years beginning about twenty-two years ago. I been married twenty-two years."

"Would you say the two of you were friendly?"

"No. I wouldn't say we were friends. No."

"Enemies then?"

"No, of course not. I just didn't like him, that's all."

"And why do you say that?"

"I disapproved of some of the things he did."

"And what were some of those things, if we may ask?"

"I'm a carpet salesman at Hechts now. Carpets and furniture. We sell reproductions of Oriental rugs, fine quality but not handmade. Those would be too expensive for our customers. But I have a respect for good-quality rugs. I been educating myself about them ever since I been in the business, and I don't mind telling you what Mr. Finnemeyer did to some of his own rugs was truly a sin."

"Can you please be a little more specific? Exactly what did Mr. Finnemeyer do to these rugs that you found objectionable?"

"He ran over one with his car, for starters. Back and forth and back and forth right there in the alley. Must've been a couple hours he kept at it."

"And to what purpose do you suppose he did that?"

"Objection. Calls for speculation."

"I'll allow it."

"Why, to age it, of course. Couldn't be no other reason."

"Go on."

" 'nother time he hosed down a perfectly good Turkistan and left it in the sun for nigh on a month. Left it there till it faded like you wouldn't believe. It's truly a sin what he did to some of those things."

"Did you ever ask him what he was doing?"

"Objection."

"Sustained."

"All right. Mr. Tribordella, how many times did you observe this sort of behavior on the part of Mr. Finnemeyer?"

The serious-faced man paused to think. "Two, no, three times with rugs. He put out lots of other linens and things, but it was the rugs he mistreated the most. I sell carpets, as I said, so naturally they were what I noticed."

"By any chance did you ever express your feelings about the treatment of the rugs to Mr. Finnemeyer?"

"No, sir. I did not."

"Why not, if I may ask?"

"I figured he was doing something shady. I didn't want nothing to do with him."

"No further questions." Samuel Lloyd took his seat.

Eric was scarcely at the microphone long enough for his trousers to shake out. "Mr. Tribordella," he said, "I'm sure you've noticed the rug we have here in the courtroom."

"Yes, sir. Nice looking Caucasian."

"Yes, it is. Tell us, please, was this one of the rugs you saw on Mr. Finnemeyer's clothesline?"

"No, sir. Can't say as it was."

"No further questions."

Grudgingly, I admired Samuel Lloyd's strategy. Suspecting that Muir's personality might sooner or later irritate the jurors—some momentarily, others for good—he had immediately offered an alternative: pious, indignant Oscar Tribordella, regular guy, rug lover, and back neighbor of Charlie Finnemeyer, the blatant cheat. Even if you couldn't quite figure out what Charlie had been up to, you knew it wasn't good.

All that and there was still half an hour left of the morning.

Chapter 25

Janella Piper's movements mesmerized. She glided toward the witness stand like a goddess floating through a cloud. When she lifted her arm to be sworn in, her body seemed to be without bone. Except perhaps for a spine. She certainly appeared to have a spine.

". . . so help me God." About then I was beginning to think that Charlie was the one in need of divine intervention.

The jury gaped at the television star with awe while Samuel Lloyd enumerated Piper's credentials like a host serving caviar on a silver platter.

"Now, if you will, Ms. Piper, please tell us the nature of your relationship with Professor Finnemeyer."

My lungs clenched inside my chest as I remembered the gossip Didi had elicited from Sally Shultz. I seriously doubted that Janella Piper was going to confess to an affair, but the phrasing of the question frightened me just the same.

"He was my print instructor in college."

"Your fabric print instructor?"

"Yes."

I watched the young woman's smooth, café-au-lait face for hints of hidden nuance, but her answer appeared to be the simple truth.

"How did you get along with Mr. Finnemeyer? Was your relationship cordial?"

The fascinating face segued into an even more fascinating

smile, which she directed toward Charlie. "Oh, yes. Some of my friends teased me about being his favorite student."

Charlie scowled at his hands.

"Would you say that Mr. Finnemeyer was a good teacher?"

"Oh, yes. Excellent. If it hadn't been for him, I wouldn't be where I am today."

And where do you mean, I wondered nastily—outside of jail?

"Can you please describe his teaching methods for us? Briefly, of course."

"Certainly. He was exceptionally creative. By that I mean he used all sorts of tricks to open up our minds. One week we took a field trip into a clothing store. Another time we made potato prints on paper. He mixed it up, made it interesting. Everybody loved going to his class."

Lloyd gave her a quick that's-nice nod. "Now tell us, Ms. Piper, did he ever teach you how to determine the age of an Oriental rug?"

Janella's head drooped and her softly styled hair fell forward. "Yes, he did."

"Can you please tell the jury what methods he used to teach you that skill?"

"He brought in four or five different rugs, and we had to write papers on why we thought they were genuine antiques or fakes, if we thought they were fakes."

"Was that an effective way to learn?"

Janella brightened. "Oh, yes. I can't imagine a better way."

"And were some of the examples he showed you fake?"

Janella's deflated again. "Yes."

"Do you happen to know where Professor Finnemeyer came by the rugs he showed your class?"

"I . . . I . . . no. I just thought he brought them from home."

When it came his turn, Eric tried to underscore Janella's uncertainty about where the sample carpets came from, but that proved to be a fruitless tactic. The jury was left with the original impression Janella had put forth, that Charlie had shown his students rugs he personally owned.

On the way out for the lunch break I tried to commend Eric

on his morning's work, especially his questioning of the expert from UCLA, but he vehemently rejected my compliments.

"I wouldn't say Charlie's off the hook yet, would you?"

Depression shadowed me along Market Street and into the train station. I traveled back to my car in a fog, gave myself indigestion eating a couple tacos too fast on my way through Wayne, then drove southeast toward my appointment with the Textile Conservator from Winterthur in a blue funk.

Located on Delaware Route 52 six miles northwest of Wilmington, Winterthur had been the lifetime project of Henry Francis du Pont, a fourth-generation member of the French emigrants who founded the Du Pont company. Apparently H. F.'s diligence turned what had been a working farm and dairy into a 985-acre masterpiece of "twentieth-century American naturalism," to most minds a sizable enough achievement.

But du Pont also had an eye for antiques. When his collection—some 50,000 items—outgrew his family's towering stone mansion, an expansion was built. Now the museum owns upward of 90,000 pieces and boasts of "the world's premier collection of American decorative arts of 1640 to 1860."

Aware of this, I felt awed and clumsy as soon as I turned onto the property. Only lithe, well-bred people owned antiques and strolled through spectacular gardens every evening. My good china was stoneware, and it was a lucky year if I found time to set in a flat of petunias. However, I reminded myself, that was why they sold tickets to this place.

The long driveway wound through a drab January landscape reminiscent of a giant sleeping under an old blanket. Canada geese padded around the edge of a couple of cold black ponds, and my memory saw them in warmer water. March perhaps, when there would be acres lavished with blue scilla, snowdrops, adonis, daffodils, crocus, and more—bucketsful of color splashed on the ground beneath the still-leafless trees.

I parked on a flat, paved expanse uphill from the buildings and took the diagonal path down through a woodsy garden leading to the education center, museum store, and cafeteria.

A small bus leaving from there delivered me and two late-
arriving tourists to the museum proper.

Its entrance was suitably attractive—creamy stucco, mature
trees, stone benches for summer, and a tall, glassed-in doorway. Inside the large vestibule, I politely asked someone from
the Information Desk to alert Nancy Hunt that I was there.

In no time Winterthur's Textile Conservator emerged from
a corner doorway. Her posture and long bouncing stride told
me she was a product of either dance class or finishing school.
She wore indestructible mud-brown slacks and an off-white
silk blouse with a textured leaf pattern. Practical. The outfit
would work equally well kneeling on the floor to reach a low
shelf or bounce-striding into a boardroom. Lumpy jewelry in
earthy colors suggested expensive taste, but the dust smudge
marring the woman's square jaw told me she refused to worry
much about something as trivial as dirt. I placed her age at
about forty.

"Mrs. Barnes?" she inquired with an outstretched hand.
Without the thin wire-framed glasses her face would have been
too ordinary, almost incomplete.

"Please call me Gin. You must be Nancy Hunt."

"Yes. Do call me Nancy." Her voice was reedy and her
delivery sure. I sensed that, unlike Janella Piper, Hunt withheld some of her assets from public view.

She began to lead me back through the corner door into the
working/storage area of the building. We passed through a
large room full of Oriental rugs rolled onto cardboard spools.
Supported by chains, the spools were hung in rows from ceiling to floor. I couldn't help but wonder whether any of them
were fake.

"Now, remind me why you're here?" Hunt prompted as she
opened the far door.

We entered another storage room containing stacks of what
looked like oversize pizza boxes on wheeled racks. "Textiles,"
Hunt remarked as she walked by.

I hurried to catch up, in all respects. "I'm hoping you've
remembered more about the quilt the student offered Winterthur eight years ago. Have you given it any more thought?"

End to end in the room's center aisle were two rectangular tables covered with white cloths. The tables held a miniature antique canopy bed, two cradles, and a tiny double bed—all with authentic-looking linens. A larger sample of a fancy green drape suggested that preparations for a new display were in progress. Or else these were teaching aids, I couldn't tell which.

"It was a preposterous story and we turned it down," Hunt remarked. "What else do you need to know?" She was almost at the end of the large room.

"Was the student by any chance African American?"

My guide stopped so abruptly I nearly bumped into her. "Why are you asking me that?"

"I'm trying to identify which of Professor Finnemeyer's ex-students offered you the quilt. Only one happens to be black, so I thought it would save time . . . "

"Why does her identity matter now? We dealt with the problem. It's over."

I stalled with a deep breath but decided there was no reason not to be honest. "Because I think whoever approached you committed murder to keep her little experiment with fraud a secret."

Nancy Hunt folded her arms and scowled. "Come with me," she said, and we finished the circuitous route to her office in record time.

The office was a horror of mismatched chairs—three— overflowing file cabinets, wheeled carts full of books, three desks piled high with papers, telephones, and fabric scraps. A wall of warm wooden slats with a square window standing on end was plastered with memos and pages of cloth samples. Another was covered with posters. I prayed I wouldn't sneeze and cause a catastrophe.

Nancy Hunt took the blue chair. I got the gray.

"I never actually met your student," my host admitted, and my heart sank. "I didn't like the story she gave me over the phone," she continued, "so I turned her over to my assistant as a sort of learning experience."

Assistant? I glanced around to check for such a person, but

we were totally alone. Patience, I admonished myself the way I would one of my kids. Settle down here. Let the woman talk.

"Lexie was an intense girl, but impulsive. Young. Just young. So I tried to give her as wide a range of experience as I could. I thought fielding the quilt thing would do her good."

"Does she still work here?" I had to ask.

"Now? Oh, no. She's long gone."

"Sorry. Please continue." Nancy Hunt's face hadn't weathered the interruption well, so I vowed not to disturb her monologue again.

"As you might expect, we both doubted the authenticity of the quilt—that story about Betsy Ross was just too wild. But wilder things have happened in this business, so I told Lexie it wouldn't hurt to give the item a look." She shifted in her squeaky chair while I took pains to hold perfectly still.

Hunt waved a hand. "The whitework part of the quilt seemed old, all right, although perhaps not as old as it should have been.

"To Lexie the giveaway was the stitching around the appliqués. It was too perfect, too new; and when she brought the thing in for my opinion, I agreed. But just to make sure, I picked open an inch of stitching to look at the underside of one of the print patches. None of the blue had leaked through at all, something that absolutely would have happened if the prints were genuine.

"Plus *all* of the appliquéd pieces were in Hewson's style, not just the amount you'd expect to find printed together in a block, which was how he sold his quilt designs. In other words, the piece was just as fake as we expected it to be. You seem surprised."

"Only that you messed with the stitching. I didn't think you could do that."

Hunt gave that a brief nod. "Interfering with the integrity of a piece is controversial, naturally. But in this case I wasn't taking much of a risk. The item was not a genuine antique."

"So what did you do about it?"

"Family members are often misinformed about the provenance of what they inherit, and I figured the girl fell into that

category, that she probably offered us the quilt in good faith.
I told Lexie just to say no thanks, which she did. Of course,
I hadn't heard the girl's spiel firsthand, and that can make
quite a difference."

"Of course," I wholeheartedly agreed, since that exact difference had motivated me to drive all the way down to Wilmington.

Hunt continued. "In fact, after the girl left, Lexie and I had
quite a heated discussion about the incident. She insisted that
the girl had deliberately tried to put one over on us, and she
was furious about it. She had even tried to get the young
woman's license plate number for the police."

"Did she get it?"

"No, the girl had too much of a head start. But Lexie recognized a student parking sticker on the bumper, and one of
those Philadelphia College of Textiles and Science decals was
on the rear window."

Winterthur's Textile Conservator flicked some lint off her
knee. "To humor Lexie I compromised and phoned the president of Textile. I still thought it could have been a mistake,
or maybe a student prank, some sort of initiation like sororities
sometimes do." She shook her head. "President Davidoff
didn't see it that way. He asked for the student's name so he
could take disciplinary action, but the name the girl gave Lexie
proved to be made up. After that, I don't know what happened."

I might have told her that Charlie Finnemeyer retired in
order to shield the student; but that part of the story still made
me uncomfortable, so I just sat there looking glum until Nancy
Hunt rerouted the conversation.

"Tell me again," she said. "Why do you think somebody
committed murder over this?"

Since those suspicions were exactly why I was there, I will-
ingly shared all my conclusions, probably in too great detail.

Winterthur's Textile Conservator listened patiently, but
when I mentioned Roland Ignatowski's name she jerked with
surprise.

"I'm meeting with his widow tomorrow," she confessed.

My own shock was evident. "Really?"

Hunt gave me an ironic smile and another nod. "She wants to sell off some of her husband's collection. Never was her thing from the sounds of it."

"May I come with you?" The request was out of my mouth before I thought about it.

Naturally, Hunt became wary. "Why would you want to do that?"

I forced myself to reason through my answer, but unfortunately, my request was based on the same thing Dr. Muir used to evaluate the fraudulent rug.

"Instinct, huh?" the Textile Conservator repeated. "I guess I can respect that."

"You can?" Was I mistaken or had the woman's eyes finally softened?

"Sure. It figures into what I do all the time."

Amazing. What I had assessed as potential antipathy toward my goal had finally relaxed into a tentative rapport. Hunt offered me a bemused smile and two opened hands. "Okay," she said. "You can come. It'll be nice to have the company."

After we arranged the logistics, I thanked her profusely, expecting nothing more than a handshake and a quick goodbye.

What I got was an offer I couldn't refuse.

Grinning as seductively as a trollop, Nancy Hunt asked whether I might like to see a *genuine* Hewson quilt.

Chapter 26

"Have you seen any of our displays?" Winterthur's Textile Conservator inquired as we headed out of her jumbled-up office.

I admitted I had not.

"Then I'll take you a roundabout way." Nancy Hunt glanced at her watch. "I can't show you everything, but I can get you started."

Since I needed to return home soon, I told her the whirl-wind route would be perfect; and in short order we were climbing some back stairs to the eighth floor of the former mansion. "The maids lived on the ninth."

Must have been a hundred of them, I thought after our long climb.

Hunt held the door for me to enter a warmly inviting hall-way. Immediately to our right was an assortment of miniature antique furniture displayed on the shelves of a lighted alcove.

"I guess dollhouses have been around as long as little girls," I remarked.

My guide gave me a puzzled scowl before enlightening me. "Most of these items were salesmen's samples." When I failed to come up with a response, she added, "Beats lugging around a four-poster bed, wouldn't you say?"

The next twenty minutes were a blur of exquisite decor, each room a sample of perfection. I admired lavish drapes, Chinese wallpaper, graceful furniture polished to a warm glow, silver, porcelain, lace, candlelight colors, and a swirling staircase that reminded me of a lyre.

I learned that fire screens were designed to keep wax-based makeup from melting, and that Martha Washington's favorite portrait of George was the one with him standing by the white horse. Apparently a Benjamin West painting of the signing of the Paris peace treaty—nice as far as it went—remained unfinished because the British refused to pose. And in a modest semicircle on the sideboard below—six authentic Revere tankards.

Nearly last on our route lay an especially large room Nancy told me was touted nationally for its beauty. A mirror of itself left and right, the room contained identical sitting areas, window treatments, bookcases, and accessories down to the last detail. I tried to visualize the Barnes family living with such fussy formality, but even in my imagination the kids moved everything around and Gretsky refused to stay off the sofas.

We passed through the vestibule for the corporate meeting rooms and traversed another hallway that ended at the special displays. This area looked less like a residence and much more like a museum. Items were artfully grouped, but here each one was featured for individual appreciation.

My host waved her hand toward a side wall. "That's it," she said of the white quilt hanging unobtrusively behind a spinning wheel and a rocking chair.

Struck by the history of the piece as much as its beauty, I think my mouth dropped open.

"It's lovely, isn't it?" I mumbled, but Nancy merely offered a bemused smirk.

Stitched in a tight, swirling pattern with white thread, the quilt's primary ornamentation consisted of a printed center patch surrounded by single appliquéd patches. Surrounding those were strips of pink roses arched gracefully around what would have been the top edges of the bed.

"The roses aren't Hewson's," Nancy told me. "Just the more central prints."

These Hewson designs employed the quieter colors—golden yellow, tan, brown, black, blue—suggesting a subtle,

elegant decor, while the designs were what I'd learned to expect from the colonial master—stylized birds on branches and
flowers, so imitated they seemed cliché. *Like Agatha Christie*,
I thought, whose quaint village intrigues had been replicated
so often it was easy to forget who created the prototype.

"There are only ten pieces of Hewson's work left, you
know," my guide marveled. "Known pieces, of course. The
Philadelphia Museum of Art has one too." Her remark, delivered with one eyebrow raised, helped me understand why she
had encouraged her assistant to at least look at the offered
fake. Just as Eric Allen had argued in court this morning, now
and then a preposterous-sounding story might prove to be true.

However, she had also just underscored how brazen the
Textile student had been by offering her fake to two institutions that already owned the real thing.

Nancy Hunt watched me gape at the display for a minute
or two, then lightly touched my arm. "I've gotta go," she said.
"You still want to meet me in the morning?"

"Oh, yes," I agreed. I had no intention of missing my opportunity to meet Roland Ignatowski's widow. The odds of
learning something that would help Charlie's cause were probably as slim as Birdie's when she went to ask Ignatowski to
drop his complaint; but much like her and Nancy and her
assistant, I couldn't completely dismiss the possibility.

Back home I prepared ravioli, salad, and garlic bread, which
I managed to burn as usual. My mind never stays still for the
minute it takes to broil the bread, and tonight I was busy being
pleased over my afternoon. I had met a textile conservator and
would soon get to watch her work. Eric had scored a few good
points with the jury, and tomorrow I had hopes of learning
something useful from Yvonne Ignatowski.

However, I never got to share any of that with my family.

"Danielle does *not* like Richie Knaus. And stop calling him
Mickey Mouse. He hates that." My daughter's cheeks were
chapped blotches of red, her deep-black eyes lasers aimed at
her younger brother.

Garry's sneaker heels clunked against the bench where he

was seated for dinner. "Maybe *you* like Mickey Mouse," he
taunted.

"Maybe you *are* Mickey Mouse," Chelsea returned.

"Hey!" I shouted to insist on a truce. "Take it in the backyard after dinner," I said. "Your ravioli is getting cold." That
elicited the humorless disgust I expected, but at least my children were back on common ground.

Just then Rip lumbered in from his home office and
dropped onto the end chair. His shirt sagged around his waist,
his eyes puffed from fatigue, and his scowl creases looked
about a quarter of an inch deep.

"What?" I asked, referring to his dejection.

His gaze reached for me as if climbing out of the depths
of anesthesia.

"What?" I asked again, withholding his plate of food until
I got an answer.

He relieved me of the plate and waved me into my own
chair. "Geraldine Trelawny," he said. "I'm not very good with
crying women—as you know."

I knew that tears distressed him inordinately, but he wasn't
as bad at handling emotional women as he thought. I had
tested the absorbency of his shoulder on occasion and found
the experience had its moments. However, I preferred not to
disagree with my husband in front of the children. Not on that
topic, anyway.

"What was she upset about this time?"

Rip dipped his chin and waved his fork in an ambiguous
fashion. "The same thing she was upset about before only
multiplied by a few hundred."

"What does that mean?"

"It means the whole school knows her boyfriend dumped
her."

"And how did the whole school find out?" I asked with a
spark of concern.

Rip spoke around a mouthful of ravioli. "Damned if I
know."

The spark threatened to ignite. I needed more information.
Fast, before my panic became a forest fire.

"She didn't tell anyone but you?" I inquired as mildly as possible.

"No, of course not. The thought of anyone else at school finding out mortified her. As you know, it took forever to coax her to tell me what happened. Half of what she was blubbering today was that she *didn't* tell anyone else."

"So essentially she was accusing you of betraying her confidence." An understatement, judging by Rip's instantly reddened face.

"Um-hmm," I observed. "Any luck convincing her that wasn't true?"

"What do you think?" If anything, Rip's face became redder.

Chelsea and Garry had stopped eating in order to watch us. This was better than MTV, better than an ambush talk show. This was their very own dining room drama, and it wasn't about them.

"You can't talk about this, kids," Rip cautioned.

"Why not? You did." I suppose Garry thought he had a point, but he was mistaken.

"Listen, bub," Rip lectured in his most authoritative baritone. "I did not say anything to anyone about Ms. Trelawny's problems to anyone outside this house. Did you?"

"No, sir," Garry replied with no trace of sarcasm.

Chelsea, too, shook her head in dead-serious denial. "We never repeat what you say, Dad. It's usually too boring."

Rip flicked a doubtful smile toward his daughter, while I poked the pasta on my plate without recognition. Oh, yes— ravioli.

"Exactly what details were flying around?" I asked. "Anything that could be traced back to your office?"

"Everything that could be traced back to my office, apparently. The Grateful Dead CDs, the motorcycle. Geraldine said yesterday a couple of boys walked behind her making vrooming noises, and she passed a girl at her locker humming 'Sugar Magnolia.' "

"That doesn't necessarily mean anything."

"How about if the girl was pretending to sob at the same time?"

I swore. Just the one little word I use for anything from burned garlic bread to a frozen roast landing on my foot. Since no one else knew the context of my thoughts, the kids smirked and giggled and my husband's mouth tilted down pretty far to the left. In spite of his fifteen years with me, Rip likes to believe that all women are ladies at heart, and to honor his mother's memory I try not to disillusion him very often.

"We'll talk later," I remarked as I wrinkled my nose. Then I fulfilled Chelsea's conversational expectations by initiating a discussion about rotating the tires on Rip's car.

As soon as the kids had gone off to do homework, I took my husband aside and told him, "I think we should check your office for bugs."

We were standing in the dimly lit kitchen surrounded on all sides by evening shadows. The illusion enhanced my permanent him-and-me-against-the-world mind-set, that certain sense of partnership and completion that was born the moment we met.

"Gin, I really don't think . . . Jeez, Gin. What have you been reading?"

"Nothing. I've been escorting juvenile delinquents downtown, remember?"

Rip opened his mouth, but no words came out. He tried to speak a second time and failed. Three proved to be the charm. "That would explain a lot," he admitted. "But where would Ryan Cooperman get his hands on a listening device?"

"You can buy anything on the Internet."

"Yes, you can," Rip agreed, his face darkening by the second. "What the hell? Now I won't sleep until I find out. If this is a wild-goose chase . . ."

"If it's a wild-goose chase, we lose half an hour instead of a night's sleep."

"Right." He stepped into the front vestibule and shouted down the hall toward the kids' bedrooms. "Chelsea! Garry! Mom and I have an errand to do at school. Won't take long."

"Okay," Chelsea called back. "Behave yourselves."

As the same words had been next on Rip's script, he bit them off and rephrased. "Stay off the phone, okay?"

Moans in response.

Gretsky remained behind to serve as the kids' first-alert system, but I would have loved having the dog along to scare the school ghosts back into their closets.

Only meat lockers and caves can be as cold as Bryn Derwyn Academy felt when Rip opened the front door to the lobby on that Monday night in January. The tall ceiling had leeched any warmth left from the day, the spirits of recently departed bodies stirred the air, and I shivered over the chilling realization that any clever vagrant or thief could be hiding in one of fifty darkened rooms, sleeping or plotting or waiting to turn violent if discovered. I held onto Rip's sleeve and risked running up his heels with every step. He didn't object, didn't even seem to notice. His fistful of keys rattled in his assistant's office door as they had at the outer door, but this time I was positive I saw his fingers shake.

"Can you turn up the heat?" I asked.

"Not worth it," the official head of school replied. "We'll be gone before it goes up five degrees." The system was ordinarily on a timer, and we hadn't been expected.

"How about lights?"

"Lights I can do." My husband slipped into a utility room off of Joanne's area and pulled an electrical lever. Lights illuminated every hallway throughout the entire building. I immediately felt warmer, safer.

"Thanks."

"I'll send you the bill."

We were being breezy because it was possible that we were not on a wild-goose chase after all, and neither of us wanted to address the implications of that just yet.

"Shall I take this half?" I asked, referring to the left side of Rip's office, which he had unlocked and illuminated brightly.

"Sure."

I pulled my coat collar up to my ears and started searching.

Nooks and crannies, the underside of shelves, lamps, silk plants, and ring binders—I covered every inch that might conceal even the tiniest of microphones. Behind the picture frames, the back of the file cabinets, under the chairs, along the baseboards—all I got for my efforts were a splinter and two dirty sleeves.

"Finding anything?" I asked Rip, who had more furniture to examine than I.

"A pen I lost a couple months ago."

"Big deal."

"It's a nice pen. I'm glad to have it back."

"Whatever."

We labored assiduously for half an hour checking the inside of Rip's storage closet, the desk drawers, the wastebasket. We found nothing that didn't belong, nothing Ryan Cooperman or anyone else could have planted.

Finally, with nothing left to search, we acknowledged our chagrin.

"I wanted it to be true," Rip admitted. "How scary is that?"

"Very scary," I conceded, but I wasn't listening to myself.

Because Rip had trusted me enough to actually drive over here and carry out a search, I felt compelled to dig deep for another idea.

Subsequently, I flipped on his radio—loud.

"What's that about?" my spouse inquired.

"More than one way to skin a cat."

Rip shook his head. "I've always hated that expression."

Me, too, come to think of it, but it was apt nevertheless. "Now we walk the halls."

"Why?"

"To see if we hear your radio, of course."

"Of course."

Our destination became clearer as we progressed through the building. Most all the classrooms were locked. Lab equipment and art supplies and even sheet music often disappeared if teachers neglected that basic precaution, which made their rooms illogical repositories for any spy equipment. To overhear Rip's private conversations—and not get caught doing it—required a safe haven for students, such as a little-used closet or, as I came to believe, the seniors' lounge.

True, Ryan Cooperman was not yet a senior; he wasn't even a junior. But he was exactly the type of kid to curry favor from his upperclassmen by letting them in on his risky pranks.

French, Spanish, and Latin classrooms surrounded the cubbyhole reserved for the most trusted kids, the privileged twelfth graders who had begged for a space of their own. I knew the mismatched sofas and overstuffed chairs to be cast-offs from various Main Line homes. A crooked brass floor lamp and a beverage machine—part soda, part juice—lighted the windowless twelve-by-twelve cubicle night and day.

And hidden under a rock 'n' roll magazine on a rickety end table—a small, radiolike box with one knob.

I twisted the switch expecting to hear my husband's favorite classical radio station. What I got was static.

"Guess that proves it wasn't a hidden mike," Rip lamented, but his words seemed to echo.

"Step out into the hall and say that again," I instructed.

My husband humored me one more time. "I . . . said . . . I . . . guess . . . that . . . proves . . ."

"Hey, hey," I stopped him. "What did you do with that pen?"

"Put it in my pocket. Why?"

I held out my hand, and he put a fairly ordinary black plastic Parker ballpoint on my palm.

I unscrewed the two halves. Inside, instead of a stem containing ink, was a narrow metal cylinder with a black antenna protruding from the top and red and black wires extending from the bottom.

"Ryan Cooperman is lunch meat," Rip growled as if he meant much much worse. "I've had it with that little twerp."

"What are you going to do?"

"Get a couple seniors to talk. Then I will gleefully expel the little bastard. He belongs in a nice tough public school— or maybe the army."

I almost reminded Rip that Ryan Cooperman was too young

for the army, but then I got it. The cork was out of the bottle. My husband the headmaster was delirious now that he had enough ammunition to dropkick his biggest problem into somebody else's territory.

Unfortunately, or perhaps fortunately, he didn't know the worst of it. Sadly, I did.

Geraldine Trelawny had merely been one of Ryan's victims, and although the disclosure of her private business was quite painful and embarrassing, her recovery would soon begin—as soon as she discovered that people are, for the most part, sympathetic and kind.

However, Ned Steward and Roland Ignatowski would never recover from Ryan's betrayal of them, and I feared that Charlie Finnemeyer just might be headed down the very same one-way road.

How was easy to explain. *Why* was another matter.

If I were Ryan, I would have put the microphone in place to eavesdrop on the headmaster's most recent conference with my parents—the same meeting I got invited to attend because I was currently the Coopermans' No. 1 patsy.

Attendance records indicated that Ryan had cut class during that hour, almost certainly to listen in on us; but for good measure (or perhaps for an alibi), the sophomore had also set a paint pan atop of the art room doorway. Right after the meeting Rip had been called away from his office to deal with the mess resulting from that.

And as soon as Rip left, I grabbed his phone to tell Eric Allen what I had learned from President Davidoff (via his wife) about Charlie Finnemeyer's retirement.

Standing in the seniors' lounge tonight, it took no effort to picture Ryan in the ugly overstuffed chair leaning over the receiver listening to his parents' departure, lingering in the hopes of catching one last word from Rip or me about himself.

His attentiveness was rewarded with something even better—my recital of someone else's extremely sensitive business over the telephone.

I cringed to think how fervently I had emphasized the confidentiality of Davidoff's information, how strongly I stressed to Eric my promise to Textile's president that his confidences would be used exclusively to prepare Charlie's defense.

To a boy craving attention, even negative attention, using his deep adult voice to inform the newspapers of what he heard must have seemed like great fun and a bit of justified revenge all at once.

Plus there was the added bonus of knowing his father was furious with Rip and me. Whether Ryan chose to impress Dad with the cleverness of his revenge right away or to hoard that pleasure for later didn't matter. It would be a heady power trip for the teenager either way.

Obviously, the story got approved by the appropriate newspaper editor, as hot information regarding an ongoing federal trial surely would. The facts were unwittingly verified by Birdie Finnemeyer. The article ran, and a few million people read it, including the one person most threatened by the reputation-damaging story: whoever faked the quilt in the first place.

To her, self-preservation suddenly became tantamount. Ned Stewart had been her first obstacle; Roland Ignatowski became the next. Technically, Ryan Cooperman had instigated his murder.

The question was: What was I going to do about it?

The answer: Exactly nothing. The kid was fifteen. He didn't know. For all his intelligence, I doubted that he would understand even if I explained it to him for an hour. I liked to think he would feel sorry when I was finished talking; but that was uncertain, and anyway the feeling might only last a moment or two.

It was later I worried about. Ryan Cooperman might become even sorrier as his life evolved, and his life wasn't going so well to begin with. Judging by the risks he took, he was already burdened beyond caring who he hurt, even if it happened to be himself.

Anybody who screams for help that loudly will sooner or later attract the attention he craves, but for Ryan it would not be from anyone at Bryn Derwyn Academy. Obstructing every professional overture the institution offered was a way of wasting his parents' money, and Ryan couldn't resist the symbolism of that. Yet somebody somewhere would respond to the boy's cries. At least I liked to think so.

Meanwhile, I would keep Ryan's connection to Ignatowski's murder to myself—with one possible exception.

Should the Coopermans be foolish enough to pursue their lawsuit against Bryn Derwyn (and Rip and me), then I would be forced to give Ryan's parents a private education they wouldn't soon forget.

Chapter 27

Tuesday morning at eight forty-five, I was waiting in the parking lot of a small strip mall on Skippack Pike sipping rotten coffee from a cardboard cup and running my car's engine for warmth. An egotistical morning radio personality toiled under the misconception that I would convert to his cranky view of national politics if only he could lecture me colorfully enough. Nancy Hunt drove into the lot just as I punched off the noise.

I'd only been parked ten minutes, but the thought of dumping out my liquid warmth made me shudder, so I drank it down to the last inch before I transferred into Nancy's spotless vehicle.

It was blue and comfortable with *heated* taupe leather seats and no dog hair or gum wrappers in sight. I felt completely adult riding in that car. Maybe someday I would feel that way all the time.

"How should I introduce you?" Winterthur's Textile Conservator inquired with a sideways glance.

"Good question." Roland Ignatowski's widow might not appreciate a friend of Charlie's showing up at her door. "Assistant? Apprentice?" Hitchhiker? Concerned bystander? Spy?

Nancy stopped at an intersection and peered at me skeptically. "I'll handle it," she decided.

We cruised along a two-lane country road with expansive properties on either side, fenced grazing pastures, tree-studded driveways, formidable stone homes with discreet barns—gentlemen's farms. Estates really. Gwynedd wasn't the most convenient suburb if you frequented Philadelphia's cultural offerings and worked in something hi-tech. You could get to the city or the silicon strip—even a small airport lay nearby—but I always imagined this pocket of wealth to be inhabited by the rat-race dropouts, the ones who made it and then actually slowed down to enjoy it.

The Ignatowskis' place wasn't visible from the road. Hidden behind a forest solid with evergreens, the front of the house met the curve of the driveway as it arched around the trees. To the north, our left, lay perhaps eight acres of unmown field edged with white plank fencing only along the road and the far neighbor's property line. The majority of the field consisted of frozen lumps of grass topped by wobbling stalks of blackened Queen Anne's lace, but toward the back stood the skeletons of a kitchen garden awaiting a proper spring burial.

The outside of the house wasn't especially beautiful or even very well groomed. All of gray stone—even the porch pillars—the architect's primary goal must have been longevity in the face of the elements. What little wood trim there was looked dull and flaky, and dead leaves littered the notch of ground to the side of the porch.

Nancy parked toward the back of the building in an area large enough for a small fleet of trucks. I supposed Birdie had left Charlie sleeping back here while she waited on the broad front step for someone to appear. From the ground level the grille-covered windows were set too high for anyone to peer into, so Roland's presence either dead or alive would have been beyond her view. According to her, she had met Yvonne Ignatowski on the slate sidewalk curving back toward the garage, had her brief and futile conversation, and then departed.

"Smells like snow," Nancy remarked. The sky was a pale pinkish gray, the temperature probably thirty.

Nancy and I wasted no time approaching the wide maroon front door. She operated the heavy brass knocker, and in scarcely a moment we were face to face with a tall, thin woman with spun fiberglass hair and a dried apple face.

Yvonne Ignatowski resembled a broken umbrella. I've seen black dresses hang better on a hook, shoes that gaped less on a mannequin's foot. Her crevassed cheeks were the same pale apricot hue as her hair, and her gash of a mouth twisted oddly around her crooked teeth when she spoke.

"Hello, Mrs. Ignatowski," Nancy opened in the voice reserved for church or a delicate situation. "I'm Nancy Hunt from Winterthur, and this is Ginger Barnes."

I murmured my condolences, but the widow scarcely listened.

"Call me Yvonne," she instructed. "Please come in."

The inside of the house was an industrial-size vault mitigated by oversize seating, huge Oriental rugs, and surfaces scattered with decorative objects. The uncovered third of the floor shone like "black ice," those questionable spots on the road you avoided if you could.

Nancy inquired kindly, "Are you sure you wouldn't like to wait a while longer for this?"

"No, not at all. I appreciate your coming." The widow's smile included me even if she was not sure why. "Rolly bought this pile of rocks to house his collection, and I've never felt at home here. Without him—" Her sentence abruptly halted. "I know it's going to take months for me to downsize. I thought I might as well get started.

"What would you like to see first?" Yvonne inquired of Nancy.

"Whatever you'd like me to see," the Textile Conservator replied. "I'm not an expert on all antiques, of course, but I can report anything I find interesting to my colleagues."

If I were Yvonne Ignatowski, I realized I, too, would flee this mausoleum as soon as possible, before a neighbor dropped in and found me reciting "Jabberwocky" in a closet. But that's not the sort of thing you admit out loud.

"It's really quite impressive," I told the mourning woman in my best put-your-listener-at-ease tone.

"Yes," Yvonne agreed wistfully. "Roland had excellent taste."

I hummed noncommittally and followed Nancy and our

host deeper into the living room, where the shopping tour began in earnest.

Nancy did not dawdle. She focused, examined, cataloged in her mind, and moved on. Lingering over any one thing invited a history of the piece, or rather a play-by-play of Roland's gamesmanship in acquiring it.

"Did he purchase every item himself?" I wondered aloud.

Yvonne skewered me with a skeptical "Why?"

"It's just that there's so much here. I imagine that finding this many beautiful things would have been a full-time job."

Putting it that way seemed to appease the woman. "Naturally he had dealers looking out for him, people familiar with his preferences."

So I could imagine. The way the house was stuffed with antiques, I bet he had an army of dealers eager to offer him more.

We proceeded through an old-fashioned pantry and kitchen and back around to a lengthy dining room containing a mahogany table the size of Delaware. Built-in cabinets stored enough flowing blue china to serve every Bryn Derwyn faculty member and significant other a full-course Christmas dinner. Like Winterthur's visionary patron, Roland Ignatowski seemed to have more enthusiasm for his hobby than space to store it.

Meanwhile, the museum's emissary took her time examining a thick glass pitcher, at one point holding it out for me to admire. I smiled stupidly and bobbed my head, which elicited a pitiful grimace from Nancy.

"Some assistant," she mouthed as soon as our hostess couldn't hear.

A few minutes later she asked Yvonne, "What's the history of this?" referring to a framed watercolor at the top of some stairs.

The homeowner eagerly related something about an artist I never heard of and how Rolly's friend picked up this particular item at an auction out in Lancaster. Her face still consistently deadpan, Nancy hung the piece back on the wall without further comment.

"How about this?" I asked Nancy of a silver goblet with

ribbonlike handles that reminded me of the one I'd seen at the Philadelphia Museum of Art. She merely grunted and moved on.

And so it went throughout the sizable abode, Nancy handling a pewter pitcher, fingering the bedspreads, checking the joints of drawers, reading the back of a displayed dish. She avoided ceramics but pawed through piles of linen and lace, spent an inordinate amount of time thinking about a writing armchair with a drawer, peeked under an eighteenth-century table with quarter-round molding at the corners, and listened to Yvonne's stories about each piece without revealing much of anything.

"That one's from Boston, circa 1776." "English, I think Rolly said. Came from Kent." "That's French lace from Lyons."

"Your husband must have loved to travel," I remarked at one point. I couldn't shake the feeling that Roland Ignatowski's purchasing habits might shed some light on Charlie Finnemeyer's trial.

"Oh, no. Rolly was quite the homebody."

Oh? Then how did he manage to acquire all this stuff? "But he must have loved exploring antique shops!" I pressed.

"Occasionally," the man's widow remarked so enigmatically that my curiosity multiplied.

And in pursuit of that carrot I manufactured opportunities to ask different versions of the same inane question. "Did your husband find this himself?" "How lovely! Did a dealer discover this for you?" Yvonne's expression invariably conveyed that I was a nuisance and quite possibly an idiot, but she humored me because she didn't want to appear ungracious in front of Nancy.

Still, her answers became increasingly brief. "I believe a dealer offered that to my husband" became "A friend found that" or "Rolly bought that privately." Finally she cut me off with "Friend" or "Private" before I even asked.

When I wasn't occupied being a pest, I spent my time taking in the overall impression of the Ignatowski abode, which was too much of everything crammed in too big a house.

Nothing really came together. A pleasant-enough painting would be too big for its corner, or too small, or too bright. Evidently Rolly's enthusiasm had evolved into gaudy excess, causing me to worry about his overall judgment.

Meanwhile, Nancy's professional demeanor never changed, never revealed a hint of what she was thinking.

When we finally got back to the front doorway, she thanked the tall, angular widow with her sad, wrinkled face. "There are a several pieces of interest, Mrs. Ignatowski; but as they're mostly outside my field, I'd like to return with one or two other colleagues—at your convenience, of course."

"Any time," Yvonne agreed eagerly. "I hope we can do business together. Rolly would have loved that."

Nancy squeezed the woman's hand, I added my thanks, and we took our leave by ten-fifteen.

"Well?" I prompted as soon as we rounded the trees.

Nancy Hunt scowled with concentration. "Some of the linens were nice," she said, "and the writing chair, of course. I kind of liked that covered pine cupboard, and the fluted-leg Chippendales are probably worth a second look."

That was all? She had to be holding back. "Come on," I urged. "What did you really think?"

The Textile Conservator shook her head hard as if ridding herself of the burden of good manners. "You're right," she pronounced with fervor as she steered onto the road. "Most of the stuff was crap. That watercolor was an inexpensive Wallace Nutting. And did you notice the handle of that glass pitcher? If you put anything in it, it would have snapped right off!"

"So that means . . . ?"

Nancy accelerated to about fifty, and two blanketed horses blinked as we whizzed by.

"That it was a reproduction, of course." Nancy tossed a hand. "And a bad one. Genuine antique pitchers were made to be used. The handles should be solidly attached—balanced as well as graceful. Since reproductions are just for show, nobody cares whether they actually work."

"So are you saying most of what Ignatowski bought was worthless?" Because of the overwhelming size of the collection, I had difficulty imagining that a preponderance of it was junk.

"Oh, I was serious about the linens and the Chippendales. Plus there were some other things I want somebody else to see, but no doubt about it—Roland Ignatowski was an easy mark." She shook her head in amazement. "The word must have really been out."

"Poor guy."

"Yeah, poor rich guy."

"So all those friends, all those dealers . . ."

"Either they were as clueless as he was, or they were crooks," Nancy confirmed.

"That's a lot of crooks," I remarked, then fell into a thoughtful silence.

Nancy had been exceptionally kind in allowing me to go along on her shopping expedition, and I thanked her profusely when we got back to the strip mall. But, eager to go off on our own, our eyes slid off in opposite directions as soon as we said good-bye.

The most expedient route back to Charlie's trial was the train again, and I let my thoughts follow their own path as I drove to the nearest station.

It didn't matter that Ignatowski's prized belongings had come from many far-flung places—antiques often did. However, this particular collector hated to travel and rarely seemed to venture out on his own. The only explanation was a middleman, a glorified personal shopper dedicated to ferreting out Rolly's heart's desires. True, Yvonne indicated that her husband had used a stable of dealers; but since so much of the collection was bogus, I doubted that she had been completely truthful. More than two or three cheats defied logic. One individual dedicated to abusing Ignatowski's trust seemed much more probable.

That Yvonne perpetuated the secret relationship made me even more certain that such an arrangement existed. Auction prices always soared when a person known to be well off bid

openly, and most likely a collector as avid as Roland Ignatowski had the very same problem. Unfortunately, it wasn't
his only problem. Ignorance and misplaced trust may have cost
him much more than money—his life, in fact.

As I watched snow stream by the train window like television static, it depressed me to realize that the personal shopper idea didn't eliminate even one of my murder suspects. TV
personality Janella Piper was renowned for her expertise. Sally
Schultz, the hell-raiser Didi went out with, owned an antique
shop on Pine Street, and Pamela Zenzinger apparently worked
for another dealer somewhere. Any one of them was qualified
enough to dupe the gullible Roland Ignatowski, probably even
Maxine Devon Nash. Although she wasn't officially employed
by anyone, with a couple kids and a husband in medical school
she surely would have welcomed a commission arrangement.

Yet those women were not the only possible culprits. Gordon Yeager, the dealer who purchased Charlie Finnemeyer's
rug, would probably be on the witness stand today, and I was
very eager to hear his testimony.

Yet even so, when I arrived at the courthouse after a wind-
swept five-block walk, I had a pounding concentration headache and my hand balked at opening the door. This was not
where I needed to be.

It was nearly noon, and courtroom lunch adjournments
were lengthy.

I turned and ran. If I hurried I might be able to get back
before I missed too much of Gordon Yeager's testimony.

Chapter 28

Yvonne Ignatowski took longer to answer the door this time. I suspect she had been eating lunch.

"May I come in for a minute?" I inquired boldly. "It's really quite important."

The angular woman wanted to say no but couldn't think of a reason quickly enough. "Come in," she said. Compared to earlier this morning, she looked much more withdrawn and unhappy.

"Thank you," I said, pleased as always to realize how polite most of us are. With that in mind I stood in the entranceway and made no attempt to remove my coat. I would say my piece, then quickly leave the woman alone.

Trying to be tactful, I said, "I didn't want to ask in front of Nancy, but I've been wondering whether you happen to own a whitework quilt with Hewson appliqués on it?"

Yvonne's already pasty complexion paled to the color of cement.

"Please understand that I don't care whether you own such a quilt, but if you do, it might explain why your husband was killed."

The woman made a strangled noise and steadied herself on the doorjamb.

"You do own such a quilt, don't you, Mrs. Ignatowski? It's all right, really. I just need to know."

"Yes."

"I thought as much. But don't worry. I think I know why you didn't show that item to Ms. Hunt. Your husband suspected it had been stolen, right?" The seller had to have told Ignatowski something to prevent him from bragging about the acquisition. Any uncertainty about its provenance would do.

Ignatowski's widow wobbled into her living area and lowered herself onto a seat. I followed discreetly behind and sat meekly a few feet away.

"Why do you say this has something to do with Roland's death?" the woman whispered.

I took a moment to select my phrasing, then I delivered it as sympathetically as I knew how. "I'm sorry to be the one to tell you, but that quilt was probably faked by a student from the Philadelphia College of Textiles and Science about eight years ago. Charlie Finnemeyer always had his beginning fabric print classes try to imitate John Hewson's techniques.

"For extra credit one of the young women appliquéd her samples onto an old quilt. Apparently she did an A-plus job, because the result looked authentic enough to pass off as real, which is exactly what she tried to do. Either for money or a dare—whatever—she attempted to defraud Winterthur and probably the Philadelphia Museum of Art, as well. I'm afraid that's where the murder motive comes in," I concluded.

Blood had returned to Mrs. Ignatowski's face, but I wasn't sure that was a good thing. "I'm sorry, what was your name again? I can't think . . ."

"Ginger Struve Barnes. Gin."

"Well, Mrs. Barnes, Gin," she sighed, "this is all quite shocking, but I still can't understand why this has anything to do with my husband's death."

"If I'm right, I'm afraid the quilt scheme had everything to do with it," I affirmed, settling down for a more thorough explanation. "Maybe I better start at the beginning."

"Please do."

I nodded, stalling because of what I had to say.

"You see," I finally began, "Charlie Finnemeyer is a dear old friend of mine." Minimal reaction, so I braved ahead. "I've been helping his lawyer gather some background information to aid in his defense. That's how I came across the quilt scam, and that's what appears to have prompted both your husband's death and the death of an expert witness named Dr. Edward J. Stewart. I think whoever faked the quilt is desperately trying to keep that past transgression from being mentioned during Charlie Finnemeyer's trial."

My listener eyed me carefully. "Okay. Suppose I believe you about the Hewson," she said, and I could see from the way her eyes flicked that the caution light had been blinking over that one for quite some time, "but why would anybody kill Rolly over that? He just bought the thing. He probably didn't know anything about that, that so-called past transgression."

Since the woman already had plenty to worry about, I preferred not to tell her that even the slightest reference to the previous Hewson incident might have tipped her husband off to the fact that he was being systematically swindled. Perhaps Nancy Hunt could explain that to her later.

"I know you said your husband had lots of people helping him to locate items for his collection, but did he by any chance have a close relationship with one person—an antique broker perhaps?"

Yvonne Ignatowski's lips pinched together and her cheek wrinkles colored. "Why do you ask that?"

"Did he?"

"Yes. So what?"

"A woman? About twenty-nine or thirty?"

"Yes."

I brought out that handy Textile yearbook once again. "Would you mind glancing through the seniors' photos to see whether one of them happens to be the woman your husband used?"

"All right." The widow began to study the photographs as if they were so many mug shots, which essentially they were. The process made me squirm.

"Would you like me to bring you a glass of water?" I asked hopefully.

"Yes, please." Grateful for something to do, I made my way back to the kitchen.

I had interrupted Yvonne's lunch. A glass of grapefruit juice was scarcely touched, and the last half of a grilled cheese sandwich lay stiffening on a greasy plate. The loneliness of it tightened my stomach and caused me to hurry back—with the juice instead of water. Widows need all the nourishment they can get.

When I arrived in the living room, Yvonne was staring into space, her hands fisted on both sides of the opened yearbook. I strained to see which of the suspects she had selected, which one had caused the staggering blow.

I set down the juice and hovered over the woman. Then I sat quite close on the sofa and tried to peer over her shoulder.

Yvonne turned her head toward me and remarked, "She killed my husband, didn't she?" Emotions I hoped never to feel had transformed her into a gargoyle.

I was still anxiously waiting to see which person she had singled out, but she remained oblivious to my frustration. Finally I just plain reached over and lifted her wrist.

The killer's identity jolted me, too. I rocked back in my seat and imitated the widow's stony stare.

But there was no doubt. Yvonne had scratched a gouge just below the face of one of Charlie's favorite students. Had my husband been her victim, I would have torn out the page and set it on fire.

"She did it, didn't she?" the woman repeated. She sounded battered, exhausted.

I told her yes, I was fairly certain the student she pointed out had committed murder.

Yvonne Ignatowski turned her wet eyes to meet mine. "Can you prove it?"

The question suggested some deeply buried strength struggling up toward the surface. I rejoiced over that and prayed that my answer wouldn't disappoint.

Shrugging a shoulder, I said, "I think I can get her arrested." Proving double homicide would be up to the District Attorney, aided by the police and a battery of forensic experts.

"How?" It sounded surprisingly commanding coming from a recent widow.

I couldn't keep still, so I stood and paced a little. "Now that I know she had a business relationship with your husband, I want to show her picture to the staff at Jack's Firehouse. Ned Stewart ate there just before he died. Maybe he had dinner with her."

Yvonne stood so abruptly that I teetered backward.

"I'll get my coat," she announced.

I didn't dare argue.

Chapter 29

If you faced City Hall from the art museum steps, Jack's Firehouse would be in among the side streets to the left of the Benjamin Franklin Parkway. Just look for the two-story firehouse doors in front and the prison across the street.

Cozied up to the prison walls as it was, Jack's parking lot seemed a bit foreboding, but this was midday and Yvonne Ignatowski and I were on a mission. We swept through the brass-handled doors of the restaurant like something out of the Wild West. Well, I did anyway. Yvonne looked a bit more like a cannibal mother shopping for lunch.

"Good afternoon," the drowsy maitre d' murmured, automatically reaching behind him for two menus on a shelf. He had small bones, puppy eyes, and a pencil mustache, and he wore dark denim jeans, a bistro apron, and a bright red shirt. As he turned back toward us, he noticed Yvonne's intensity and spent the next thirty seconds trying to blink his eyelashes off.

I gave him our names in an effort to put the man at ease. Then I quickly glanced around.

A rectangular bar with curved ends began soon into the spacious first room, and a copper still had been converted into a cruvinet for serving wine by the glass.

Hanging above was a sleek wooden scull, one of those slender rowing boats that always remind me of bugs skating on the surface of the water. About a hundred years ago the Philadelphia artist Thomas Eakins had immortalized rowers on the Schuylkill River, and this scull was of that picturesque vintage.

The rest of the room, with its warm wood tones and gentleman's club atmosphere, might have suited the artist's sense of mood. Not quite a pub and not typically gourmet either, the place came off as uniquely local. I knew Jack's to be renowned for its bourbon bar and the exotic menu—rabbit or wild boar, perhaps, with red cabbage on the side.

Then, of course, there was the prison across the street, which added its own undeniable flavor to the atmosphere.

"I don't want to be melodramatic," I told the restaurant's host, "but I need to show you a yearbook to see if you recognize a certain woman."

Yvonne was presently imitating a cat-o'-nine-tails, or at least something long, thin, and lethal. I was tempted to poke her middle with my elbow, anything to make her bend a little, but just then my cellular phone rang in my pocket.

"Excuse me," I apologized to the maitre d' as I extracted the instrument. "I have to take this."

On the ride here, an experience almost as harrowing as a New York cab ride, I had put a message on Eric Allen's beeper. Apparently this was the lawyer's first opportunity to call me back.

I handed Yvonne the Textile yearbook and nodded that she was free to show our man the picture. Then I turned my back on the two of them and answered the phone.

"Eric." I sighed after I heard his voice. "Listen, I know who the killer is and I'm about to get confirmation."

"What! Who?" Eric babbled, plus some more shocked utterances before I could calm him down.

"Just listen, will you?" Then I told him who it was, quickly adding, "I'm terrified she'll leave the trial before I can convince the police to arrest her. Can you do something? Hold her there? Please?"

"What's your evidence?" Eric demanded. Not much he could do without knowing that.

I moved farther away from Yvonne before I answered. "She

faked that Hewson quilt just the way I thought she did, and Ignatowski bought it from her along with a lot of other junk. She's been bilking him for years, and that's what she was desperate to hide.

"She probably killed Stewart to keep him from recognizing her at Charlie's trial. Then when the quilt story leaked to the papers, she had to kill Ignatowski before he started to question everything else she sold him. This woman really does not want to go to jail."

"Makes sense."

"Yeah, I know." Not that I was happy about it. "So can you do something?"

"I'll give the police a heads-up. The judge, too. She's not going anywhere."

It felt safe to breathe again. After I hung up, I turned back to Yvonne and the maitre d'. They were staring at me, the maitre d' with huge eyes and a look of panic. Guess he'd overheard some of what I told Eric.

"I showed him the picture," Yvonne reported. "I think he knows her. Ask him." She gestured with the open yearbook, and the man actually jumped back.

Like Yvonne I was chafing inside my skin, but I knew better than to frighten our potential witness further. I deliberately turned on the sweetness and gracefully raised an eyebrow.

"Is that true?" I asked. "Have you seen this woman before?"

The maitre d', whose name tag read "Manuel," sidled toward me and away from Yvonne. Then he held out his hand for the yearbook, which the widow relinquished as soon as she realized what he wanted.

As if for warmth, the man moved closer until our shoulders actually touched. Then he sheepishly tapped the picture with the scratch under it. A short distance away Yvonne sniffed with indignation.

"She looks familiar," he told me, tapping the yearbook again and monitoring my companion with his eyes.

My heart pounded until my ears buzzed. "Any chance you can be a little more specific?"

Manuel blushed and turned me away from Yvonne. I shot her a conspiratorial glance over my shoulder.

"I don't want to cause any trouble," the headwaiter began with his own nervous glance back at Yvonne.

"I understand."

"The young lady came in with an older man."

"When?"

"Last week."

Surely my face was throbbing visibly. Pretty soon I'd begin to bounce. "And how do you remember this?" I inquired.

Another glance back at Yvonne, who was admiring the scull.

"The man died right after."

Bang, boom, bam. My ears practiced their twenty-one-gun salute. "Really," I remarked. "Right in the restaurant?"

Manuel laughed uncomfortably. "No. Oh, no. Thank the Lord. In his car along the street. Otherwise . . ." A high hand wave and an eye roll suggested that had that happened Jack's might have vaporized into oblivion from the bad publicity. "Just a heart attack, but most unfortunate, wouldn't you say? Surely the anticipation."

"I beg your pardon?"

"The young lady. I think they were . . . you know." He checked his distance from Yvonne once again.

"Oh. Did they look as if they were . . . you know?"

"Perhaps a first date," Manuel decided. "But when she left, she, she stroked his face."

"Like how?"

Manuel came around to face me, thinking hard. Then he cocked his head to the side and gently ran his hand down my left cheek. It could have been either a gesture of affection or of good-bye, and at the very least it told me Ned Stewart's murderer was right-handed.

"Is she?" Manuel asked, jerking his chin toward Yvonne.

"Is she what?"

"The wife?" he whispered.

My thoughts were so much further down the road that I almost said yes, but then I realized he thought Yvonne was Ned Stewart's nearly betrayed wife rather than who she actually was.

"No. Don't worry. She's somebody else's widow." That confused him; but he made an effort to keep up.

"Listen, Manuel," I said. "You've helped us more than you can imagine. Would you mind repeating exactly what you told me for the record?"

"You're a detective, aren't you? One of those women who carry a gun." I had been wondering what he made of my hold-that-suspect conversation with Eric, and why he had been drawn to me and away from Yvonne—not that that was so hard to understand. To Manuel, what I had told Eric made me a private investigator and Yvonne my client. Two separate cases—one a murder, one merely an infidelity.

"No," I said. "I'm just helping out somebody's lawyer, and he's going to be thrilled with your information. You'll give him a statement for me, won't you?"

Manuel smiled with good humor. "For you? Of course."

Maybe he was into redheads or mysterious women in general. I didn't care. I had what I wanted—someone to give the police for the two murders other than Charlie or Birdie Finnemeyer. I kissed Manuel on the cheek and said, "Someone will be in touch."

He hastily wrote his name and the restaurant's phone number on a slip of paper, and this time I squeezed his hand to thank him. A second kiss probably would have procured his home number, but that I didn't need.

This time entering Courtroom 6-A felt even more like entering a church during the sermon. Almost as if we were expected, everyone, and I mean everyone, noticed us. The court stenographer; the roving jurors Jack and his pal Joe; Samuel Lloyd, who stopped talking into the mike and turned to see what was causing the stir; even the judge.

Due to an apparent scheduling switch, Pamela Zenzinger was on the witness stand. With the same dark eyes, the same cheekbones, the same soft, auburn hair as her yearbook photo, she might have won the "Who hasn't changed a whit?" category at her tenth college reunion.

Today she wore dangling silver earrings that touched her shoulders, and her striking deep-red hair hung in a long braid down her back. Her dress was black knit, showing off a full figure and long graceful hands adorned with silver rings, an outdated style but not objectionable. She was simply an arty person advertising her interests.

An arty person who had killed two men.

Stupid she was not. She recognized immediately that Yvonne and I had to be who Eric Allen and the others were watching for, and she put everything else together in a flash. The very next instant she swung her booted legs over the edge of the witness box, jumped down, and actually began to run.

In three strides two federal marshals caught up with her and proceeded to hustle her down the side aisle and out into the hall. As she exited the room, Zenzinger held her chin aloft like a modern-day Joan of Arc on some imaginary holy mission. Two deadly serious men from the audience also rose and joined the entourage, no doubt the homicide detectives Eric had alerted.

Naturally, the audience had been jolted onto their feet, and now they were babbling. Judge Bjorn hastily declared a recess. The courtroom deputy with the big blond hair guided the jury toward their side door, and Yvonne and I went to join Eric out in the hall.

From there he led us to the witness room, which was empty of witnesses but full of law enforcement types, Pamela, Eric, Yvonne, and me.

One of the detectives, a square-faced man with straight blond hair, approached and asked us, "What do you two know about this?"

I tried to speak, but Yvonne Ignatowski cut me off. "That woman killed my husband and Ned Stewart, too."

Pamela struggled forward to yell "You lying bitch. How dare you . . ." and so on until her outburst degenerated into mostly spits and curses. Eric finally had to stand directly in front of the woman and shout "Hey" to get her attention. Then he strongly suggested that she keep quiet.

Even considering her widow weeds, fiberglass hair, and red gash of a mouth, I thought Yvonne Ignatowski looked unimpeachably dignified. She put forth her case against Pamela Zenzinger in about five well-chosen sentences, ending with a flourish. "I wouldn't be surprised if half the items this woman sold my husband turned out to be fake."

The detective rubbed his chin and nodded. "We'll certainly look into all that, Mrs. Ignatowski. But right now we need more than your word to hold her on."

Behind him Zenzinger was once again yelling. "See! See! She's lying. Make her stop lying about me."

"Settle down," the blond detective told her. "You'll get your turn."

Unsure of who should hear what, I jerked my head to draw the homicide detective aside. Then as discreetly as possible I told him, "There's a maitre d' at Jack's Firehouse—Manuel—who's willing to make a statement. He saw this woman having dinner with Dr. Stewart just before his death. And the Textile Conservator from Winterthur can tell you which of the items Ms. Zenzinger sold the Ignatowskis are fake. She examined almost everything in the house just this morning."

The detective glanced at Yvonne, who had been near enough to hear.

"That's true," she confirmed.

The man's face didn't exactly brighten, but it did take on a resolve. "All right, folks," he said with a clap of his hands. "Let's take Ms. Zenzinger over to the roundhouse for questioning." Philadelphia Police Headquarters, literally a round building, was less than a two-block walk away.

"Mrs. Ignatowski, would you care to join us?" the detective asked the widow in a gentlemanly fashion,

Jurisdictions had to be straightened out, statements taken, rights read, lawyers summoned. Quite a lot of people would be questioned over the next few days, Didi and me included. Mostly based on the statements given by Yvonne Ignatowski and Nancy Hunt, Pamela Zenzinger was arraigned for fraud on Wednesday. The murder charges took a little longer.

That afternoon, my satisfaction was minimal.

Charlie Finnemeyer was still in danger of going to jail.

Chapter 30

Amazing!" my buddy the roving juror exclaimed. A mistrial had just been requested and denied. "Right back on the horse," Jack muttered into my ear with a puff of chocolate breath.

I grunted and nodded once. In my opinion, adjusting to Pamela Zenzinger's arrest deserved more than the time it took for a deep breath. Yet Judge Bjorn had just verbally swept the incident under the courtroom's industrial-strength carpet. ". . . nothing to do with the present proceedings . . . jury is instructed to disregard . . . Please call your next witness."

On a rational level I appreciated that court time was precious and life-altering events its daily fare, but the pure pragmatism of Bjorn's get-over-it attitude sunk me into a heavy funk.

Disappointed by my silence, Jack turned to his prodigal chum, and the two elderly gents chittered at each other like a pair of wrens until the woman in front of us turned around and shushed them.

Unfortunately, Jack and Joe weren't the only ones amped up by the arrest. Like a ballpark watching a no-hitter, the slightest movement made everybody in the room flinch. Standing in his customary place in front of his microphone, Samuel Lloyd appeared to be flushed from his receding hairline to the edge of his collar, yet all he was doing at this point was establishing his new witness's identity.

"Gordon Yeager, 1172 Twinlyn Pike, Fort Washington, Pennsylvania."

"And is your place of business also on Twinlyn Pike?"

"Yes, I have an antique shop in my barn."

Throughout this riveting revelation His Honor shifted on his seat as if a cheek had fallen asleep, and his hands twitched as if they were upset about it.

Yet Bjorn's eyes left no doubt. He remained in charge of this domain, even if it was a very different domain from what it had been before the Zenzinger incident. With few exceptions, the spectators had tasted blood and anticipated more—Charlie Finnemeyer's, most likely. He must be guilty of something or he wouldn't be here. Right?

Depressing beyond words.

"Please tell us, Mr. Yeager, how you came to purchase the Oriental rug you sold to Mr. Roland Ignatowski."

The upper half of Yeager's face reminded me of a junior-high boy who pursued me relentlessly. Blond, with an ingenuous moon-face and eyes so ordinary they almost looked blank, Dan, I think he was called, walked me to every class daily for a week and picked me up afterward. One day I agreed to accompany him to his parents' house, a short two blocks from school, and he presented me to his mother with such fanfare that I finally became suspicious.

Free of his smothering attention over the weekend, I managed to dope out what was wrong. In his excessively self-involved junior-high fashion, young Dan had stalked and bagged me as surely as if I had been the objective of an African safari. Who knew what was really on his agenda, but the point was—he had had one. I've questioned surface impressions ever since.

"Mrs. Finnemeyer stopped into my shop one afternoon and asked if I was interested in purchasing an especially fine Caucasian carpet."

"And how did you initially respond?"

"I said I wasn't interested."

"Why did you say that, Mr. Yeager?"

"Because I'd never bought anything from the Finnemeyers

before, and I had just made a fairly expensive purchase."

"In other words, you were low on cash."

"Objection."

"I'll rephrase. Were you low on cash, Mr. Yeager?"

"Yes, I was."

"But obviously, the situation changed. Can you tell us what happened?"

Yeager contemplated Lloyd's left shoulder. "Two things, really. I sold a very valuable desk inlaid with ivory—giving me a cash surplus—and a very good customer of mine inquired about an Oriental of approximately the same size and style as the one the Finnemeyers were offering."

"You anticipated a quick turnover."

"Yes."

"I don't suppose you related this turn of events to Mrs. Finnemeyer."

The moon-face clouded slightly, perhaps with a combination of embarrassment and modesty. "I wouldn't be much of a negotiator if I did, would I?"

"Probably not. How did the negotiation proceed?"

"I called Finnemeyers and spoke to the wife, asked her a few more questions about the rug."

"What sort of questions?"

"I verified the pattern, colors, quality, that sort of thing."

"Did you discuss price at that time?"

"No. I tried, but she put me off. Said her husband was calling for her."

"What, if anything, did you make of that?"

"Just that they were playing the same game I was."

"Game?"

"Sort of holding their cards close to the vest. You know, keeping up my interest."

"What happened next?"

"Mrs. Finnemeyer brought the rug over for me to see."

"Once?"

"No, a couple times. We settled on a price, then I resold the rug to my customer."

"Mr. Ignatowski."

"Yes."

"All right. Now, I've been listening carefully, as I'm sure the jury has, and I've noticed that you usually referred to both the Finnemeyers rather than just saying *Mrs.* Finnemeyer or *she*. Why is that?"

Apparently Yeager hadn't heard that question during his preparation. He blinked his boring eyes and rubbed his round boring chin. Then he flipped up his gaudy geometric tie and smoothed it down. "I suppose because I felt I was dealing with both of them."

"But something must have given you that impression. Can you tell us what that was?"

The witness considered his answer. "Probably that Mrs. Finnemeyer didn't know much about carpets."

"Kindly explain."

"Well, for example, I asked her how old the rug was, and she just shrugged."

A couple of laughs erupted from the audience, causing Judge Bjorn to scowl and tap for order.

"Thank you, Judge," Samuel Lloyd commented before returning his attention to the witness. "And yet, Mr. Yeager, you paid quite a handsome price for the item. Sixty-five thousand dollars, I believe?"

"Yes, that's correct."

"It's my understanding that antique Orientals are rarely worth that much. Why did you agree to such a high price, if I may ask?"

"By then I'd determined that it was exactly what my customer wanted, and Birdie, uh, Mrs. Finnemeyer told me she had another buyer lined up if I didn't take it."

"I see." Lloyd tossed the jury a knowing look.

I had been squirming on the hard surface of the pew like a tadpole out of water. This was worse than sweating out Chelsea's ear operation. Worse than hurting my father's feelings. Worse than waiting to hear if Rip got his headmaster's job. This was somebody I cared about being unfairly accused and wrongfully convicted. This was *injustice*, and it was taking place right in front of me in a federal courtroom.

Or was it? Maybe I was squirming because I, too, was beginning to lose faith in Charlie. Again. How many times this week had I doubted him, then trusted him, then doubted him again? It didn't help that I knew the crux of it all was that honesty lecture Charlie had delivered to Karen and me way back when.

We're flawed—all of us. Who knows why? Dad smokes two packs a day. He doesn't want to pass his dangerous habit along to his son, so he rattles off the Do as I Say/Don't Do as I Do lecture. Maybe Junior trusts the words for a minute or a week, but sooner or later he catches on and internalizes the real message. It happens all the time.

Still, I preferred to believe that the Charlie Finnemeyer I loved as a kid would only lie out of desperation. Unfortunately, no reason—not even exorbitant medical bills—would keep him out of jail if Samuel Lloyd won the day. And that was looking more and more probable.

Permission or no, my lip begin to quiver, so I pouted hard before finally hiding my face behind a tissue and pretending to blow my nose.

From my left Jack Armstrong observed this production with a skeptical tilt of his head; but I was too busy giving myself a sobering cold shower to respond.

I reminded myself that just because my soft, sentimental female *heart* had decided Charlie had to be innocent to preserve some soft, sentimental *idealized* notion of my childhood didn't mean he wasn't guilty as sin.

The judge was right. Pamela Zenzinger's arrest had nothing to do with Charlie's trial. He could be guilty of antique fraud. Probably was.

Nuts. I could lecture myself like that all day, but I would never convince myself that Charlie Finnemeyer was a crook.

And yet I saw no way to extricate him from this mess. Either because the Finnemeyers trusted the jury to be every bit as softhearted as I, or (I had to admit) because Charlie was guilty as charged, the couple had hog-tied their own defense attorney. As a result, Samuel Lloyd was scoring with the jury every time he opened his mouth.

I wiped my eyes for real this time, then put the tissue away. I trusted juries, really I did. But much like a doctor basing his diagnosis solely on information provided by the patient, what they heard and who they heard it from were critical to their decision.

How nice it would be if someone came up with an alternate explanation for everything that had been said so far, preferably one that left Charlie out altogether, perhaps even placed the blame on somebody else. Maybe . . .

I straightened up so fast that Jack Armstrong yipped with alarm.

"I've got it," I stage-whispered to explain myself. "I really think I've got it."

Jack's non-eyebrows lifted so high they rounded his eyes. "Got what?" he asked with boyish eagerness. Joe, too, leaned forward to hear my revelation, and most of the nearby spectators seemed to be eavesdropping.

"I've got an important question for Eric Allen to ask this guy." I jerked my thumb to indicate Gordon Yeager, the current witness.

Joe and Jack exchanged thoughts with a glance. Then, in gleeful harmony, they both dove for their pockets.

Joe came up with a ballpoint pen about the time that Jack handed me the wrapper from a Skor bar, which he opened flat and smoothed on his knee. The printed side of the paper was dark brown, but the inside was clean and white. My printing came out clearly enough if I wrote on the hard wooden bench. Jack read my note upside down as I wrote it, then showed it to Joe.

The professional spectators were now cats delirious on cream, but I had sunk back into dejection. "Now what?" I muttered, never expecting an answer.

"Now you give the note to Eric Allen," Jack remarked as if he had wanted to end the sentence with "dummy." Beside him Joe nodded vigorously.

"I don't know, guys," I demurred. The thought of disrupting a federal trial with a ridiculous television antic seemed presumptuous, absurd, and, at the very least, terminally embarrassing.

Both men frowned their opinions of my cowardice and urged me toward Eric with finger wiggles and jerks of their chins. Jack finally poked me in the thigh with the pen. "Go on," he prodded. "It's a really good question."

Up front Samuel Lloyd had finished with Gordon Yeager and was back at his seat. Eric Allen had risen from his chair and stood sideways buttoning his suitcoat—as usual. In a second he would turn his back to the audience. Then he would walk toward his microphone several feet from the pews and that much farther out of my reach.

He was scarcely into his turn when I bolted upright and pushed my way to the aisle. Ignoring the murmurs and stares, I hustled up to the front opening.

"Pssst, Eric. Here."

Censoriously the judge said, "Just a moment, miss. What is the nature of this interruption?" A federal marshal moved his hands to his hips and sidled toward me.

And Eric finally turned his head.

I waved the note in front of me. Some of the audience giggled. The judge made another remark, and Eric replied, "I beg your pardon, Judge. Mrs. Barnes is a colleague of mine. Excuse us just a second."

The defense attorney came over and relieved me of the note, which looked exactly like a folded candy wrapper.

"What's going on, Gin?" Eric asked soto voce. "You can't just do this. It's not a fucking *Perry Mason* show, you know."

Oh, sure, I thought. As if I went around making an ass of myself just for fun. But I merely snapped "Read the note," without adding any of the nasty names that came to mind. Most likely, he was more mortified by my behavior than I.

But he did read the note. Then he did meet my eye. And I got to watch his face transform into a grin that made all the stares and glares worth it.

Blushing and beaming with total abandon, I hurried back to Jack and Joe, who were bouncing on their seats and punching the air and high-fiveing each other like schoolboys.

"Sorry, Your Honor," Eric apologized. "Something my colleague forgot to give me earlier."

"Can we get back to business now?" The judicant's square Scandinavian face effectively conveyed that all theatrics had better be over.

"Yes, sir."

"Proceed."

Eric strolled back to his microphone and paused, allowing everyone's attention to return to the witness.

"Mr. Yeager," the defense attorney began with feigned neutrality. "Will you please tell us who set the price for the rug you bought from Mrs. Finnemeyer?"

I couldn't help it. My heart rose with pride as Gordon Yeager's head sank down toward his collar.

"Take your time," Eric told the antique dealer. "You are still under oath."

Yeager waffled. "I'm not sure I know what you mean."

"Oh, come on now. It's a simple enough question. How did you settle on the amount you paid for the rug? Did Mrs. Finnemeyer ask you for $65,000?"

"No, not exactly."

"Speak up, please."

"No, not exactly."

"I see. Did Mr. Finnemeyer ask his wife to ask you for $65,000?"

"No."

"He didn't? Are you sure?"

"Yeah, I'm sure," but grudgingly so.

Eric glanced quickly in my direction, then back to the antique dealer.

"Mr. Yeager, is it possible that Professor Finnemeyer didn't even know that his wife was selling the rug?"

Yes! I sang to myself. That just might do it.

Yeager squirmed. "Mr. Lloyd did get me thinking about that."

"Oh? And what have you decided?"

"He knew." This with an accusatory glance toward Charlie.

"Are you sure?" Eric pressed, his disappointment clear.

"You did say that Birdie never answered your question about the rug's age. Could it be because she was selling it behind his back?"

Yeager contemplated Charlie for a moment. "No. I still think he knew. Mrs. F was always saying things like 'I gotta check that with my husband,' 'Let me ask Charlie about that.' Stuff like that. So I think he knew."

Idiot. The oldest stall in the book and men invariably fell for it, I suppose because it flatters their sex. To me it now seemed perfectly obvious that what Eric suggested was true—Birdie never told Charlie a thing about selling the rug until the police came knocking.

But my beliefs and the jury's were still two different things.

"All right," Eric conceded. "We'll leave that and return to my original question. You still haven't told the court how you settled on the price of $65,000."

Yeager sighed into his microphone so loudly that the audience jumped.

"You have to understand," he said. "I really thought the rug was a genuine tribal Caucasian dragon rug, two-hundred-forty knots per inch, wool warp, all the right colors. The pattern was exactly what my customer wanted. I thought I couldn't lose." He shrugged eloquently. "Then Mrs. Finnemeyer told me about the other buyer and I panicked."

"What do you mean, you panicked?" Eric asked sternly.

"I made a simple mistake," the dealer admitted while defensively puffing his chest. "I thought I was going to lose the deal if my offer wasn't high enough."

"Are you saying what I think you're saying, Mr. Yeager? Are you saying that you *offered* $65,000 for the rug, and Mrs. Finnemeyer accepted?"

"Yes. There was a little haggling; but yes, that is essentially correct."

The reluctant answer sparked much murmuring and rustling around the room. Judge Bjorn quickly tapped his gavel, and Eric took advantage of the ensuing silence.

"And you in turn resold the rug to Mr. Roland Ignatowski for $110,000. Is that also correct?"

"Yes, it is."

"But then something went horribly wrong, as we've all heard. Why don't you tell us in your words, Mr. Yeager?"

"Ignatowski got the rug appraised."

"And?"

"And the appraiser told him it was only worth $15,000 . . . at the most."

"I imagine Mr. Ignatowski was rather irate about that. Was he, Mr. Yeager? Irate?"

"Yes. He . . . he actually called the police."

"Which we all realize led to this trial. But that aside, I think we need to know how you personally dealt with Mr. Ignatowski's anger, some of which was surely directed toward you."

"I didn't do anything. I was as surprised as he was."

"So you didn't accept blame for the error and offer to make restitution?"

"No."

"No? Why not?"

Yeager seemed intent on rubbing the joint of his thumb. "I . . . I couldn't. I'd already used the money to purchase something else."

"I see. So you allowed Mr. Ignatowski to think that you had been duped by Mr. and Mrs. Finnemeyer."

"Yes. I guess I did."

"Which we now have learned is not true."

"Well . . ."

Eric Allen pivoted abruptly, dismissing Gordon Yeager and squarely facing Judge Bjorn.

"Since the charges against Professor Finnemeyer seem to have been caused solely by Mr. Yeager's failure to admit an error of judgment, I move that the government's case against my client be dropped."

"Motion granted." The gavel wacked, and the room went wild. Jack and Joe and I danced our way into the aisle while all around us might as well have been midnight of New Year's Eve.

Minutes later, as the courtroom finished emptying, the Finnemeyers, Eric, and I clustered together out in the hall. Tears coursed down Charlie's cheeks into his beard while Birdie glanced from Karen to Eric to me and back.

"I don't understand any of this," she told our euphoric faces. "What happened?"

"I'll explain it on the way home," Karen told her mother. "Let's get out of here."

Chapter 31

That night we skipped Mme. Mimi's painting class. After two days of baby-sitting, all my mother wanted to do was to go to bed with a book.

As a result, the following week we chose to ignore the afternoon's inch of snow and the evening's fifteen-degree temperature just to get there. Cynthia wore thin pull-on Totes over two-inch heels and felt like a pioneer woman trekking through a mountain pass toward the Promised Land. I wore Timberland work boots and felt like Annie Hall's mule. Neither of us was in danger of stepping on much more than shoveled macadam or salted cement, but we felt prepared for adventure nevertheless.

The weather shrunk the art room to an intimate cluster of acquaintances temporarily behaving like friends. Mimi corralled us around the radiator and darkened the far end of the room. Instead of her ten-minute lecture she played ice-skating music on a portable CD player—Strauss with lots of strings. One of the women had brought a large Thermos of hot chocolate, which we drank from cardboard cups. I didn't care if I painted a stroke, and neither did anyone else. Yet we each dabbled at our work while we talked, and I'd say we all progressed much further than we expected.

"What's going to become of Ryan Cooperman?" Mother asked as she dusted a spot for her napkin with her hand. After completing his interviews the morning after we found the Cold

War surplus spy equipment, Rip had expelled Ryan. Krystal, stunned mute by the blow, finally managed a tear.

"How did you remember that name?" I queried my mother with pretend surprise, for she always remembered exactly what she wanted to remember.

"He reminds me of a young man your uncle worked with. A draftsman, I think, but not a very good one. He was let go, of course, and a year later he came back to thank his ex-boss for firing him."

"And something about this guy reminds you of Ryan Cooperman?"

"Yes. Don't you see? The draftsman said losing his job had put him onto himself."

There was a thought—Ryan Cooperman figuring out what a brat he was and then doing something about it.

I informed her that Ryan's parents were sending him to Valley Forge Military Academy. "They asked Bryn Derwyn for his transcript."

Mother paused in her painting to visualize the Ryan I had described fitting into such a rule-infested environment. While I watched her dress our boy in a uniform, teach him to march and figure calculus, to play football and plan battles, I did the same.

VFMA (and Junior College) used to be viewed as the local last resort for incorrigible boys. Except that was never strictly true. All schools have personalities, especially private ones founded for a particular purpose, such as preparing boys for the military. It's an admissions officer's job to match students to their institutions, and I could easily imagine Valley Forge's seer recognizing Ryan's blatant craving for discipline.

And if Ryan lived long enough to adapt, the structure of the place would probably teach him to channel his talents into something society would welcome.

Then again, Ryan Cooperman would also be learning how to shoot.

"Best thing for him," Mother concluded.

I was still stuck on the image of Ryan Cooperman with a gun, so I replied, "Lord, I hope so."

We pondered Monet and Marlboro country respectively for
a couple minutes while listening to the "Winter Wonderland"
rendition commissioned by The Weather Channel for its corporate "hold" button. Middle-age Mrs. Keller refilled our cardboard cups, and this time I detected a hint of sherry in my
cocoa.

Mme. Mimi strolled among us and for once kept quiet
about our lack of progress and/or skill. Judging by her conspiratorial smile, the silver flask peeking out of her pocket had
been the source of the sherry.

"Tell me again how you got Charlie Finnemeyer off,"
Mother prompted during a pleasant lull. His acquittal had
made all the local papers, so everyone else's eyes—six sets—
drifted toward me with degrees of tactfulness ranging from
some to none.

"Not me, Mom. I explained this before." I spoke through
clenched teeth the way teenagers try to shush their parents in
front of their friends, with about the same success.

"Yes, I know Eric got that dealer to admit he made a mistake, but I'm still not entirely sure how that helped Charlie."

Birdie had had the same problem, I recalled. However, it
was equally possible that Cynthia Struve meant to entertain
the troops with how clever I was.

Then again, maybe she really didn't understand. The question was, could I answer her question without coming off like
a dog performing in a tutu?

I decided that walking that tightrope was better than embarrassing my mother by refusing her in front of acquaintances
(even though she had no similar compunction).

So the erstwhile artists of Ludwig settled back to sip tepid
cocoa and listen to my edited tale of murder and fraud. Pamela
Zenzinger played the villain to Gordon Yeager's fool. Samuel
Lloyd and Eric Allen served admirably as jousting knights,
and Charlie and Birdie Finnemeyer rose in the room's eyes as
beloved monarchs.

"But . . ." Mother protested.

"Nobody really set out to cheat anybody else," I explained,
finally responding to Mother's original question, "so no fraud

was committed. Birdie just wanted to catch up on Charlie's medical bills by selling off something they didn't need. She knew the Caucasian rug was valuable because of the way Charlie protected it, but she really had no idea what it was worth. Naturally, she haggled with Yeager because she knew a dealer would expect that, but I think she intended to accept whatever he offered all along. Of course, she was overjoyed by her windfall, and for a while Yeager was probably happy with his profit, too. But then Ignatowski got the rug appraised, Yeager found out what a fool he'd been, and you know the rest."

In a lucky break, Dr. Stewart's car, which had been impounded after his death, had not yet been claimed by his family. Technicians were able to lift Zenzinger's fingerprints from the passenger door and interior. They also found trace fibers from Zenzinger's overcoat and a few strands of her hair. It was hoped that an exhumation and autopsy would reveal the same sedative in Stewart's system as that found in Ignatowski. And Eric, my informant, assured me that the police were collecting enough other physical evidence from Zenzinger's apartment and the Ignatowskis' living room to secure an indictment against her for murder.

Mom's face glowed in the light cast off by a good story. "When Ignatowski called the cops, Yeager was afraid *he'd* be sent to jail, right? So he let Charlie take all the blame."

"That's about it," I agreed. Lots of money involved, lots of fear flying around. Two men dead.

Surprising everyone, Mrs. Keller set her cardboard cup on the windowsill with a resounding *thock*.

"I think it's all a bunch of nonsense," she groused at me, her wrinkled lips forming a line of disapproval. "You're copying a Monet. Your Mom's copying a cigarette ad." She waved her hand wildly and glanced around for support. "Some Textile student appliquéd her own prints on an old quilt and made it prettier. That Tuduc guy messed up a rug he made himself. What's the big deal? If something's beautiful—it's beautiful. Who cares about anything else?"

My lungs deflated, and my eyes met the wry gaze of Mme.

Mimi/Mary Gothwald. It appeared that our thoughts matched exactly.

"Where to begin?"

"Where to begin?"